SURPRISE PARRY

Remo grinned as he saw the ~~oldier~~ figure assume a praying mantis kung fu stance. Remo no more feared kung fu than he did flying Popsicle sticks.

"This will be over in a second, Kung Fu," Remo taunted.

It was.

Remo let fly with his fist. But there was nothing to connect with. Remo landed on his hands and knees. The guy was unbelievably fast.

"You're good, pal," Remo said tightly.

"I'm the best," the other returned.

"Got a name?" Remo asked.

"Yes. Death!"

Remo had thrown his best punch—and now he had to face the worst danger of his life. . . .

#83

The Destroyer

SKULL DUGGERY

Created by
WARREN MURPHY & RICHARD SAPIR

Ⓞ
A SIGNET BOOK

SIGNET
Published by the Penguin Group
Penguin Books USA Inc., 375 Hudson Street,
New York, New York 10014, U.S.A.
Penguin Books Ltd, 27 Wrights Lane,
London W8 5TZ, England
Penguin Books Australia Ltd, Ringwood,
Victoria, Australia
Penguin Books Canada Ltd, 2801 John Street,
Markham, Ontario, Canada L3R 1B4
Penguin Books (N.Z.) Ltd, 182-190 Wairau Road,
Auckland 10, New Zealand

Penguin Books Ltd, Registered Offices:
Harmondsworth, Middlesex, England

First published by Signet, an imprint of New American Library, a division
of Penguin Books USA Inc.

First Printing, January, 1991
10 9 8 7 6 5 4 3 2 1

 REGISTERED TRADEMARK—MARCA REGISTRADA

PRINTED IN THE UNITED STATES OF AMERICA

PUBLISHER'S NOTE
This is a work of fiction. Names, characters, places, and incidents either are the
product of the author's imagination or are used fictitiously, and any resemblance
to actual persons, living or dead, events, or locales is entirely coincidental.

BOOKS ARE AVAILABLE AT QUANTITY DISCOUNTS WHEN USED TO PROMOTE PRODUCTS OR
SERVICES. FOR INFORMATION PLEASE WRITE TO PREMIUM MARKETING DIVISION, PENGUIN
BOOKS USA INC., 375 HUDSON STREET, NEW YORK, NEW YORK 10014.

For Van Williams, who wore the green mask

And the Glorious House of Sinanju
P.O. Box 2505, Quincy, MA 02269

1

More than a year after Tiananmen Square, the tanks still rolled through Zhang Zingzong's dreams.

They lunged at him, their caterpillar-tread teeth seeking his feet, his hands, his frail human bones, and he would run. But there would be no place to run, for Zhang was surrounded by T-55 tanks.

It was not the sound of their treads clawing for his bones that awoke Zhang Zingzong at twelve minutes past midnight on a Tuesday evening in the city of New Rochelle, thousands of *li* from Beijing.

Even as he bolted from sleep, his ears rang with their clatter and the terrible *pong pong pong* sound that, more than the T-55's, haunted his waking hours.

The room was too bright. Moonlight washing through the thin window curtains was like white neon. It made a distorted triangle pattern on the bedspread and wall.

Blinking his almond eyes, Zhang Zingzong fumbled a pack of cigarettes off the nightstand. He speared out a single one. He took it in his dry mouth. The fibery taste of the American filter scratched his tongue. In disgust, he spit it out and threw off the covers.

Zhang Zingzong perched on the edge of his bed, his brain thick with unresolved dreams, his lungs like concrete wings. As he pulled the nightstand drawer open, he saw why the moonlight was so intense.

It was snowing outside. The flakes fell thickly, like scabs of lunar dust.

A spidery cedar was already heavy with accumulation. Beyond it, housetops were pristine sugar-dusted fantasies.

Zhang Zingzong found his last pack of Panda cigarettes, which he kept sealed in a plastic sandwich bag.

He pulled apart the seal and fished out a single cigarette, noting he was down to four.

He lit it with a Colibri lighter and sucked down the coarse, aromatic tobacco smoke. After two puffs, his head felt clearer and he went to the window.

The ethereal beauty of New Rochelle wrapped in a midnight snowfall held his attention, all thought of Tiananmen Square dispelled by the swirl of countless white flakes.

Then Zhang Zingzong saw the footprints.

They were ordinary footprints. One pair, they broke the even snow on the safe-house walkway like well-spaced intrusions. Although they were fresh, the falling snow was already beginning to soften their cookie-cutter edges.

Something disturbed Zhang Zingzong about the footprints. They appeared to lead from his front door to a long black car that was parked out front. For a moment his concentration shifted from the footprints to the silent car.

Obviously a limousine, it was a model he had never seen. It was not a Lincoln Continental. One had whisked him from the San Francisco airport to the first of many safe houses strung across the United States. He wondered if it was an official car and why his guard had left the house to go to it.

For Zhang Zingzong jumped to a logical conclusion. Except for a single FBI guard, he was the only person in the house. There were footprints leading from the house to the mysterious car; therefore, his guard had gone to the car.

Why had the driver not come to the house? he wondered.

Was something wrong? Would they have to move again, as they had in Paris, San Francisco, and again in that cold ugly city with the odd name, Buffalo? Zhang Zingzong had thought he would be liquidated in Buffalo. Only quick action by the FBI had extracted him from that situation.

Zhang Zingzong was considering getting into street clothes when he took another look at the footprints. His sharp eyes told him something was not right. He looked harder, his eyes squeezing against the harsh moonlight reflecting off the snow until they were like black slits in his white-brown face.

He saw it then. It made the skin of his bare back gather and crawl. He involuntarily worried the short hairs at the back of his neck with a nervous hand.

For the accumulating snow was quickly filling the footprints. Soon they would be obliterated. That was not the thing that made a thrill of supernatural fear clutch at Zhang Zingzong's heart, a heart that had not quailed at the sight of tanks rumbling through Tiananmen Square, a heart that had seen what the cruel steel treads could do to human flesh and bone.

What impelled Zhang Zingzong to jump into his jeans and throw on a shirt was the indisputable fact that the footprints furthest from the black limousine were freshest.

Zhang Zingzong did not know what it truly meant. The footsteps were plainly going toward the car. But those nearest it were fast blurring in the gentle downfall. There was no wind, so drifting would not explain the phenomenon.

Except that it meant the owner of them had come to the house from the car. Someone unknown to Zhang Zingzong, perhaps someone unfriendly to Zhang Zingzong.

Zhang Zingzong shoved his sockless feet into his Reeboks and stuffed his wallet into the tight jeans pocket. He breathed through his mouth, in gulps like a beached fish.

Creeping to the closed bedroom door, he put one ear to it. He heard no sounds at first, and then he detected footsteps. Padding footsteps, not like the American FBI agent. Six months on the run had made everything about the man, from his stale breath to his heavy-footed walk, as familiar to Zhang Zingzong as the rose-petal scent of his own wife, who was still in Beijing.

These were not his footsteps. They moved unsurely. Once, a lamp wobbled on a coffee table and stopped suddenly. A leg brushing a table and two quick hands reaching out to prevent the crash of an upset lamp. The image leapt into Zhang Zingzong's mind as clearly as if the bedroom door was transparent.

That settled the last of Zhang Zingzong's wavering indecision. He leapt to the bed and got down on his stomach. Reaching in with both hands, he found his khaki knapsack, the same one that had borne his meager supplies on the long trek to Canton. He yanked it out by the straps, felt the square-edged shape inside, and went to the window as quietly as possible.

The pack on his back, he undid the window latch and shoved the pane up. It rose with barely a scrape, for which Zhang Zingzong was silently grateful.

The storm window was another matter. He did not instantly fathom its construction. Did it lift or pull out? He felt around the edges, seeking a clue, his smoldering Panda dangling from his tight mouth.

He sucked in a breath, tasting tobacco smoke. It reminded him of those precious last four cigarettes.

Zhang Zingzong rushed to the nightstand and grabbed his last pack of Pandas. It was a foolish thing to do, but as it turned out, very fortunate.

Turning from the nightstand, Zhang Zingzong saw the line of light spring to life under the bedroom door.

The boldness of that act told him instantly that his FBI guard was no more.

Zhang Zingzong picked up a wooden chair, and holding it legs-out as he had been taught by the FBI to ward off knife-wielding assassins, charged the stubborn storm window.

The stout legs splintered going through the thick glass and the chair back knocked the breath from Zingzong's smoke-filled lungs. But it worked. The impact of the chair carried him safely through the glass and into the soft snow.

He jumped up, throwing off shards of glass and dusty dry snowflakes.

His eyes went everywhere, seeking a safe escape route.

The driver's door of the limousine popped open, and an apparition stepped out.

It seemed to be a man garbed entirely in a black uniform. He wore a peaked cap, military style. Its brim shadowed his face as he walked slowly and catlike toward Zhang Zingzong.

He moved with an easy-limbed grace, as if he were in no hurry.

And as he approached, his head lifted, revealing a cruel, certain smile—but only gleaming black where his upper face should be.

"Ting!" Zhang cried. "Stop! Come no closer!"

The man in black quickened his pace.

Zhang stood frozen, transfixed by the half-hidden gaze of the approaching man. His fear was palpable. Unlike the blind tanks, he felt there was no escape from this black devil.

A shot broke his paralysis. It came from inside the house. Hoarse shouting followed. The FBI man! He lived!

"Tom! I out here!"

Another shot. A window broke, and from within the house another voice, guttural and harsh, spoke one word in Chinese: "Sagwa!"

Zhang Zingzong's eyes were pulled from the house back to his stalker. Abandoning his sure pantherlike approach, the man in black raced for the front door, going through it like an ebony arrow.

That was all Zhang Zingzong needed. Slipping and sliding, he ran down the streets of the foreign land of America, where he had thought he would be safe, and was not.

As he stumbled around a corner, he wondered why the guttural voice had called him *sagwa*. He was a college student.

2

His name was Remo and he really, really knew his rice.

"Let me have a bag of that long white, and some brown," he told the blond at the health-food store. "Got any Blue Rose?"

"I never heard of Blue Rose," the blond admitted. She was tall and willowy. Her long straight hair looked as if it had been ironed. Remo didn't think anyone ironed her hair anymore. Not since Janis Joplin.

"Grows only in Thailand," Remo told her. "Has kind of a nutty taste."

"Really?" the blond said, her deep brown eyes growing limpid. "Maybe I can special-order some."

"In that case, put me down for as much as you can get."

"You must like it a lot."

"I eat a lot of rice. A *lot* of rice. When you eat as much rice as I do, variety is important."

"I'll bet."

"In fact, it's critical," Remo went on. "If I had to go on just domestic Carolina, I'm not sure my sanity would survive."

"Sounds *très* New Age," the blond prompted.

"It's not," Remo said flatly. "How about Patna? Got any of that?"

"That's another one I never heard of," she admitted. "Are you some kind of rice connoisseur?"

"I didn't start out that way," Remo admitted glumly, his eyes scanning the shelves of glass containers with their heaps of hard rice grains. Most of them contained the usual boring domestic lowlands, California Carolo's and Louisiana Rexoro's and Nato's. "Let's see . . ."

"How about wild rice?"

Remo frowned. "Not really." He was going to say that wild rice was no more rice than white chocolate was true chocolate. But why bother? Only another rice connoisseur would appreciate the distinction.

"Guess I'll take some short-grain white," Remo said. He pointed at one container and said, "Let me see that one."

The container came down off the shelf and Remo lifted the lid. As the blond watched, he took a pinch of grain to his lips and tasted it carefully.

"Pearl," he pronounced with the authority of a wine taster. "Grown in Java."

The blond's eyes widened in surprise. "You can tell that by *tasting*?"

"Sure. It has that iron tang. Goes away in the cooking—unless you undercook it, of course."

"I'll bet your wife never, ever undercooks your rice."

"Absolutely correct," Remo said, disposing of the tasted grain in a wicker wastebasket.

The blond acquired a slightly sad pout.

"Since I don't have a wife," Remo finished.

The pout jumped back into her mouth and her lips curved into a smile.

Her reaction was not lost on Remo Williams. He pretended not to notice it as the blond busied herself scooping quantities of rice into clear plastic bags, tying them with twister seals and making small talk.

"Hope you're not planning to carry all these home on foot," she quipped.

Remo jerked a thumb over his shoulder. "That's my car out front."

The blond looked up, her brown eyes curious to see what kind of car a rice authority would drive. Her curiosity froze.

"What car?" she asked.

"The blue one," Remo said absently, scanning rice labels.

"Shouldn't it be waiting for you?"

Remo turned. There was no blue car parked out front.

Came a screeching of tires and a blue Buick Regal suddenly jumped into view, going in the opposite direction it had been pointing when Remo had parked it minutes before.

Hunched behind the wheel was a black man Remo had never seen before.

"Damn!" he bit out. Remo raced for the door as the car picked up speed. The blond followed.

"Should I call 911?" she gasped, her eyes fever-bright.

"No," Remo said grimly. "I'll handle it."

"You will?"

Remo Williams began running. He started off with an easy, joggerlike pace, his bare forearms up, fists not loose-fingered, but tight. His thin, just-this-side-of-cruel mouth was grim.

He hit his stride at forty-five miles an hour, his mouth slightly parted. If he was exerting himself, there was no sign of strain on his high-cheekboned face. Only tight determination showed in his deep-set brown eyes.

He caught up to the Buick at a stoplight.

The driver wore a pea jacket and his hair was razored close at the temples. The name "Shariff" was shaved in bare scalp. He pretended not to notice Remo tapping on his window, so Remo planted his feet the way he had been taught and grasped the door handle firmly, waiting for the red light to change.

The driver—he looked about twenty-two—continued to ignore him as he fiddled with Remo's radio. The arrogance of the youth's nonchalance made Remo's blood boil. He calmed himself, thinking that he was not going to be ignored much longer.

The light turned green.

The driver hit the accelerator.

The rear tires spun, throwing off rubbery clouds of smoke.

The Buick stayed in place. A station wagon directly behind started to honk. With his free hand, Remo waved the car to go around him. His other hand held on to the driver's-side door handle, his feet rooted on the asphalt street as if by Super-Glue.

Remo waited patiently for Shariff to notice him. It was taking a while. The guy jammed the accelerator to the floor. The rear tires spun faster, shaving hot rubber off his treads. They were winter tires, so Remo didn't sweat the loss of tread. Besides which, he'd get satisfaction from the car thief soon enough.

Finally the driver released the gas. He put his nose to the glass and looked up at Remo.

Evidently he was not frightened by what he saw, a skinny dude of indeterminate age wearing—despite the winter chill—a black T-shirt and black chinos, because he rolled down the window.

"You mind?" he said.

"Yes, I do mind," Remo said pleasantly. "You are sitting behind the wheel of my car."

"This?"

"Do you see any other wheel you're sitting behind?"

"This *your* car?"

"I answered that. Now, you answer this: Why are you driving my car?"

"You weren't using it."

"So you just felt free to steal it, is that it?"

"I ain't stealin' it! Get outta my face with that shit!"

Remo leaned down. He bestowed a friendly disarming smile on the tough's scowling face. "Correct me if I'm mistaken, Shariff, but isn't that a screwdriver where my ignition used to be?"

"What you expect? You forgot to leave me the keys." His tone changed. "How you know my name?"

"ESP," Remo said.

"ESP? How you do that?"

"Do what?"

"That thing you did before. Had the pedal to the metal and I wasn't goin' nowhere. You shoulda been yanked along for the ride. Instead, I'm wastin' time talkin' witchu."

Remo made his voice contrite. "Sorry about that."

"You gonna tell me how you do that, or what?"

"Sinanju."

"Spell it. I wanna buy it, learn it, or steal it. Whatever it takes."

"Actually, it takes about fifteen years and seventy tons of

rice just to master the basics. Then you *really* have to buckle down."

"Don't have that kind of time. Now that I got this fine car, I plan on moving up in the world, Jim."

"The name's Remo."

"Thought you said it was Sinanju."

"I can see why you're stealing cars," Remo sighed. "Sinanju is what I do. It's kinda like . . . *fahrvergnugen*."

"Say what?"

"You know the TV commercials about being at one with your car?"

"Mighta come across it once or twice," Shariff allowed.

Remo waved another car through the intersection. "Well, Sinanju is kinda like that, except you don't need a car."

"That's good," Shariff said, "because you ain't got a car no more. Now, if you don't mind, I'll be gettin' on my way."

Shariff hit the accelerator. Remo was ready. The black car thief had telegraphed his intentions so loudly he might as well have shouted them.

This time, Remo didn't hold the car in place. He let it accelerate. But he stood his ground, keeping hold of the door handle.

As a result, the Buick described an arc in the slippery snow until it spun into the opposite lane, pointing back toward the health-food store where the blond stood watching him, clutching herself against a shivery wind.

"Why you do that for?" Shariff complained. "Now I'm pointin' the wrong way!"

"Because that way's where my car was parked before you interrupted my life with your sociopathic intrusion," Remo said without malice.

"Was that *farfarnugat*?"

"You must mean *fahrvergnugen*, and no, you weren't paying attention. Sinanju is what I do. *Fahrvergnugen* was only a metaphor."

"Yeah, well, metapor *this*, sucker!"

A machine pistol jumped into the man's hand.

"Nice Uzi," Remo commented.

"You stupid? This here's a Mac-10. Drive-by heaven."

"All guns look alike to me," Remo said, "and don't tell

me you're going to shoot me simply because I want my car back."

"No, I'm gonna shoot you because you're holdin' up my life."

"That's even less of a reason," Remo said, and stuck his index finger into the muzzle of the weapon. It didn't quite fit.

"You think I'm jokin'?" Shariff spat.

"Try me," Remo invited.

Shariff hesitated. There was something in the deep eyes of the skinny guy with the thick wrists, something that said he was not afraid.

"*Fahrvergnugen* work against guns too?" he wondered.

"Ask Volkswagen," Remo said, forcing his finger into the barrel with sudden violence.

With a *crack!*, the steel gun barrel split along its top seam clear back to the breech, changing the black man's hesitant expression to one of soul-disturbing doubt. His eyes got wide, then narrowed, then widened again as his thinking processes methodically considered and rejected various explanations for the impossible calamity that had befallen his weapon.

Finally he opened his mouth.

"You broke my Mac!" he wailed. "Why you do that?"

"You were about to shoot me," Remo said politely. "Come back to you?"

"Says who?"

"Every telltale muscle in your dishonest body."

"Prove it. It's your word against mine!"

"And it's my car," Remo said, withdrawing his steel-hard but unexceptional forefinger from the burst gun barrel and placing it to the teenager's forehead.

"What you gonna do with that?" Shariff wanted to know, his eyes trying to focus on the threatening digit. He was getting cross-eyed with the effort.

"That depends."

Shariff gulped. "On what?"

"On how fast you return my car to where I left it."

"Six seconds do you?"

"Make it five."

"Done. Hop in. Give you a lift."

"I'll meet you there. I've seen you drive."

"You got it!"

Remo withdrew his finger. The black man's head snapped around. He fixed his slowly uncrossing eyes on the empty parking space and hit the accelerator.

Four-point-nine seconds later, he screeched to a slippery halt before the store and jumped out of the car as if it were on fire.

He looked back up the street.

"I don't see the dude," he muttered to the blond. "Do you?"

A very, very hard finger tapped him on the shoulder once. He jumped, turning in place.

Standing on the sidewalk, not appearing winded at all, was the white dude whose name was Remo Farfarnugat, or something like that.

"Nice parking job," Remo complimented.

"Thanks."

"You only got one wheel up on the sidewalk."

"I'm going now," Shariff said, starting off.

"Not so fast," Remo said, arresting the youth with a hand on his shoulder.

"Hey, I did whatchu said."

"Let's take it a step further. I need help loading up."

"What do I look like—Jimmy Friggin' Hoffa!"

"Want to compare expressions face-to-face?"

"What you need loaded?"

"In there. Rice. Just put it in the trunk."

The black man went into the store. He came out with his arms full of rice in bags.

Remo opened the trunk for him. He went in for another trip.

"I saw what you did," the blond said.

"No, you didn't," Remo said. But he smiled when he said it.

"Okay, I didn't see what you did. But how did you do it?"

"You've heard of *fahrvergnugen*?"

"Sure. I drive a Jetta."

"Well, this is super-*fahrvergnugen*."

"Amazing. Teach it to me?"

"No," Remo said flatly.

He felt her hand on his half-bare bicep. "Please?"

Remo looked at her uptilted face, her half-parted, appealing mouth, and considered changing his mind.

He exhaled a long sigh instead.

Gently Remo disengaged the blond's fingers as the youth came out with the last of the rice.

"You sure must eat a lot of rice," Shariff muttered.

"I do," Remo returned. "And if you're standing there with your hand out for a tip, you're gonna freeze in place and the pigeons are going to redecorate your 'do."

"That's the thanks I get for luggin' your stuff all the way to your damn car!" Shariff snarled.

"If you hadn't come along, pal, I'd have done it myself and been home by now."

"Point taken. I'm going."

"Don't stop till you come to a state line or an ocean," Remo called after him.

As they watched Shariff turn a corner, the blond turned to Remo and said bravely, "Where were we?" She bit her lip, waiting for a reply.

Remo said without a trace of feeling one way or the other, "I was about to drive home with my rice and you were about to inventory your cash register for missing twenties."

One hand flew to her mouth. "My register! Oh, my God!" She bolted into the store.

When, after a moment, she didn't scream, Remo slid behind the wheel and pulled away from the curb. The car bounced violently as the front tire dropped off the curbstone.

Remo pulled into traffic, his face a frown of unhappiness.

He wasn't sure what bothered him more—walking away from an attractive blond or losing a convenient source of rice.

Either way, Remo could never set foot in that store again. She had seen him perform impossible stunts. That made her a security risk. He couldn't jeopardize her life by becoming friendly. Not here in Rye, New York, where he lived and where his boss and the organization for which he worked was headquartered.

There was no telling what Dr. Harold W. Smith would do if Remo Williams started dating a Rye girl. Probably have her eliminated in the name of national security. Anything was possible.

As Remo left the shopping area, he drove past the car thief, who was grumpily trooping down the street. Remo gave him an angry blast of his horn as he drove past, causing the man to jump. Shariff turned, and upon recognizing Remo, dived for cover. His maimed Mac-10 skittered out from under his pea coat.

And that was another thing. Normally Remo would have killed the thief too. But that might raise a ruckus, and the last thing Remo wanted to do was cause problems in Rye. Smith would probably force him to sell his house and relocate. He had had two decades of relocating. He was settled now. Forever, he hoped.

Once, Remo's aspirations had been simple.

He had been a Newark, New Jersey, beat cop. His dreams were limited to a sergeant's desk, a wife, and a nice suburban house with a white picket fence.

Harold W. Smith had changed that forever. It was Smith, in his capacity as director of CURE, a supersecret government organization that Remo had never heard of then and which virtually no one knew of today, who had engineered a frame so perfect that no one dreamed that Remo Williams, honest foot-slogging Remo Williams, had not killed a certain pusher in a certain alley and dropped his badge beside the body so very long ago.

Remo landed on death row so fast he thought the world had been turned upside down. And that was only the beginning. His life—his true life—began after he'd walked the last mile at Trenton State Prison and sat in an electric chair that sent a jolt through every jumping fiber in his body.

It did not kill him. He woke up later in a place called Folcroft Sānitarium with a new face and a choice so stark he wondered if he had died and gone to some sinister catch-22 hell: Join CURE as its enforcement arm or fry for real.

And although Remo Williams had gotten a second chance in life, his dreams of a wife and family and white picket fence were irretrievably lost.

It had taken most of the twenty years he'd worked for CURE to realize—or accept—it.

Twenty years of training in Sinanju, the *fahrvergnugen* of martial arts. Twenty years that had taught him to conquer all physical limitations, including absolute mastery of the opposite sex.

Under the tutelege of the Master of Sinanju—the last of a
long line of professional assassins going back five millennia—
Remo had discovered the thirty-seven steps to bringing a
woman to blissful ecstasy. The same knowledge that unlocked the power to hold a car in place despite the best
efforts of six sparking cylinders sent out subtle sexual signals
that most woman responded to on an instinctive level. And
that while Remo simply stood there trying to read rice
labels.

The earliest steps could bring a woman to exquisite climax—
and leave Remo listening to his bed partner's snores.

This was only another reason why, as the years went on,
Remo had stopped bothering. What was in it for him?

Pulling into the driveway of the suburban house he had
finally acquired after two decades of anonymously liquidat-
ing America's enemies, Remo wore an unhappy expression.

He carried the expression into the kitchen, along with the
first two bags of rice, thinking he would gladly trade in part
of his abilities for a measure of sexual satisfaction and get
back a tiny spark of that old dead dream.

From the other room came the sound of a TV. The
Master of Sinanju, enjoying his leisure.

Remo went out to the car, his hurt eyes glancing over to
the Tudor-style house next door. The home of Harold W.
Smith. It reminded him that this was all Smith's fault.

The thought struck him as he lifted the trunk. He shut it
with a metallic slam.

Grimly Remo walked up to Smith's front door and rapped
the imitation-brass lion's-head knocker against the door.

The door opened, framing a stoop-shouldered man of
advanced years and rimless spectacles. Harold W. Smith
looked indecisively in both directions, knuckles tightening
on the door. "Remo!"

From behind him, a woman's voice asked, "Harold, who
is it?"

That decided Smith. He closed the door behind him.

"Remo! What is this?" His croak was anxious.

"I just have one thing to say to you," Remo told him.

Smith adjusted his glasses. "Yes?"

"This is all your fault."

And with that, Remo turned on his heel and went back to
finish carrying rice into his empty home. His supersensitive

hearing picked up the frumpy voice of Mrs. Smith asking Harold who had been at her front door.

The answer infuriated Remo: "Just the paper boy, dear."

Remo finished putting the brown rice in the brown-rice cabinet, the white rice in the white-rice cabinet, and the exotic varieties in the others. There were five cabinets over the sink. Four of them were packed with rice in various containers.

With any luck, Remo thought glumy, the supply would last three weeks.

Remo left the kitchen to break the bad news to the Master of Sinanju.

"Little Father . . ." he began.

A spindly arm lifted, dropping a silken sleeve.

"Hush," a squeaky voice said. The figure of the Master of Sinanju occupied a floor space no greater than might a German shepherd.

Before a big-screen projection TV, he sat, his legs tucked under one another in the classic Asian lotus position. His kimono was like a monarch butterfly's wings replicated in silk—orange and black and iridescent.

Remo looked to the screen. He was surprised to see, not a British soap opera—Chiun's latest passion—but a documentary of some sort.

And because the Master of Sinanju was not watching a soap opera, Remo knew he could interrupt without risking a minor rebuke such as a compound leg fracture.

"Little Father, we need to talk," he said firmly.

"Remo!" the Master of Sinanju snapped. His wizened face glanced around, his clear hazel eyes annoyed. They were the only youthful aspect of the dusty lunar map of his features. "Not now!"

Remo folded his arms, his face a thundercloud of unhappiness. He thought about storming out, but he knew better than to escalate an argument he could never hope to win.

He wondered what Chiun, reigning Master of Sinanju, found so interesting. As Remo watched, scratchy archival footage from another time flickered on the screen. A crisp narrator's voice was saying, "Amelia Earhart left New Guinea on her fateful voyage on July 1, 1937, and was never seen again. Many theories have been put forth since her plane was lost over the South Pacific, but the mystery has never been solved."

From the Master of Sinanju came a derisive snort and a butterfly fluttering of his exquisitely long fingernails.

The announcer's overfed face appeared on the screen, looking serious. "We at *Ten-Thousand-Dollar Reward* believe there is no mystery that cannot be solved," he continued. "Somewhere out there is someone who knows what befell the brave aviatrix on her flight into the unknown. The producers of this program have placed ten thousand dollars in a trust fund to be paid to the first person to provide a credible documented account of Amelia Earhart's fate. If you are that person, call the eight-hundred number on this screen. Now!"

Twin puffs of hair floating over the Master of Sinanju's tiny ears like volcanic steam quivered in anticipation.

Remo detected that tiny warning subliminally. He stepped back in time to escape the explosion of butterfly silk that was the Master of Sinanju coming to full boil.

"Quickly, Remo!" Chiun cried, whirling about. "Fetch the telephone device. We must call this number!"

Remo eyed the Master of Sinanju, his arms flung out like wings, his wispy beard barely visible under his anguished mouth.

And he did not move.

"Did you not hear me, deaf one?" Chiun squeaked. Even with his arms upraised, he looked tiny.

"I hear you fine," Remo said calmly. "Just as you heard me when I wanted to talk to you."

"But the reward!" Chiun cried, his squeaky voice twisting with imminent loss.

"You know where the phone is," Remo said casually.

"But I do not know how to work it properly!"

"Just press the buttons, like any lesser mortal," Remo offered, his hands sweeping to the telephone on a tiny table, the only bit of furniture in the bare room other than the big TV.

"Very well, I will," said the Master of Sinanju, lowering his saillike arms. He shrank to his normal height, which was barely five-feet-five. He padded toward the telephone on white sandals. His feet made an audible sound only because the Master of Sinanju wished to make his unhappiness known to his pupil.

"But I will not share the reward with you," he warned as he lifted the receiver to his face. Remo noticed with a smile-suppressing tightening of his lips that Chiun placed the earpiece to his prim mouth.

"Don't tell me you actually think you can convince the TV people you know what happened to Amelia Earhart," Remo said.

"I do and I will," said Chiun, stabbing push buttons with a long-nailed forefinger. The nails kept getting in the way—the true reason Chiun did not like using telephones.

"They won't believe you," Remo warned.

"I know where the body is."

"You do?" Remo said, a perplexed frown eradicating his smug expression.

"She was not lost, as many believe," Chiun retorted, one eye on the treacherous, nail-snagging keypad. "No storm claimed her craft—unless the sweet wind that has blown through the centuries is a typhoon."

"Sweet wind? I don't think I like where this is going. . . ."

Chiun stabbed the O-for-operator button. He pressed too hard, making three zeros and not two. When he finished dialing, a feminine but mechanical voice said, "The number you have called is not a working number."

"But it was just on the television!" Chiun screamed into the earpiece. "I demand that you connect me!"

The voice repeated the message and the Master of Sinanju hung up huffily.

"These devices are impossible!" he shrieked. He turned to Remo, pointing an accusing finger. "You! I must claim that reward! Name your price!"

"Half," Remo said.

"Too much!"

"Three-quarters!"

"You are going high when you should be going low!" Chiun cried in exasperation. He grabbed his decorative hair puffs as if to yank them out by the roots.

"The more you stall, the higher my price goes," Remo told him, enjoying the rare experience of having leverage over the other man to bring him to this sorry sexless state in life.

"Bandit!" Chiun accused.

"Sticks and stones will break my bones, but names will cost you ten percent more," Remo sang out.

Chiun turned his back. "I will not be dragged into this insane negotiation," he said huffily.

"Suits me. You'll never see the reward anyway."

Chiun spun about like a fury. "I will so!"

"Prove it to me," Remo invited, folding his arms. "I'll be the judge."

The Master of Sinanju hesitated. His lifted chin dropped, making the wispy tendril of a beard jump out against his orange-and-black kimono. "How do I know you will not call these people when my back is turned, and claim the reward for yourself?"

"Good point," Remo said. "Why don't we just forget the whole thing?"

Chiun stamped one foot like a petulant child. "I will not! The reward is rightfully mine."

"Why?"

"Because we eliminated the dirty spy of a woman."

Despite the earlier hint, Remo was taken aback by the Master of Sinanju's venomous pronouncement.

"One of your ancestors killed Amelia Earhart?" he blurted out.

"No," said Chiun.

"That's a relief," said Remo. "For a minute I—"

"I did," added Chiun.

"You!"

"It was during a prelude to the Second Idiocy of the Barbarians," Chiun explained. Remo recognized the oft-used euphemism for World War II. "This woman was a spy, working for the Americans."

"Who did *you* work for?" Remo wondered.

"Why, those she intended to spy upon, of course."

"Not the Japanese?" Remo demanded.

"Possibly," Chiun said in an evasive voice.

"You worked for the Japanese?" Remo said, aghast.

"I said possibly," Chiun admitted in a quieter voice. "It was many years ago."

"The same sneaky, treacherous, unworthy Japanese you revile at every opportunity?"

"Not all Japanese are to be described so harshly," Chiun allowed. "There are a few who are worthy—for Japanese."

"I thought you hated the Japanese."

"I do not hate their money," Chiun retorted, gathering up his autumnal kimono sleeves.

"You don't hate anyone's money," Remo snapped. "You worked for the Japanese. The people who conquered Korea, so-called land of eternal perfection?"

"It was a special case," Chiun said, tight voiced.

"So tell me the story," Remo invited, toeing a tatami mat in front of him. He sat down, folding his legs, and assumed a patient expression.

The Master of Sinanju looked to the telephone. His many wrinkles bunched together in frustration. Then he stalked back to the television and assumed his own mat. He sat down with his back to his pupil.

Remo vented a sigh, got up, and brought his mat around. When he resumed his seat, Chiun wore an inscrutable expression, but his eyes gleamed with his minor victory.

"This was in the starving years," began the Master of Sinanju in a doleful voice. "There was little food. The babies were hungry from sunup to sundown. The Chinese were at war with the Japanese and the Japanese vexed the Chinese. For the House of Sinanju, the finest assassins known to history, there was no work from either of them. I was young then—not that I am not young still—but younger, not yet having seen the majority of the years I have so far enjoyed."

"Get to it," Remo said.

"The emperor of Japan had heard of an American woman who sought to spy in his empire. Word was sent to the village of Sinanju. A man came on foot, and because he was Japanese, he was not allowed to tread our sacred soil."

"Mud, you mean," said Remo, who had been to Chiun's ancestral home, a pitiful mud flat on the West Korea Bay, where the men fished and the fish hid. The women did most of the work of feeding the village. The Masters of Sinanju—a line that stretched back five thousand years—supported them all by working as royal assassins to the great thrones of history.

"I treated with this man and accepted the gold that paid for the flying woman's life," Chiun continued. "That was the difficult part. Accepting Japanese gold. I was forced to wash it. Twice."

"Cut to the chase, will you, Chiun?"

"It was a simple matter then to journey to a place where the aircraft was being refueled and gain passage."

"You were a passenger on Amelia Earhart's last flight?"

"She did not know that—until it was too late."

Remo winced. "So what happened?"

"She experienced what might be called mechanical difficulties and, in the parlance of that time, ditched in the ocean."

"Then?"

"The unfortunate woman drowned, along with her craft."

"And you?"

Chiun's feathery eyebrows shot up. "Need you ask? I did not drown, and therefore I am here to pass on the heritage of the House of Sinanju to you, its latest heir. Ingrate."

"You killed Amelia Earhart," Remo whispered in shock.

Chiun shook his aged head. "No, *we* killed Amelia Earhart, for it is written in the Book of Sinanju that each Master builds on the work of the Masters who came before him, and each Master's achievements are a gift to later generations. You are Sinanju, Remo. Therefore you have claim to the credit, and the reward. Ten percent and not a penny more!" Chiun said quickly.

"No deal," Remo shot back. "And let's stick to the subject."

"This *is* the subject."

"No, it isn't. I came in here to talk about my lousy sex life."

"How can something that does not exist be lousy?" Chiun pointed out.

"Exactly."

"I am prepared to talk to you about your lousy sex life, Remo," Chiun offered. "Within the bounds of good taste, of course."

"And for a price," Remo said acidly.

"Five percent of your ten percent. Agreed?"

"No. I don't want to talk about my sex life anymore."

"Your *lousy* sex life," Chiun corrected.

"My lousy sex life," Remo growled. "I want to talk about you, and what you did before you worked for America."

"I do not work for America. I work for Emperor Smith. Remember this. One does not work for nations, for they shift boundaries with the changing times and speak with no single voice. But an emperor is a different matter."

"Before America, who?"

"Immediately before America, I worked for no one. You know that story, Remo. There was no work. I had no heir, for my wicked nephew, Nuihc, had become a renegade. The village of Sinanju had fallen on evil times. I could find no worthy heir and so I resigned myself to living out the natural span of my years knowing that I was the last Master of Sinanju."

"It wasn't always that way," Remo countered. "If you worked for the Japanese in the thirties, you must have worked for other clients. Fess up. Who?"

Chiun stroked his wispy beard. "Why do you suddenly wish to know this, Remo? We have known each other for many years. Never before have you asked me about my past."

"I never gave it much thought before," Remo admitted. "So who else did you kill?"

"We," Chiun corrected.

"Who? Gandhi?"

"The price was too low and I was too proud to work cheap," Chiun said flatly. "Amateurs got that one."

"Who else?" Remo pressed.

"There were so many. I cannot recall their names," Chiun said evasively.

"Okay, let's try it from another angle. Other than the Japanese, who did you work for?"

"I had clients in my young days, it is true. Some minor princes. No one you would know."

"Hitler?"

"That posturing Austrian?" Chiun spat. "Too late, I was assigned to eradicate that one. I was cheated of my fee."

"By the British or the Russians?"

"By the victim. He heard of my approach and immolated himself. The coward."

"I'm not hearing names," Remo said evenly.

"You would not recognize many of them. You are too young. They were before your time."

"Names. C'mon. You're hiding something. For years you've

been regaling me with stories of previous Masters, but hardly any of your own. Who'd you work for before America?"

"A Chinese," Chiun admitted.

"Not the thieving Chinese, scourge of the Sinanju collection agency? The one who defaulted on a fifteen-dollar fee in 1421?"

"Not the Chinese. A Chinese. An individual. A mandarin."

"Not an emperor?"

"He was ambitious. This was before the Communists, of course."

"Would I know of him?"

"Not under his true name. But he was known to the West under a silly name, Fu Achoo, or some such nonsense."

Remo made a face. "Fu . . . you can't mean Fu Manchu?"

"See? Even you understand what a ridiculous name it is. It was that lunatic British scribbler's fault. He disseminated all manner of lies and slanders about me."

"You? What are you talking about? I read those books as a kid. I don't remember any Korean assassins in them."

"Precisely, Remo. He changed everything willy-nilly. Where the Master of Sinanju was at work, he improvised Dacoits. I think that was in *The Ears of Fu Achoo*. Dacoits are always cutting their own fingers off by accident. Poisonous spiders, venomous scorpions, and other insects abound in those ridiculous books. But not one single Korean. I ended up on the cutting-room floor."

"You're mixing your media, but I get what you say."

"It was that so-called author who was mixed up. Imagine a Chinese named Fu Manchu. The Manchus are not even Chinese. They are nomads, like the Mongols. It would be like naming you Remo Apache."

"Little Father, I think you're pulling my leg. Fu Manchu was a fictitious character. He never existed."

"His gold existed," Chiun shot back.

"I don't believe you. You're just telling me this to hide the truth."

"Then do not believe me," Chiun sniffed. "Your lack of faith does not change the truth, only your perception of what is truth and what is falsehood."

"So what happened to this alleged client?"

"He died. Then the hard days began. It was very long ago, and the memories unpleasant. Not like the bird woman,

Amelia. Now, that was a magnificent assassination, the first in the Sinanju line to extinguish both an aircraft and its pilot with a single blow. You see, I attacked the—"

"Save it. It's a depressing thought."

"To the victim, perhaps. But we are Sinanju, Remo. We are never the victim."

Remo's eye sought the floor. He was quiet for several minutes. Presently he lifted his head.

"I am unhappy, Little Father."

"Yes?"

"I am unhappy with Smith."

"The purpose of an emperor is not to make his assassin happy," Chiun intoned solemnly, "only wealthy. It will pass."

"I am unhappy with Sinanju."

"What! Unhappy with the near-perfection of existence? How can this be so?"

"Sinanju has given me many gifts, Little Father," Remo admitted. "The gift of oneness, of correct breathing, of knowing myself more fully than I ever dreamed possible."

"For which you should fall to your knees before me."

"It has also robbed me of my dreams."

"Dreams are for those who sleep," Chiun said joyously. "You have been awakened, Remo Williams. Rejoice in that." His arms lifted in benediction.

"Once I dreamed of a house such as this," Remo said quietly.

"Which you now have—thanks to Sinanju."

"And a wife."

"Take as many as you wish. But keep them in the attic, for they will undoubtedly prattle and complain all day long."

"And children."

Chiun touched Remo's knee tenderly. "You have a daughter. True, this is not exactly a cause for rejoicing, for if the lean times come again, she will be among the first to be sent home to the sea. For as you know, in times of approaching famine, the female babies are always drowned first. The males only after the famine has struck. This way—"

"A daughter born to me by a woman who will not have me because the work I do is too dangerous," Remo interjected. "A daughter I haven't seen in years."

"When you have a son, it will be different. We will train him together, you and I."

"How can I have a son if there is no pleasure in sex for me? How can I have a wife or a family with the work we do, the dangers we face?"

"These are problems each Master must solve in his own way," Chiun said with a dismissive wave.

"But what is my way? I feel empty. I met a woman today, at the rice store. She was interested in me. But I had to walk away from her. She saw me do stuff. And you know how Smith is about security."

"This is bad," Chiun grumbled.

"You understand?"

"Of course. This means I will have to buy the rice from now on. Oh, Remo, how could you be so careless?"

"Somebody stole my car," Remo said, annoyed.

"An unworthy excuse. You could have walked the fifteen miles home."

"I walked away from love because I knew it would be too much trouble," Remo said with intensity. "I walked away because I knew the sex would be boring. I need someone to fill the emptiness in my life, and I walked away. Don't you see? I've given up."

"Do you think a woman could fill that void?"

"If I stop believing that one could, I lose my dream."

Chiun considered. "I might be able to show you how to enjoy sex once more."

"For a price," Remo and Chiun said together. Neither man laughed.

"I'll make the call," Remo said instantly.

He got to his feet, but before he took a single step, the phone rang.

Frowning, Remo picked it up. It was either Harold W. Smith or an insurance salesman, he knew. He hoped it was the latter. Smith was a really dull conversationalist.

"Remo," Harold Smith said peevishly. "I need you. At once."

"You have me mistaken for the paper boy." Remo slammed the receiver down. It rang again before he could dial the eight-hundred number.

"Cut it out, Smith!" Remo snapped, hanging up again. This time it ran again instantly. Remo hung up again and the phone kept ringing.

"How are you doing that?" Remo demanded hotly.

"Phone trap."

"What's that?"

"A lever on the side of my telephone," Smith explained. "It prevents the connection from being severed at your end. The phone company uses them to trace obscene phone callers."

"So you're going to hold my phone·hostage until I do what you say, is that it?"

"I have an assignment for you," Smith said, his voice like lemons being tortured of their inmost juices.

"Stuff it!" Remo said, pulling the phone cord from the wallboard.

"*Auugh!*" cried the Master of Sinanju. "My reward!"

"Damn!" said Remo, suddenly remembering why he had gone to the telephone in the first place.

"For that," Chiun cried, flouncing toward the door, "you will suffer from a lousy sex life to the end of your miserable days!"

"Where are you going?" Remo called after him.

"To see Emperor Smith. I will have him place the telephone call. I should have considered this in the first place."

"Don't forget my ten percent," Remo called over the sound of the slamming door.

3

Zhang Zingzong was holding a pair of queens.

He took a drag on a Panda, expelling smoke out of the side of his mouth. He had lost all his pocket money to the corpulent dealer in the first ten minutes of the poker game. His traveler's checks had gone next. The last one lay in the pot.

Zhang Zingzong eyed it narrowly, his heart racing. The checks had gotten him as far as New York's noisy Chinatown, where he blended in with these alien Chinese who spoke Mandarin in Hong Kong accents or no Chinese at all.

A waiter at the Golden Pagoda restaurant told him where to find the poker game when Zhang Zingzong doubled his tip. It proved to be in the back of the very same Division Street restaurant. Zhang had only to flash his traveler's checks to be admitted.

Now, scarcely an hour later, his throat burning with a combination of anxiety-produced heartburn and pepper chicken, Zhang looked from his two queens to the last traveler's check, without which he would starve, even in Chinatown.

Zhang gave up three cards, hoping for a full house.

He got a jack, a deuce, and a four back.

Spitting out a harsh curse, he slapped his hand down on the table.

The dealer eyed it with humor. The others broke into amused laughter, displaying gold-filled teeth. It made Zhang wonder if Chinese-Americans had been born with ivory teeth that wore away, revealing their gold hearts.

"You fold?" the corpulent dealer said gruffly.

"I have no more money," Zhang admitted.

"What in sack?"

Zhang's eyes went to the knapsack hanging off the back of his chair so fast the others exchanged glances, taking note of his expression.

"All I have in world," Zhang said quietly, attempting to keep his face stiff.

"Then you fold?"

A drop of hot ash fell from the Panda dangling from Zhang's loose mouth as he considered his answer. With a hoarse cry, he brushed the ash aside before it burned through his jeans.

The cigarette dropped from his mouth. Reflexively, Zhang reached for the pack in his shirt pocket.

The bicycling panda on the package front caught his eye as he fished a cigarette out.

"I have these," Zhang said suddenly. "Genuine Chinese cigarettes. Brought from Beijing." Which was a lie. He'd got them in Hong Kong.

"You are Beijing man?" the dealer asked intently.

"Yes," Zhang admitted.

"You were in Tiananmen?"

"I was."

"You very brave man. These cigarettes not worth squat. But we let you play one more hand."

"Thank you," Zhang said in his formal English. He had found it easier to communicate with the men in English, not their odd Chinese. It was an irony not lost on Zhang Zingzong.

The dealer shuffled the cards. Zhang cut the deck. The cards started whispering around the table, forming four silent piles.

When the remaining deck was laid down, Zhang picked up his cards. They had fallen in order, by suit, which Zhang took to mean good fortune. The king and queen of clubs nestled in his hand.

He got rid of two, picking up a pair of kings. That gave him three of a kind.

"I call," Zhang said.

The dealer folded. So did the man to his right. Zhang grinned. Then the man on the left laid down a royal flush.

Zhang quietly placed his cards on the table. His face was a mask of old tallow.

"You fold now?" he was asked.

"I fold," Zhang said sadly.

"Too bad, Tiananmen man. But you live. Consider that the gods have smiled upon you. You survive Tiananmen and are in US now. Very good fortune."

Smiling woodenly, Zhang reached for his knapsack. He stood up, and noticing the fallen Panda, stooped to pick it up.

The winner reached out to claim the pot. He grabbed up the pack of Pandas with one hand. The soft pack crushed too easily, and his winning smile fell apart.

"Hey, you! Tiananmen man! Only two cigarettes here."

"Sorry. All I have left."

"No good! No good! You cheat!"

"I do not cheat," Zhang snapped back. "Those all I had."

"Maybe sack have something I like," the winner said, getting to his feet. He was tall and reedy, his muscles hard from physical labor.

Zhang backed away, clutching his knapsack. "I go now."

"No!"

Zhang bolted for the beaded curtain that led back into the restaurant dining area.

Behind him, chair legs scraped. Feet made whetting sounds on the tile floor. High singsong shouts followed him.

Zhang Zingzong raced into the restaurant, nearly colliding with a busboy. A waiter reached out for him. Zhang swerved just in time, but a dangling knapsack strap snagged a chair. The chair tripped Zhang. He went down.

Fiercely he jerked at the strap. It tore. He bounced to his feet, looking everywhere, seeking the quickest escape. Fear disoriented him long enough for a thick-bodied Chinese behind the cash register to grab him by the shirt collar.

Zhang tried to punch him back, but he kept Zhang before him.

The others caught up and surrounded Zhang Zingzong, hurling abuse at him.

"Cheat!"

"Robber!"

"*Chark!*"

Zhang Zingzong hung his head and said nothing. Tears started to flow.

The knapsack was pulled from his fingers. He did not resist. What was the use of resisting? He had no money. Where could he go?

The dealer snapped open the flap and rummaged through the knapsack, pulling out and dropping to the floor odd bits of Zhang's clothing.

Then his eyes went wide with interest.

"Ah," he breathed. He pulled out the ornate teakwood box.

The others stepped closer, their faces trembling with excitement. They recognized that this was no tourist-shop knickknack. The workmanship was exquisite, the carvings fine, delicate.

"Where you get this?" the dealer demanded.

Zhang said nothing. He brushed a tear from one downcast eye.

"It is very fine," the dealer said quietly.

"It belongs to China," said Zhang Zingzong.

"It is mine now," the winner said, grinning.

"This is not fair!" Zhang burst out. "It is worth much more than pack of cigarettes!" As soon as he had said it, Zhang regretted his hasty words.

The dealer nodded to one of the others. He went into the

back room and returned with the crumpled pack of Pandas. He stuffed them into Zhang's shirt pocket.

Zhang paid no heed. He was watching the dealer fiddle with the lid of the teakwood box. His blunt fingers pressing and worrying at different carvings, coming close to the secret catch, but never quite engaging it.

"How does this box open?" the dealer demanded, looking up in frustration.

"It does not open. It is solid," Zhang told him flatly.

The dealer looked back to the box. He shook it. It felt solid. Still, he refused to accept Zhang's word and resumed fingering the designs, seeking for the box's secret.

The catch click was like a knife in Zhang Zingzong's stomach. The lid popped up unexpectedly.

The dealer almost dropped the box, he was taken so much by surprise.

He peered into the box, his black eyes like oblique knife wounds in his waxy face.

Only the dealer was in a position to see the contents of the box. He saw them for less than a second. The image of the box's contents registered and his thin eyes seemed to explode like twin blasts of surprise.

This time he did drop the box.

Zhang Zingzong dived for it, his captured shirt collar tearing free with the violence of his lunge, leaving the man who had been holding him with only a ragged strip of cloth.

Zhang scooped up the box, pushed the contents back inside, and locked the lid in one breathless motion. He rolled out of the reach of grasping hands. A foot lashed out, scraping skin off his temple. The glancing blow barely slowed him down.

Zhang Zingzong plunged for a table. He upended it. The others recoiled from the crash of platters and flying knives and forks and chopsticks.

Zhang was halfway to the door when it suddenly opened and he found himself looking into the deadliest eyes he had ever seen.

They resembled gray agates, hard and clear. They were not Chinese eyes, although they were Asian. The face that served as their setting was like a parchment death mask.

Zhang stopped dead in his tracks, uncertain what to do.

"You are Zhang Zingzong?" the vision asked in queru-
lous but flawless Mandarin.

"*S-Shi*," he breathed.

"I am the Master of Sinanju," the Asian intoned, lifting
his arms as if in blessing. His draperylike sleeves expanded
like wings. He resembled a monarch butterfly emerging
from the chrysalis of a human mummy.

"I . . . I do not understand," Zhang stuttered.

"Know this, Zhang Zingzong," the being who called himself the Master of Sinanju said. "As long as you are under
my protection, no harm will befall you."

Zhang Zingzong had nothing to say to that.

Behind him, the others were stepping around the up-
turned tables, their padding feet cracking broken platters
into smaller pieces of porcelain.

A voice called out. The dealer's smoky voice.

"Who are you, old turtle?"

In perfect Cantonese, the Master of Sinanju replied:

"I have spoken my title. My name does not matter."

"This isn't your quarrel," he spat. "Go now!"

The Master of Sinanju beckoned to Zhang, saying, "Come
to my side, Zhang Zingzong."

Zhang took a single step forward. A fist grabbed a bunch
of his shirtback, stopping him.

"I cannot," Zhang whispered.

"Then I will come to you," said the Master of Sinanju.

And with a cry like a screaming bird of prey, the Master
of Sinanju spread his monarch wings further and took to the
air.

Later, Zhang Zingzong realized that the Master of Sinanju
had not sprouted wings. But the combination of outspread
arms and wild cry created the illusion of a descending winged
creature.

Zhang recoiled in fear of the flapping apparition.

The fist at his back released him. A man grunted. Another screamed in pain. A table splintered under the sudden
impact of a falling body. Glass broke.

Zhang looked toward the sounds. He caught a sudden
vision of a man flying toward himself at full speed. The
man's two converging faces met in a splintering of suddenly
red glass.

The man had been sent into a wall mirror, Zhang realized.

Zhang straightened slowly, his jaw hanging open. All around him, his erstwhile captors sprawled in various states of ruin.

The butterfly-garbed Master of Sinanju stood before him, his hands seeking one another in the closing sleeves of his kimono.

"Who are these men?" he asked coldly.

"Cheaters!" Zhang said quickly. "They took all my money in a crooked card game."

"He lies," a voice mumbled brokenly. "He cheated us."

A sandal whipped out, silencing the voice that had spoken.

"Gather your things," instructed the Master of Sinanju, eyeing the clumped form he had just silenced.

Hastily Zhang Zingzong found his knapsack. He stuffed the teakwood box inside, covering it with discarded bits of clothing.

"You have all your possessions?" the Master of Sinanju asked.

"Not my money. In the back."

"Then get your money, Zhang Zingzong."

Zhang went to the back. There he scooped up the pot, taking not only his money but also that belonging to the others. He hesitated, his eyes furtive.

Then he slipped out the back way, into an alley, and pelted toward the street.

He did not know who this Master of Sinanju was, but he could trust no one and would trust no one.

As he ran, some inner voice caused him to look behind him.

Like some vampire, the Master of Sinanju was pursuing him. Panting, Zhang ducked into a stinking alley. He slid on the packed snow, pulled himself up, and kept running.

There was an opening at the other end.

He looked behind him. There was no sign of the black-and-gold-silk-clad figure. But Zhang knew he would never relent. His own footprints in the snow betrayed the route of his escape.

He redoubled his efforts, but then, at the alley's opposite end, the Master of Sinanju floated down, silent, majestic, and so utterly inescapable that Zhang Zingzong simply gave up.

He stopped in his tracks and watched as the diminutive

figure of the old Korean approached him, saying, "Why did you run, Chinese? Are you so ignorant that you do not know that there is no escape from Sinanju?"

Zhang had nothing to say to that. He wondered who had betrayed him this time.

4

Remo Williams calmed down after the first hour. He spent the second watching TV. By the end of the third hour he was beginning to wonder what was keeping Chiun.

Maybe Smith had let Chiun make his call. He couldn't imagine security-conscious Harold W. Smith allowing the Master of Sinanju to make a call that would undoubtedly lead to Chiun going on television, confessing to the assassination of Amelia Earhart, and probably making cryptic allusions to his secret work for America. But anything was possible these days.

Well into hour four, Remo couldn't resist pulling aside a living-room curtain and looking across the carport to the window of Smith's dining room.

Smith and his wife were seated at a table, eating. Smith looked more like he was taking castor oil by spoon, but that meant little. It was a permanent Harold Smith expression.

Remo saw no sign of Chiun.

Concerned, he reached for the telephone, remembered it was out of commission, and went out the front door instead. He crossed over to Smith's front door, his foorprints barely denting the snow.

Remo hammered on the brass lion's-head knocker until the paint began to crack around the its edges.

The door opened a crack. Harold Smith peered out like a spinster with recurring nightmares of the Boston Strangler.

"Remo!" he whispered. "What are you doing here?"

"Looking for Chiun. Where is he?"

Smith paled. "He's not with you?"

"No. Last I heard, he was about to barge into your life."

"That was hours ago. I gave him his assignment."

"Damn," Remo said. "He must have gone without me." Responding to Smith's puzzled expression, Remo added, "We had a fight."

"He mentioned you've been acting up."

"Acting up!" Remo exploded. "Last Chiun was talking, he wanted to go on the *Ten-Thousand-Dollar Reward* show and confess to bumping off Amelia Earhart."

"He did mention it," Smith admitted. "Do you suppose it was true?"

"I don't know. He also claimed he'd once worked for Fu Manchu."

"A fictitious character, if I remember my childhood reading."

"You read them too?" Remo asked in surprise. "I always thought spreadsheets were your idea of literary excitement."

Smith said nothing.

"Where can I find him?" Remo said at last.

"New Rochelle. There was an attack on a safe house overnight. A Chinese student who escaped the Tiananmen Square demonstrations is missing, his guard murdered. You and Chiun were to look into it."

"Give me the address," Remo said in exasperation.

Smith rattled off an address from memory, then said, "This is very important."

"It must be, if Chiun didn't nail you for that reward," Remo said sourly.

"I promised to match it if he dropped the matter."

"Let me guess—he made you double it."

"Actually, it was three times the amount. I considered it cheap under the circumstances."

"It would have to be, if you agreed to it," Remo said acidly, walking away. He got behind the wheel of his car and sent it squealing out of the driveway. It was his way of saying good-bye to Harold Smith, the architect of his troubles.

The front yard of the house was cordoned off with yellow barrier tape marked with the letters "FBI."

Remo fumbled through his wallet for an FBI ID, glanced

at it to fix his new last name in his mind, and presented himself at the front door.

"Who are you?" A crew-cut agent demanded. He looked like an extra from a 1950's cop show.

"Remo Quiller, special agent."

"Since when?" the agent said, noting Remo's casual attire.

"This is my day off. Had a call to get right over here."

"We've already processed the scene."

"Fine," Remo said, pushing the man aside. "I won't have to keep you long. What happened?"

There was an outline on the floor, in white tape. No blood.

"We had a Chinese student stashed here," the agent told Remo. "Name's Zhang Zingzong. He was snatched last night. Perpetrators unknown. We lost a good man."

"Shot?" Remo asked.

The agent shook his head. "No obvious wounds. Forensics has him now."

Looking around the room, Remo said, "We had a special expert brought in from Washington. I thought I'd find him here."

"You mean the gook?"

Remo turned. "You call him that to his face?"

"Of course not."

"That explains why you're still breathing," Remo said. "Where is he?"

"Don't know. He looked around, then left in a hurry."

"Say where he was going?"

"No, but he was very interested in the agent's body."

"Interested? How?"

The agent unwrapped a stick of Beeman's gum he took from a pocket. "Looked him over quite a while. I tried to stop him, but he nearly took my head off."

"He say anything that would give me a direction to look?"

"Yeah. Whispered something while he was feeling Tom's throat."

"Who's Tom?"

"Chief agent on the detail."

"So what did he say?"

The gum went into his mouth. "Nothing. He was dead."

"I meant Chiun."

"It sounded like 'Sin Achoo.' "

"You wouldn't mean 'Fu Achoo,' would you?" Remo asked slowly.

"I might," the agent said, his words tangling in his gum. "Sounded like 'Sin Achoo' to me."

Remo started. "Not 'Sinanju'?"

"That might've been it. Hard to say. He talked funny."

"I thought you FBI agents were supposed to be trained observers," Remo challenged.

"And I thought you were supposed to be one of us," the agent said, his voice hardening. "Let me see that ID again."

"Here," Remo said, flashing his FBI ID. He lifted it to the agent's face. The FBI man leaned into the card, never seeing Remo's hand reach around to the back of his neck. If he felt the steellike fingers that paralyzed critical spinal nerves, he said nothing about it on the way down to the polished pine floor.

Remo left him snoring out of one nostril. The other was mashed flat against the floor.

Remo drove around the neighborhood aimlessly, wondering what the heck was going on. Chiun had let slip the word "Sinanju" while examining a dead FBI agent. That was not like Chiun. Had it meant he was going back to the village of Sinanju without Remo? It hardly seemed likely. He was upset, but not that upset.

Finally Remo pulled up at a Seven-eleven and plunked quarters into a pay phone. He pressed the one button until he heard ringing. After twenty years of using codes and phone numbers that changed every week, it was a relief to finally have a constant code that Remo couldn't forget. Just press one until a connection was established.

Smith answered. His voice was low and furtive.

"Speak louder," Remo shouted. "The connection must be bad."

"The connection is fine," Smith whispered back. "I'm in the bathroom."

"Sorry to intrude," Remo said dryly.

"It's not that. I am home, so I am using my briefcase phone."

"Oh, right," Remo said, rolling his eyes. "Look," he continued, "I've just been to the so-called safe house. Chiun isn't there. No one knows where he went."

"The missing student must be located," Smith said urgently.

A dim voice intruded, calling, "Harold. Who are you talking to in there?"

"No one, dear," Smith called guiltily. The sound of a flushing toilet drowned out Smith's next words.

"What did you say?" Remo asked wearily.

"This is an important assignment."

"America is full of Chinese students," Remo retorted. "What's so special about this one?"

"Later," Smith hissed. "Find Chiun or find that student."

"How about I find them both?"

"Yes, yes, of course."

"Any ideas where I should look?"

"None."

"I can't drive in circles for hours," Remo pointed out.

"And you will not find them talking to me from a pay phone," Smith rejoined.

Remo hung up. He got no satisfaction from it, the click of Smith's line going dead a split second before his receiver exploded all over the pay-phone station.

Remo got back behind the wheel of his car and pulled out of the parking lot, wondering where the hell Chiun had gotten to.

5

It began to snow again.

The snowfall started gently, but soon quickened into a furious windblown storm, freshening the already gray snow of the previous night's fall and then resculpturing its undulant planes into sharp, angular drifts.

Disgusted, Remo abandoned his pointless cruising of the New Rochelle streets and pointed his car toward the safe house.

Maybe Chiun had returned there, Remo thought.

He drove at a seemingly reckless pace, skidding into turns on locked wheels, bringing his car out of numerous skids with controlled elegance. He was one with his Buick, Volkswagen notwithstanding.

Less than twenty minutes later, Remo pulled up before the safe house. He noticed the low-slung black limo parked out front, and immediately a frown gathered in wrinkles on his brow.

Remo had once been a police officer and still had a cop's habit of noting the makes of suspicious vehicles.

He didn't recognize the limo, even though its massive square grille was pointing toward him. There was no front bumper—just two banks of headlights.

Remo stepped from his car, glancing toward the driver's side of the windshield.

The driver quickly lowered the sun visor, cutting off a clear view of his face. Then he honked his horn. Twice, in an obvious signal.

Remo strode up to the driver's side of the car and peered in, noticing the shiny black buttons of a chauffeur's uniform. Then he saw the man's face.

"Hate to break this to you, pal," Remo said dryly, "but Halloween was two months ago."

The driver looked up, displaying a polished black domino. It was molded to his features so that only his lower face showed. He looked like Dracula's chauffeur. Remo almost laughed in his face.

"Go away," the driver said in a thick Asian accent.

"C'mon," Remo said impatiently, knocking on the glass.

"I said, go away!"

Remo's retort froze in his mouth. There was something familiar about the man's voice. He looked closer. The eye holes in his onyx mask were cut in oblique slashes. The dark eyes behind them were almond-shaped. Chinese, Remo thought.

"I don't suppose you're the missing student?" Remo ventured.

Behind Remo, the safe-house door opened. Remo started to turn.

The driver's door opened so quickly Remo had to dance out of its way. He landed on one toe, the other poised to regain his balance on the slippery snow.

His arms went up automatically, ready to defend himself. His foot never touched the ground. Before Remo could react, he was flying.

There was no preattack warning, no jolt of impact. Whatever had happened, Remo had been taken at the absolute moment of imbalance.

He landed headfirst in a snowdrift.

Furious, Remo pulled his head free, shaking off wet snow. He leapt to his feet and whirled, ready to reply to a follow-up attack.

Instead, the chauffeur was calmly closing the rear limo door on a stooping figure. Remo caught a momentary image of a tall, lean man in a greatcoat and Russian-style fur cap before he disappeared into the limousine interior. The door closed.

Grinning with fierce anticipation, Remo flashed for the chauffeur's jet-black back.

Sensing Remo's approach, the limber figure turned. He dropped into what Remo instantly recognized as a praying-mantis-style kung-fu stance. Remo's grin widened. He no more feared kung fu than he did flying Popsicle sticks.

Remo raised a tight fist. His other hand, straight-fingered as a spear, floated up to parry any thrust.

"This will be over in a second, Kung Fu," Remo taunted.

It was.

Remo let fly with his fist. But there was nothing to connect with. His fist slashed through thin air, and kept going. It carried him with it.

Remo landed on his hands and knees. He rolled into his back, his feet up to ward off an overhead attack.

The kung-fu man was coming out of his crouch. The splash of trampled snow at his feet told Remo the story. The diminutive man had slipped between Remo's legs as he had attacked.

It was unbelievable. No kung-fu dancer was that good.

"You're good pal," Remo said tightly.

"I'm the best," the other returned arrogantly. His voice carried a familiar lilt. Remo tried to place it. Somehow, it fit the man's masked look, bizarre as that seemed.

Remo got to his feet in a hurry. The two men squared off, Remo standing tall, the other crouching, his hands weaving invisible patterns in the air before him. His movements were smooth and graceful. He wore a red button over his heart, but Remo had no time to read the slogan on it.

"Got a name?" Remo asked, circling his foe.

"Yes. Death!"

And, venting a high-pitched cry, he executed a flying kick.

Remo saw it coming. Not as soon as he should have, but there was a lot of driving snow in the air.

The kick flashed by Remo's twisting head. He reached out to snag the polished shoe as it slashed by his cheek. Remo took hold and twisted sharply.

Like a worm on a hook, the driver squirmed in the air. The other foot became a piston. It drove against Remo's open chest in a pounding flurry of blows.

The attack was elemental in its fury. The guy had no fulcrum except thin air, but his kicks were as hard as if his back was braced against a stone wall.

Remo kept his ribs tense, protecting his lungs and the precious empowering air inside them.

Inevitably, his opponent lost his balance. Remo spun him by the foot. The guy turned over in midair like a tightly wound rubber band unraveling.

He landed on his stomach in the snow.

Quickly Remo set his heel on the back of the guy's neck. He reached down for the mask.

From within the car, a shrill voice spoke a single word: "Sagwa!"

And while Remo's attention was drawn to the voice, the prostrate chauffeur turned into a tiger once again.

"Hey!" Remo said. It was a stupid response. But he had underestimated his foe. He should have immobilized him with a fast kick while he was down.

Black-gloved hands grabbed Remo's ankles. Remo set himself. But instead of pulling, the little guy lifted Remo straight up.

There was no countermeasure possible. Remo went into the air. Not high, but high enough for his opponent to gain his feet while Remo was registering his predicament.

Remo received three rapid-succession kicks to the face as he came down. They blurred into a drumlike tattoo, and Remo landed on his face in the snow. Again.

A fourth blow to the back of his neck made him taste snow.

Later Remo realized he must have been out for four, possibly five seconds. But as he experienced it, he spat out wet snow at the same time he sprang to his feet.

The limousine was already backing away.

"Hey, we're not done," Remo called, moving for the retreating grille.

The car stopped suddenly. The driver leaned down behind the wheel, and a tiny section of the grille popped open, disclosing a silvery nozzle.

It began squirting greenish vapor.

There were not many things Remo Williams feared, but gas was one thing he had no Sinanju defense against. You either breathed it and suffered the consequences or you didn't breathe it and escaped them.

Remo had no idea whether it was nerve gas, tear gas, or laughing gas billowing toward him, and he couldn't know until it attacked his respiratory system. Which he definitely did not want.

It was a vomitous green and that was enough.

Remo backpedaled inches ahead of the spreading cloud. When he gained a few yards, he turned around and broke into a dead run.

Behind him, the car shifted into reverse and sped away.

Remo kept going. He ducked around a corner. Somewhere a dog barked and then made a high-pitched *yip* of a sound. Then it whined and made no more sound.

A car came in Remo's direction, forcing him to leap off the road.

The driver honked once and gave Remo the finger in passing.

"Same to you, buddy!" Remo called after him.

Then, seeing his blinkers indicate a turn onto the gas-filled street, Remo waved his arms and called after him.

"Hold it! Don't go down there!"

The car kept going. It pushed swirls of green gas aside and the driver's honk of response turned into a long wail of a sound. The car struck something with a tinny crump.

Remo took a deep breath and ran back up the street.

Batting away clouds of green, he found the car. It was joined at the bumper with a parked van. Remo got to the driver. Yanking the door open, he reached and found a pulse. It was strong. The man's breath tickled Remo's palm when he held it up to his nose.

When Remo pulled him off the horn, he detected the faintest of snores.

That meant the gas was an anesthetic, not a nerve agent.

Satisfied on that point, Remo ran to his car and gave chase.

The snow was pelting his windshield. As fast as the wipers pushed it aside, more scabrous flakes collected on the glass.

The tracks of the limo were fresh. Few drivers were out in the storm, so Remo had an easy time following the car.

The distinctive tread wove in and around the upscale New Rochelle neighborhood. Remo followed at a decorous pace. As long as the tracks were visible, he figured it was best if the masked driver didn't know he was being followed.

Eventually, the trail led to a side street and turned into a driveway.

The tracks disappeared under a closed garage door.

"Bingo," Remo said. He coasted past the house and around a corner, where he parked.

Remo stepped out into the blinding snow, making unusually faint tracks through several backyards and to the garage.

There was a door on the side of the garage. Remo tried it. Unlocked. He slipped in after listening and detecting no sounds from within.

Remo froze just inside the door.

He was not surprised to find a car in the garage.

What made his mouth suddenly hang open in astonishment was that the car was a white convertible. The top was down. The body was as dry as an enameled bone.

Remo drew a line along the hood with one finger. He picked up grime.

"What the hell?" he muttered.

He dropped to his knees to check the tires. They were also dry. Not only that, but the tread was not the tread he had followed. The limo tread had been serpentine.

"Musta got confused," he muttered. "Damn."

He left the garage and slipped around to the front.

There Remo was further surprised to find the same garage door he had earlier seen and the identical limousine tread vanishing under the door.

Remo went back into the garage.

The white convertible sat there, dry and slightly grimy. Remo went around to the back of the car.

On the stone-tiled floor were the faint wet tracks of the limo's distinctive snakeskin tread. They stopped three feet short of the convertible's rear tires, as if the limo had driven into the fifth dimension. The only other line of demarcation was the edge of one of the stone flags.

"This is ridiculous," Remo muttered in the dim light. He walked around the convertible. There was enough room to pass on all four sides if he turned sideways when he passed a tool-festooned workbench, but definitely no room for a second car.

Frowning, Remo stood in the dimness of the garage and said, "I've heard of locked-room mysteries, but this is a freaking garage and it isn't even locked!"

He made another circuit of the convertible, and finding nothing, hopped into the passenger seat.

There was no black limousine in the glove compartment, not that he expected to find it. But he wasn't about to let any possibility get by him. There wasn't even a registration.

The trunk was empty of everything but a spare tire bolted into a recess. There wasn't even a loose jack or tire iron.

Remo popped the hood and examined the ordinary six-cylinder engine. The radiator was cold to the touch.

Gently closing the hood, Remo ran a Sinanju-sharp fingernail on the paint job. He got a flat gray line under the white enamel. He had hoped for black. But the convertible was not the black limo with a seven-second paint job and a new front end.

Remo Williams left the garage scratching his head. He went around to the front and looked at the tire tracks again. They were the same rattlesnake tracks, all right.

"None of this makes sense," Remo said half-aloud. He reached down and grabbed the garage door handle. It turned. He lifted the door carefully and once again beheld the white convertible's rear deck.

The rattlesnake treads continued as wet smears on the garage floor, stopping short of the white car.

Slowly Remo closed the car door and thought about what he should do.

Knocking at the white house was a tempting possibility,

but what was he going to say? Excuse me, sir, but have you seen a black limousine drive into your garage and vanish into thin air?

Tearing down the garage walls also tempted him.

Remo decided he wasn't going to do that. Maybe later. It was possible he had gotten confused and followed the trail of the wrong tires. Not that that would explain the vanishing car, but if it wasn't the limo, it wasn't his problem.

Dropping to one knee, Remo scooped up a section of snow-captured tire tread. He carried it back to his car with both hands, trying not to crush it.

He drove back to the safe house with the section of snow melting on the seat beside him, following the rattlesnake tread all the way back to the semicircle of tire tracks that had been laid when the limousine had first spun into a reverse spin after ejecting a cloud of greenish vapor.

The gas cloud had dissipated. The sleeping man was still at his wheel. Evidently it wasn't a very curious neighborhood. Either that or everyone had been knocked out by the gas.

Remo set the captured section of snow next to the tracks. The diamond-shaped scales were a perfect match.

Remo stomped on the tracks in frustration. When that didn't solve the mystery, he decided to further investigate the safe house.

Halfway up the walk, he noticed something strange.

The driving snow had nearly obliterated a set of footprints along the walk, but they were still visible as rounded outlines.

Remo noticed that there where two sets of fresh footprints on the walk. Both were going away from the front door. Remo looked back. They stopped exactly short of the spot where the limousine had been parked.

He bent down. One set of prints was large, the other small. Remo fixed the smaller set in his mind and went back to where he had battled the diminutive chauffeur. The prints were the same. That meant the other prints would have been made by the tall man in the Russian fur hat.

The problem with that, Remo realized after he returned to study those prints, was that the toes pointed toward the house. Not away from it.

Yet clearly the man had left the house. Remo had seen

him do exactly that. At least, he had seen him enter the car after hearing the sound of the opening safe-house door.

There were no other tracks on the walk, but the snow was falling so fast that earlier tracks—say, those made an hour or so before—would have been long covered up.

Remo looked back toward the closed front door, his expression falling into its natural frown lines.

Two sets of tracks. One going, one coming, but not the same man. That should mean that someone had entered the house in the last few minutes. However, the collection of snow in the chauffeur's departing tracks meant they had been made before Remo arrived on the scene. There had been no time for the man to enter or leave the house after that. He had been in Remo's sight all along.

"Unless they doubled back while I was chasing phantom tire tracks," Remo muttered aloud.

That didn't fit either, Remo decided. Because the snow hadn't yet obliterated the footprints made during his fight with the chauffeur. These were from about the same time, judging from the filling snow. And there wouldn't have been time for the snow to bury the passenger's tracks.

Yet the only tracks that could have been that man's were pointing toward the house, not away from it.

It made no sense.

But sense or not, Remo knew better than to stand here exposed any longer. He slipped around the side to the back door.

There were no tracks of any kind at the back door, so Remo made some of his own.

Breaking the FBI barrier tape, he eased open the storm door and carefully tried the inner doorknob.

It turned and caught. Locked.

Remo put his ear to the panel. There was no sound at first. Then he heard the sound of a furnace kick in, the dull roar of an oil burner firing up, and a desultorily dripping sink.

No heartbeats, no lungs in respiration cycle, no voices.

No nothing.

Remo popped the knob. It shot out of its socket, driven inward by the hard heel of his hand.

Remo stepped in, every sense alert. He drifted from room to room, finding nothing at first.

In the kitchen, a man sat at the kitchen table. His eyes were open, but his head lolled to one side. His arms were arranged so that his hands dangled between his akimbo knees.

He looked dead. He was the gum-chewing FBI agent Remo had talked to earlier.

Remo touched the agent's carotid artery with a forefinger. Definitely dead.

Noticing a faint discoloration over the man's windpipe, Remo touched it. The trachea felt mushy, as if it had been jellied.

"Sinanju?" Remo whispered in the stillness of the kitchen. His voice shook with disbelief.

He finished checking the rest of the house.

Drawers lay open. Here and there things were noticeably out of place or upended. The house had been searched. Not wildly and carelessly, but methodically and with patience.

Remo went out the front door, snapping the FBI barrier tape with a careless flick of one hand. He wore an unhappy expression as he walked down the walkway.

He was puzzling over the inexplicable footprints, trying to figure them out.

"Let's see," Remo muttered to himself. "The chauffeur came out before I got here. Okay, he's accounted for. But his passenger came out after him. So where are his tracks? And whose are these?" Remo snapped his fingers. "The FBI agent's!"

The thought sent Remo back into the house, where he removed the agent's right shoe.

Returning, he pressed it into one right-shoe mark of the unidentified footprint.

The agent's sole lines overlapped. They were too long and broader at the heel. Disgustedly Remo tossed the shoe into a drift.

"Okay, it's not him," he said. "So it's gotta be someone else." He rubbed his chin, unmindful of the snow collecting in his thick dark hair. It was melting and drops were starting to rill down the back of his neck and behind the ears. He ignored the shivery sensation.

"Let's say they doubled back," Remo said. "The tall guy with the fur hat goes in. But where does he go? He doesn't come out the back. Therefore he's still in the house. So it's the chauffeur who comes out. Trouble is, he never went in—unless he went in over an hour ago. And if he did that, how could I have fought him? Unless he's twins."

The thought caused Remo's eyes to gleam. The gleam faded.

"But if he's twins," Remo muttered in disappointment, "where is the other one? And where are the tracks of the guy I saw get in back of the limo?"

Remo was roused from his puzzle by the distant sound of sirens. He looked up and saw sleepy-eyed people emerging from their homes. They pointed to the unconscious motorist at the wheel of his crashed car.

Remo decided this would have to be a police matter. He wasn't going to solve it.

He got into his car and took off. As he turned a corner, he saw a dog sleeping in a snowbank as if it were a perfectly natural thing for a dog to be doing.

"That explains the dog," he mumbled. "But not the footprints."

6

Less than an hour after his mysterious experience in New Rochelle, Remo pulled into his own driveway in a foul mood.

He went around the front, noticing no footprints on his walkway.

"Chiun's not here," Remo muttered. "Damn."

But as he fumbled for his key at the front door, the chatter of British-accented conversation drifted through the wood.

"What!" Remo keyed the lock open and pushed the door in.

"Chiun! What are you doing here!" he demanded.

Chiun, Reigning Master of Sinanju, did not deign to turn

his eyes from the big TV, acknowledging his pupil only with his voice and a tightening of his seamed mask of a face.

"I live here, graceless one," he said. "Now, be quiet. I am occupied."

"I've spent half the afternoon looking for you," Remo shouted back hotly.

"I would think that pleasure would attend the successful conclusion of so arduous a quest, but the white mind is forever a closed book even to one as perceptive as I."

"Don't get snotty with me. Smith said we had an assignment."

"*I* had an assignment," Chiun sniffed. "You were not a part of my latest agreement with Emperor Smith."

"He told me you soaked him for triple the ten thousand dollars," Remo said, his hands resting on his hips.

Chiun's face wrinkled in disgust. "I would not use the word 'soaked,' " he said haughtily. "I bargained."

"Well, you can leave my ten percent on the kitchen table."

"You are not entitled to ten percent of my labor."

"Why the hell not?" Remo want to know. "No, don't tell me. That's why you went off on your own."

Chiun allowed a faint smile to wreathe his paper-thin lips. "Perhaps next time you will not hesitate to place important phone calls when I ask this of you," he said sternly.

"Fat chance," Remo retorted.

"Spoken like a true fathead. Now, be silent."

"It's on tape. You can shut it off for a minute."

"It will dispel the mood the players have so deftly striven to create," Chiun pointed out.

Remo looked at the screen. A group of people was gathered in a typical upper-middle-class British drawing room, chatting on in refined tones about a variety of oblique subjects. The word "utterly" was repeated three times by three different actors.

"How can you watch this tripe?" Remo demanded.

"Because the characters keep their clothes on their bodies like civilized persons," Chiun sniffed.

"What about Smith's all-important Chinese student? I assume you were chasing around after him. And where were you all this time?"

"Where any sensitive person who seeks a missing Chinese person would have gone."

Remo looked his question.

"Chinatown, of course," Chiun explained.

"Oh, of course," Remo said archly. "Everyone knows the Chinese are drawn to Chinatown like freaking lemmings to a cliff."

"Something like that," Chiun said vaguely.

"Go on," Remo invited, folding his arms.

Chiun watched the screen as he spoke. "Knowing that this man was Chinese," he continued, "I knew that if he were abducted, it would have been by another Chinese—for who else would place any value in such a person? And if he had become lost, I knew that, even lost in a strange land, he would go there to be among his kind. And being Chinese, he would seek out a Chinese gambling den."

"How'd you figure that?"

"Everyone knows the Chinese are notorious gamblers."

"Well, I don't."

"I do. It is in their nature, along with laziness."

"That's the worst load of crap I ever heard. So you didn't find him and you gave up, and the assignment is unfinished, is that it?"

The door to Remo's bedroom opened and a frightened Asian face poked out uncertainly. He looked at Remo.

"Master Chiun, who this person?"

"What's *he* doing in my room!" Remo demanded.

"Master Chiun, who is this *lofan*?"

"What did he call me?" Remo demanded of Chiun.

"He called you a white man," Chiun explained. "Do not be insulted. He is new to these shores."

"I'm not insulted."

"I would be," Chiun said aridly.

The Chinese man repeated his question. "Master Chiun, who is this *lofan*?"

"This is Remo," Chiun answered, adding, "my valet."

"My ass!" Remo exploded. "You get out of my room! Right now!"

The Chinese man hastily slammed the door shut.

"You have frightened my houseguest," Chiun complained.

"Guest! You brought him here? What about security? What about—"

"Smith knows. It was his suggestion."

"Now Smith is giving away my bedroom to any old vagabond who strays into trouble," Remo complained.

"That is not *any* person," Chiun countered. "That is Zhang Zingzong. He is very famous, even if he is Chinese."

"Never heard of him."

"That does not mean he is not famous. May I finish watching my program now?"

"You know," Remo said, putting his hands back on his hips, "of all people, I thought you'd be the last one to let a Chinese guy stay under his roof."

"One makes certain exceptions for the privileged."

Remo growled. "Are you by any chance charging him rent?"

"Of course not," Chiun said in an offended tone.

"Good."

"I am charging him room and board," Chiun added. "It is not the same. There is no lease, for example."

Remo threw up his hands. "This is ridiculous. Look, we gotta talk. I just came from that safe house."

"It is improbably named."

"Tell me about it. The FBI guard is dead."

"They are paid to fall in the line of duty. Soldiers love their glory. Who are we to criticize them if they wish to throw away their lives will-nilly?"

"He was taken out by a larynx stroke. Clean, too."

"Many have copied the larynx stroke of Sinanju," Chiun intoned, video-screen light washing his attentive face. "It is regrettable that we do not get royalties."

"Yeah, well, the guy who did it did it almost as good as me."

"Have I not always said your bent elbow would bring you to ruin?"

"Almost as good as you," Remo added.

The Master of Sinanju wrinkled his offended nose. "I will not be insulted."

"I speak the truth, Little Father," Remo said with quiet earnestness.

And hearing the suddenly respectful tone of his pupil's voice, the Master of Sinanju lifted a long-nailed finger. The remote control clicked. The VCR ceased its quiet whirring, the picture frozen in distortion.

Chiun rose to his feet.

"The larynx was crushed throughout?" he inquired.

"Like a sponge. There was a small bruise. But it was very small."

"A fortunate amateur," Chiun pronounced sagely. "He has no doubt squandered his entire life practicing that one blow. It is all he knows. In other situations, against a worthy opponent, he would stand helpless."

"I tangled with the guy—at least, I think he's the guy."

"And?"

"I musta had an off day," Remo admitted, quiet-voiced. "He ran me ragged."

Chiun's mouth formed an O of surprise. "Truly?"

"I am ashamed to admit it, Little Father."

"And you should be ashamed," Chiun admonished. "This man was not white, was he? For if he was white, my shame would know no depths."

"I think he was Chinese."

Chiun shook his head sadly. "Almost as bad. Are you certain he was not Korean?"

"The eyes were not Korean. I'm sure of that. His voice sounded familiar, but I couldn't place it."

"You knew him?"

"He wore a mask. The funny thing was, even so, I thought I recognized him."

Chiun cocked an inquisitive head. "You recognized the eyes, or perhaps the lips?"

"I don't think so. If you want the truth, I thought I recognized the mask."

Chiun waved a dismissive hand, saying, "Any idiot may wear a mask."

"This was special," Remo countered. "It was molded to his facial contours. Doesn't make sense, does it?"

"You seldom do."

"There's more."

Chiun lifted thin eyebrows and Remo launched into a long recitation of all that had happened to him since he encountered the black limousine. He went into great detail regarding the mystery of the garage, and then told the Master of Sinanju about the impossible footprints.

"Can you explain any of it?" Remo concluded.

Chiun's eyes grew narrow and steely. He said nothing for many uncomfortable minutes.

"I am not making this up, Chiun," Remo said to break the silence.

"You are mistaken," Chiun said solemnly.

"About what?"

"About everything."

"Those footprints are still there," Remo pointed out.

"You are mistaken," Chiun repeated. "You saw no such thing."

"Who are you to tell me what I saw?" Remo asked testily.

"What you saw is impossible," Chiun lectured. "Therefore, you could not have seen it."

"Which are we taking about—the tire tracks or the footprints?"

"All of them. I do not understand this vanishing car of yours, but no one leaves such footprints. No one living, that is."

"Are we talking ghost?" Remo asked suddenly.

"No, we are talking the dead. And the dead do not walk."

"I saw what I saw," Remo said stubbornly.

"And I say to you what I say to you—do not disturb my sleep with such trifles."

"What's sleep got to do with anything?"

"Sleep," said the Master of Sinanju, "has to do with everything." He got up without another word and padded into his room.

Remo reached out and shut off the VCR. He wondered what the heck was going on.

After a few minutes the smell of incense drifted from Chiun's bedroom. From within, Remo heard the quavering sounds of his master singing. He recognized the old Korean prayers, though not all of the words were understandable. These were very old prayers handed down from the early days of Sinanju. They were prayers beseeching the protection of the village of Sinanju from the great Void.

They made Remo shudder.

He decided to do something about the situation. He went to his own bedroom door and flung it open.

"Rise and shine!" Remo called. "Time for answers."

The Chinese man was seated on Remo's sleeping mat, his head bowed as if in meditation.

He turned at the sound of Remo's voice and reached out for his knapsack, hugging it close to him. He slid around on the mat so Remo couldn't see his face.

Noticing the man's back, Remo frowned. "Do I know you?"

"I do not think so. Not know you."

"There's something familiar about you."

"I do not know you."

"You wouldn't by chance have been driving a black limousine this afternoon, would you?"

"Black limousine!" he said excitedly. "Where you see black limousine?"

"Back at the safe house. What do you know about it?"

"Nothing," Zhang Zingzong said quickly.

"Oh, bullshit!" Remo retorted. "You know something."

"Know nothing."

"No, it couldn't have been you. You're too tall," Remo decided.

"Not know what you mean."

"Screw you," Remo said, slamming the door shut after him.

Remo went to a closet and pulled out a handful of straw sitting mats and scattered them on the floor of a spare room. The spare room was completely bare of furniture, although one end was cluttered with fourteen stacked lacquered trunks. Chiun's precious traveling luggage.

Remo stretched out on the mats and ran the events of the afternoon through his mind. They were no clearer than before.

From the other room, Chiun's prayers continued like a singsong dirge.

Because he felt tired, Remo drifted off to sleep.

He didn't know how long he slept. He had wanted only to nap, but was awakened by a high-pitched argument in progress.

Remo rolled up onto one elbow. The argument was between Chiun and the Chinese student. It was in Chinese. Remo couldn't make out a word of Chinese.

The argument escalated from a kind of husky back-and-forth to a high-pitched volley of accusations and response.

Chiun was doing the accusing. The Chinese student was hotly denying something. Or everything.

"A little less noise out there, huh?" Remo called through the door.

The arguing subsided for a pregnant minute.

Then it started up again, low and intense, but swiftly escalating in violence and heatedness.

Finally Remo got to his feet and stormed past the suddenly quiet pair and out the front door.

"If this is how it's going to be all night," Remo barked, "I'm going to check into a motel."

He was not stopped by Chiun's voice on his way out, which both surprised and disappointed him.

The shouting resumed. It was going hot and heavy as Remo pulled out of the driveway. He laid down a hundred yards of rubber, hoping it would awaken Harold W. Smith, the architect of his misery.

7

Remo Williams tossed on the mattress pad.

It was too comfortable. He had left home without his bed mat, which the Chinese student was using anyway. So he had gone to a Motel Six, which he knew from past experience put mattress pads on their beds. And they had left the light on for him.

Remo had stripped the lumpy bed of its coverings and laid the pad on the rug. There, he went to sleep. Years of Sinanju training had made sleeping on an elevated surface as unrewarding as sex.

The pad was too thick, so Remo tossed and turned through the night. His thoughts were of the Master of Sinanju.

Remo had worked with Chiun for two decades now. They had grown close in that period of time, although their relationship had been very rocky, especially during the early

years, when Chiun had considered the training of a white an
odious task. In those days, CURE security was crucial. As
its enforcement arm, Remo was an experiment, one which
might be terminated at any time by presidential decree.

In those days, it had been Chiun's responsibility to execute Remo if the order came from Smith. The relationship
between Master and pupil had nevertheless flowered under
this dark cloud, in part because of the great promise that
Remo had shown and in part because of the respect each
man had developed for the other.

Until the day, in the midst of a grave US-USSR crisis in
which the President had ordered CURE disbanded, Smith
had given the termination order to Chiun. Remo had never
forgotten that he was partnered with a man who considered
assassin's work a high calling, one who would kill anyone
anywhere on orders or for the correct amount of gold, and
not think twice.

But when the order came, Chiun had refused to execute
it. His logic was Byzantine—something about Remo not
being the same Remo he had started with—but Remo knew
that their relationship had reached a turning point: Chiun
would never kill him, no matter who gave the order or what
the provocation.

For Remo had progressed beyond simply being a human
instrument of US political policy. He had joined the ranks
of the House of Sinanju. In truth, he had become one with
Sinanju many years before, but it was not until that day that
Remo understood he had been fully accepted by Chiun.

But that acceptance hadn't meant getting along. If anything, they fought more frequently, and about less important things. But after that, the edge had been blunted.

Remo thought he knew and understood Chiun.

He had thought the same about Smith until recent events
had reminded him that Harold W. Smith—despite his professional demeanor—could be as ruthless and cold-blooded
as the Master of Sinanju himself.

Remo decided he could live with Smith.

But still it was a shock to think, as he did now, lying
awake on the too-comfortable mattress pad with the pale
winter sun peeping through the chinks in the motel curtains,
that as long as he had known Chiun, he had not known him
fully.

In two decades, he had never thought to ask the Master of Sinanju about his history prior to coming to America. Certainly, Chiun had often spoken of the grim days of World War II, when Sinanju had no clients, and the decades after that, when clients stopped coming to the rocky shore of his ancestral village. North Korea had become inaccessible to outsiders, thanks to the Communist regime. The last potent monarchy had long since fallen. The emerging nations had resorted to guerrilla warfare or mercenaries. Assassins could be gotten anywhere, Chiun had said bitterly, even at open-air markets and Western malls, like so many melons.

Remo had never thought beyond the lesson—and there was always a lesson in Chiun's tales of Sinanju Masters—that this latest Master of Sinanju suffered to train a white only because he had no better offers. But Chiun had had an early career, one that went back to the dying monarchies of Europe and the pre-Communist days of China and the Orient. He must have had clients in those days.

Remo wondered if Chiun had in fact assassinated Amelia Earhart. It was certainly not the worst blot on the Sinanju house, which had liquidated popes and rulers down through history. As long as the gold took teeth marks, the work was worthy. It wasn't for nothing that the motto of the House was "Death Feeds Life."

But those were the previous Masters. It bothered Remo that Chiun had personally done Amelia Earhart. It made him wonder who else he had eliminated.

Remo sat up. He wasn't going to get any sleep anyway, so he padded over to the curtain and drew it open.

The sun was making tiny diamonds on the previous day's snowfall. The snow had been blown into drifts and rills like a desert sandscape of powdered sugar.

Remo noticed a young woman walking through the parking lot toward a red car, jingling her car keys. She noticed Remo standing there and smiled up at him.

Remo smiled back.

She gave him a friendly little wave.

Remo waved back. To his chagrin, she broke into uncontrollable laughter. And at that moment he realized he was standing in the big window stark naked.

Remo lost his smile and ducked into the bathroom, where he showered furiously.

Twenty minutes later he was behind the wheel, navigating through the snow-clogged streets, contemplating that he was a Master of Sinanju now. One day, the village might depend on Remo's ability to terminate a target without regard to the victim's deserving of death.

As long as he and Chiun were technically American agents, that was not a problem. But CURE was only thirty years old. The House of Sinanju had nearly five thousand years' head start. It would outlast CURE. It would probably outlast America. Remo's ultimate duty lay with the man who made him whole, not the nation which had wrenched him out of his comfortable existence and turned him into an expendable element in a global conflict that might mean nothing in a mere thousand years.

Remo grunted as he swerved to avoid an oncoming snowplow.

He was starting to think like Chiun—in the very long term.

The snow-draped hills of the Folcroft golf course hove into view, signaling that Remo was approaching his neighborhood. His house had been built, like Smith's, on the edge of the fairway.

Remo decided it was time he learned more about Chiun's past. He hoped it wouldn't be too painful.

Who knew, if he showed enough interest, the Master of Sinanju might teach Remo how to enjoy sex again.

It was a tempting possibility and it made Remo press the accelerator harder. He leaned into the turns, the big blue Buick literally skiing at times. In other hands, it was a recipe for disaster. In Remo's trained hands, he and the car were one.

The Buick went into a controlled skid at the bottom of Remo's street, came out of it as if pulled by an invisible cord, and Remo suddenly noticed the distinctive rattlesnake tread on the mushy snow before his bouncing hood ornament.

Remo slowed down. He was not surprised to see the predatory black limousine parked in front of his house. He couldn't explain it, but it didn't surprise him.

He braked and popped out from behind the wheel grinning with fierce anticipation.

"Rematch time!" he sang. He strode up to the limo. Unhappily, the driver's seat was vacant.

Remo shifted direction without even pausing and bounded to his front door. He noted two pairs of footprints. One entering the house and the other coming away. The Asian chauffeur had gone in. The other prints matched the inexplicable tracks back at the safe house.

"Good," Remo muttered. "It'll be just him and me."

Grinning, Remo rang the front doorbell so the chauffeur wouldn't know it was him. He could hardly wait to take another crack at that arrogant little guy.

There was no answer after the first ring, so Remo leaned into the buzzer, holding it down.

A voice called through the door.

"Who is there?"

"Avon lady," Remo called back, smiling in recognition of the chauffeur's distinctive clipped accent.

"You lie!"

"Try saying that to my face," Remo called.

The door flew open. The black-masked chauffeur stood there. He looked exactly the same as he had the previous day, down to the red button over his heart. Remo saw it clearly this time.

In black pseudo-Oriental slash letters it said: BRUCE LEE LIVES.

Remo's grin almost burst into laughter.

A fist started for his face. But Remo was ready for it. He ducked to one side and let the force of the blow carry the chauffeur past him.

Just to be sure, Remo kicked at one of the man's moving ankles.

The chauffeur couldn't stop himself. He went right into the mushy snow.

Remo slammed the door after him, locking it. He caught a flash of purple silk from the half-open spare-room door.

"Okay, Chiun," he called, "what the hell is going on here?"

The figure in purple was bent over an open lacquered trunk, ignoring Remo's challenge. Remo had no time to think about what that meant because an unfamiliar voice hissed, "Sagwa! *Jiu ming*!"

Remo started to whirl, his surprise on his face. He hadn't

detected another person in the house—no heartbeat, no respiration.

Before he could complete his turn, the locked front door exploded off its hinges and came toward him like a flying wall.

Remo stopped it with a hand, braced by a stiff arm. The impact forced him back a half-step, and while the energy was pushing at his stiffened arm bones, he redirected it back toward its source.

To an observer, it looked as if the door had attached itself to Remo's palm as if by static electricity. It hung on his hand for measurable seconds, then rebounded with no apparent force applied. In fact, Remo's hand had suddenly pushed it back.

The door flew back the way it had come. It met the stiff fingers of the black-masked chauffeur's right hand.

The door split as if precut and the halves slammed away. One struck on a corner and bounced like an eccentric wagon wheel.

Remo was already in the air. One foot snapped out in a flying kick.

His opponent copied the action.

The heels of their shoes collided like irresistible force meeting immovable object. They bounced off one another, neither man having gained an inch.

Remo hit the floor, recovering. His eyes sought the third man in the room. He caught a momentary glimpse of a tall figure in a long purple gown in the spare room. He wore a Russian-style fur cap. It wasn't Chiun after all!

There was no time to see more. The chauffeur was circling toward him, body crouched, gloved hands weaving cryptic designs in the air.

"Chiun!" Remo called. "Where are you?"

Remo's voice bounced off the walls. There was no answer.

And then the domino-masked chauffeur made his move.

It was a high leap, executed with a blood-chilling scream.

Remo knew the scream was a device to paralyze him. He laughed. In Sinanju, one attacked in professional silence, not like a banshee.

Remo aimed a fist at the descending crotch. Let the little guy do all the work, he thought.

But the wiry chauffeur reacted to the sudden fist. His

gloved hands grabbed a dangling ceiling light, arresting his plunge.

One foot slashed out at Remo's head. He parried it with his waiting fist and danced out of the way of a follow-up kick. The guy had incredible kicking skill. Not Sinanju, but powerful. It was as if his legs were driven by automatic pistons.

Remo looked for an opening. He got one ankle and simply yanked. The ceiling cracked. The light tore free like a molar coming out of a petrified gum.

Remo stepped back and let the man fall with the plaster debris. He taunted him with a laugh, which was a thousand times more unnerving than any high-pitched battle cry.

Off in one corner, the hissing voice said, "He is good."

Remo heard this in the moment the chauffeur took to untangle himself from the ceiling light. It made him pause. He should have taken the chauffeur out then and there, but he wanted to see who was at Chiun's trunks.

Remo turned to the sound of the voice, and in that half-turn, the black-masked chauffeur came at him, low and fast.

Remo backpedaled three steps to give himself kicking room. He miscalculated by a single step. He hit the wall with his back. He cursed.

A foot slashed up for his solar plexus. Remo braced for the impact by stiffening his abdominal muscles, simultaneously bringing his arms down protectively.

The foot never made contact. In midair, the chauffeur had turned like a spring-wound dervish and launched a pile-driver punch at Remo.

He brought his hands up and out, fending off the hammering fist. The chauffeur landed and sent an open-hand blow suddenly knifing for Remo's temple.

Remo moved to counter it.

In that moment, the other hand struck his abdomen once—hard and deep, fingers stiff. Remo felt the thrust clear back to his spinal column. The air blew out of his lungs and Remo doubled over, clutching himself, his face naked and defenseless.

In the split second before the grinning face of the masked chauffeur floated before Remo's going-gray vision and a black fist started to travel in his direction, Remo searched the room with his eyes. He caught an imperfect glimpse of a tall purple-silk-clad figure moving closer. For a moment, Remo thought it was the Master of Sinanju.

But he stood watching the tableau with absolutely no emotion on his sere-parchment countenance.

The blow knocked Remo's head back into the plaster wall. The top of his skull went in clear to his nose, and his body went lax, as if all the strength had gone from it.

Then slowly his head began to pull free of the hole, carried by the deadweight of his limp muscles, until he came loose. Remo made a clumsy pile of arms and legs on the bare floor.

The worst of it was that Remo was not unconscious. His eyes were closed, but he heard every sound in the room.

Most of all, he heard the arid voice of the purple figure as he left through the front door.

He was saying, "To think, Sagwa, all that training squandered on a barbarian *lofan*."

The chauffeur laughed grimly. The door shut after them.

Remo felt himself starting to lose consciousness. He fought it. Waves of darkness seemed to wash over his brain, but he reached into his inmost essence to hold on to consciousness.

It was a struggle. He wanted to surrender to the sweet peace that tried to claim him.

Remo refused. Deep within him, a fire began to burn and a voice from some inner reservoir intoned, "I am created Shiva, the Destroyer; Death, the shatterer of worlds."

For a moment Remo wavered between surrender and consciousness. His eyes burned with a smoldering light. The fire flickered. It was brief. His face warped into a mask of hellish agony.

Then he gathered himself together. He climbed to his feet. Every joint ached.

But when he stood erect, the burning-ember gleam in his eyes subsided, and he was Remo again.

He stumbled to the spare room. Shock was like a kick to his stomach when he saw that Chiun's steamer trunks were gone—all except an empty spare in need of repair. Remo plunged for the door, one arm across his bruised stomach.

Outside, he saw the limousine leave the curb like a silent black shark fleeing a coral reef.

Remo pelted for his Buick. He squeezed in behind the wheel, inserted the ignition key, and got the car started.

He roared after the limousine. It screeched around a corner. Remo slid into the turn right behind it. His maneuvering was ragged. He almost sideswiped a fireplug.

Coming out of the turn, he found himself on a long narrow street.

"You're good, pal," he said, gritty-voiced, "but not that good."

He floored the Buick, gaining on the limo's rear deck. On its jet-black bumper was a sticker: BRUCE LEE LIVES.

"You're dreaming, pal. When I get through with you, you're going to join him."

As Remo closed in, a silvery nozzle extruded from the limo trunk. Remo prepared himself for the expected jet of vapor. It squirted something dark and viscous instead.

Remo saw the spreading patch of oil splatter on the snow, and with a wrench of the wheel he sent the Buick up on the sidewalk.

His right-rear tire hit a patch of the gunk and he had to wrestle to keep the car straight. Every exertion made his stomach muscles cramp. He grimaced and fought to stay behind the wheel. His head began to pound.

The limo took a side street and then a street off that.

Remo did his best to keep up. The snow made it tough. Whereas before, he could use it to his advantage, literally skiing the car, now he was too badly injured to be the absolute master of every turn.

He slipped around corners, once swapping ends and finding his car suddenly pointing the opposite way in a drift.

Remo wrestled the wheel around and resumed the chase. This time he took it more slowly. The rattlesnake tracks were going to lead him, and he began to get a sense of where they were going.

They took a ramp onto Route 95, and Remo followed suit.

On the highway, he began to catch up. Remo stayed in the left lane to avoid any more oil slicks. Whoever had designed the car had built it to thwart pursuit.

The miles flashed by. Once the limo drifted into Remo's lane and he simply slithered out of the way into the right lane.

In response, the limo straddled both lanes, and suddenly greenish gas began streaming from its skin.

It looked like the engine had caught fire, except the vapor was green. Remo hastily shut every vent on the car. He took a deep breath and held it.

He hoped it was the same kind of gas as before. A nerve agent—especially the kind that worked through the pores— would kill him within seconds, he knew.

Remo held the road and his breath as the greenish streamers tore past his windshield.

A thin haze of green vapor seeped into the car. Remo ignored it. He felt no telltale skin tingling.

Eventually the gas gave out. When it was gone, Remo ran down every window and waited until the cold air had scoured the Buick's interior clean of gas before finally inhaling fresh air.

The limo picked up speed.

"Looks like you're out of tricks, pal," Remo said tightly.

Remo settled down for the ride. The overhead signs started to say "New Rochelle." Remo wasn't surprised.

The limo pulled onto an exit marked "Glenwood Lakes."

There the chase turned frenetic again. Once, Remo caught a glimpse of stern almond eyes in the narrow rear window. They regarded him without mercy or care.

On an angular turn, Remo lost control of his car, piling into a drift. He raced the rear wheels, and the car refused to budge.

Angrily Remo got out and simply lifted the car's rear tires onto better traction. His efforts transformed his face into a mask of pain-induced sweat.

He had lost sight of the limo. He decided that might be a good thing. It probably meant the driver thought he had lost Remo.

Remo took a side street. He recognized the neighborhood from the day before. With luck, he might beat the limo to the garage.

He hoped it was heading toward that same garage.

It was, Remo saw as he came up a parallel street. Through the breaks between the houses, he saw the limo slide around a corner on Storer Avenue. It had made better time than he had anticipated.

Remo pulled around the corner just as the limo nosed up

to the garage. The door began opening automatically, obviously activated by a radio command.

The limo lurched inside. The garage door began to accordion down like a Japanese bamboo curtain.

Remo parked, got out, and ran for the door.

Three steps told him that he wasn't in running shape. He slowed to a trot, his lungs burning with transmitted pain.

The garage door clicked shut. Remo grasped the handle, feeling the last vibrations of an electric motor.

The door wouldn't budge. Remo went around to the side.

That door was unlocked. He pushed it in.

Inside, he was confronted by the taunting sight of a white convertible sitting dusty and inert.

There was no sign of the black limousine.

Remo didn't waste time. He plunged out and hit the side door of the adjoining house like a cannonball on legs.

He found the house sparsely decorated, but in an unmistakable Asian decor. He ran through the house, ready for anything.

There was nothing. Every room was empty.

Remo made three circuits of the house before he finally gave up.

The garage was as he had left it. He checked for tracks. As before, faint wet smears of fresh rattlesnake tread stopped short of the convertible's rear bumper.

Remo stood looking at those tracks for a long time.

Then all life, all energy, seemed to drain from his hard face. Woodenly he stumbled back toward his own car.

He squeezed in behind the wheel and reached for the ignition key.

He lost it then.

His eyes rolled up in his head and his bruised face hit the steering column.

The horn gave out a long blast that startled the entire neighborhood, but Remo Williams didn't hear it.

He was dead to the world.

8

Remo Williams knew where he was before he even opened his eyes.

The smell gave it away. It was a combination of hospital disinfectant and Pinesol.

Folcroft Sanitarium, the cover for CURE.

A familiar lemon-lime after-shave was sour in Remo's nostrils.

"Hi, Smitty," he croaked.

"Remo, it's Smith," Harold Smith hissed.

"Would I say, 'Hi, Smitty,' if your name was Jones?" Remo retorted without humor.

Slowly he opened his eyes. The light hurt like needles.

"How long?" he asked the hovering face of Harold Smith.

"You were brought here four hours ago."

"Chiun?"

"I tried to notify him. He is not at your home. In fact, it has been vandalized."

"I know," Remo said. "I was one of the vandals."

"Remo, before the doctor returns, I must have your report."

Remo shut his eyes again. A kaleidoscope of images tumbled in his mind's eye—the vanishing limousine, the inexplicable footprints, and the tall man in the fur hat.

"I don't know where to start," he admitted.

"Where is Zhang Zingzong?" Smith demanded.

"With Chiun."

"And where is Chiun?"

"For all I know, he drove a big black limo straight into the Twilight Zone."

"I do not appreciate your humor at normal times," Smith lectured, "and especially not now."

"I'm not joking, Smith. I don't know where Chiun is. The

70

last I remember, I was getting into my car outside that weird garage."

"You were found on a residential street in New Rochelle."

"Yeah, there. I followed the limo. It went into the garage. But it wasn't there when I went in. That was the second time that little kung-fu acrobat pulled that trick on me."

"Who?"

"The chauffeur with the mask," Remo said.

"Are you delirious?"

"Check the garage if you don't believe me. The limo isn't there."

"You are not making any sense," Smith clucked. "I will come back when you are again yourself."

Remo opened his eyes. He reached out and took Smith by the wrist. He squeezed. Smith's face twisted with the pain.

"No time," Remo said tightly. "You gotta take me back there. I gotta find Chiun. I think he's left."

"Left CURE?" Smith said huskily.

"CURE. America, everything. I don't know yet. We had a fight, but I can't believe he'd throw everything we had away over a lousy fight. It must have something to do with that dingdong Chinese student."

"Zingzong," Smith said. "His name is Zhang Zingzong."

"Whatever. He and Chiun were fighting all last night. They made such a racket I checked into a motel. When I went back this morning, the limo was there, but most of Chiun's steamer trunks were gone. You know he never takes that many unless he's planning to go back to Sinanju. Then I got the stuffing kicked out of me by that kung-fu bozo."

"You, Remo?"

"Hate to admit it, but he was good."

"I will undertake a search for Chiun. Please let go of my wrist."

"I said," Remo added, squeezing so hard Smith's forehead broke out in a sweat, "there's no time. Screw your computers. Take me back to that garage. The limo went in there. It's gotta still be there, or it's not anywhere."

"Very well," Smith said stiffly. "The doctor thinks there is no internal organ damage. But are you up to walking?"

"Help me up."

Unhappily Smith allowed his shoulder to be used as support. Slowly he eased Remo up to a sitting position.

"Where are my clothes?" Remo asked, grimacing.

Smith handed him a pile of clothes and primly turned his back while Remo painfully slid into them.

"Lead the way," Remo said, getting to his feet with arthritic difficulty.

"Are you certain this is wise?" Smith asked doubtfully.

"Screw wise. We can't waste time."

Remo let Smith drive. He regretted it as soon as they pulled into traffic. Smith drove like a maiden aunt. He slowed down at every yellow light, stopping dead and looking both ways before proceeding through stop signs, and observed the speed limit as if his car would self-destruct if the indicator touched the fifty-six-mile-an-hour mark.

"Will you please pull over and let me drive?" Remo pleaded.

"No," Smith said firmly. "I do not wish to be ticketed."

Remo was sprawled in the back seat of the old car, trying to stay comfortable. It hurt to shout. So he stopped shouting.

Finally Smith called back.

"I believe it is this street," he said.

Remo sat up, looking around.

"Yeah," he said. "Dead ahead. The white garage by the Spanish-style house."

Smith brought his battered car to a crawling stop.

Smith got out and opened the door for Remo. Remo had to be helped out. He hated letting Smith help him, but saw no choice.

Remo walked to the garage door on his own.

"See the tracks?" Remo said, pointing.

Smith nodded, seeing the rattlsnakelike treadmarks in the snow. It looked like two rattlers had slept side by side.

"Okay, let's go around the side," Remo suggested.

"Is this safe?"

"Screw safe. You'll understand when we get inside."

Remo pushed in the door and waved Smith into the cool dim garage interior. The windows were grimy, cutting off outside light.

What little light there was fell on a tiled stone floor, and there was no sign of any car, black or white.

"You mentioned a black limousine," Smith pointed out.

Remo's expression was loose with doubt. "I meant a white convertible."

"Well, which is it?"

"You don't understand, Smitty," Remo said. "The black limo drives in here, the door closes, but by the time I get inside, it's turned into a white convertible. Kinda like Cinderella's pumpkin."

"I see no car."

Remo walked toward the garage door.

"There were tracks here. You can still see them. They were the limo tracks, not the convertible's. I compared the treads."

Smith said nothing. He looked at Remo through his rimless spectacles as if in pity.

"Don't look at me like that!" Remo shouted. "I swear it happened twice. The limo goes in and vanishes into thin air."

"I see no evidence of any such phenomenon," Smith complained.

"No shit," Remo said testily. "That must be why the dictionary lists 'disappears' as a synonym for 'vanishes.' "

Smith was looking at the floor. He knelt and felt the ground. His hands came away with a smear of oil.

With a disdainful expression he extracted a white handkerchief from one pocket and dry-wiped them clean.

"There must be a light somewhere," he said absently.

He found one and turned it on. Weak yellow light washed the garage interior. It came from a dangling bare bulb.

"That helps," Remo said sourly. "Now we can see the limo that isn't here better."

"Did you notice the floor pattern?" Smith asked severely.

"How could I?" Remo snapped back. "The convertible took up most of the interior."

"Look."

Remo looked. The floor was broken into rectangular sections. But certain crisscross lines were deeper than the others. They formed a long rectangle slightly larger than an automobile.

"Why didn't I figure this out before?" Remo said acidly. "It just slid through the cracks like an unemployed cockroach."

Smith looked at those grooves. "If what you claim is true," he told Remo, "and not hallucination—"

"It is. True, that is."

"Then there is a logical explanation for this," Smith added grimly. "And I intend to find it."

Smith began to move around the garage, looking at the walls and feeling under the workbench.

"What're you looking for?" Remo asked.

"A secret catch or button or some similar device," Smith said absently.

"You're joking. Didn't that stuff go out with dime novels?"

Smith said nothing. He found nothing, either.

"Maybe it's behind the tool rack," Remo said, pointing to a perforated pegboard on which tools were hung.

Smith joined Remo at the panel. They tried to lift it free of the wall but it wouldn't budge.

Smith began removing the tools and placing them on the floor. One refused to budge. A torque wrench.

"Here, let me help," Remo said, reaching for the torque wrench. It wouldn't budge for him either.

"How the hell is it attached?" Remo wondered, twisting at the ratchet. It made a clicking sound, but refused to lift free.

Then, from far below them, a great motor started to whine.

"Now what?" Remo blurted, stepping away from the open floor.

For the rectangular outline in concrete started to tilt upward. The far side dipped into the ground. The near lip lifted free. It was a section of the floor and it was revolving.

As they watched, the reverse side of the concrete slab presented itself like a shark rolling to the surface.

It brought with it the white convertible.

The hidden servomotor ceased its deep-throated whir. The convertible sat there mutely.

Steel claws extending from floor slots released its bumpers, front and rear, and retracted into the recesses below. Camouflaged panels snapped flush with the floor.

When the last clicking died, there were no seams showing, except the deeper outline of the slab itself.

"Incredible," Smith said huskily.

"I've seen something like this before," Remo muttered.

Smith turned doubtfully. "You have?"

"Yeah. But I just can't place it."

Smith looked at Remo with concern.

"The answer is obvious," he said. "The black limousine entered the garage and then the device was activated. The cars merely switched places, possibly with the passengers still inside."

"You make it sound so simple."

"It *is* simple," Smith returned. "Once you apply logical thinking to the matter."

"Yeah. Well, come on."

"Where are we going now?" Smith demanded.

"I have these really fascinating footprints to show you."

Smith followed Remo out of the mysterious garage, which was mysterious no longer.

9

Dr. Harold W. Smith could not explain the footprints in the snow of Remo Williams' front walk.

"Well, come on, Smith," Remo taunted. "You can do it. Just apply a little logic."

Smith absently wiped his glasses with a handkerchief. He lifted them to the pale winter sky and winced. The right lens was smeared with engine oil. He found a clean spot on the handkerchief and scoured it again.

Remo had led Smith into the house upon their arrival, taking care to approach by the lawn, not the walkway. The house was empty. There was no sign of Chiun or the Chinese defector. And with the exception of a single empty steamer trunk, all of the Master of Sinanju's belongings were gone. There was no note.

"Start from the beginning," Smith said thoughtfully.

"It's just like it was at the safe house, only here there are two sets of their tracks, both coming and going."

"Yes," Smith said slowly, drawing out the word.

"This is the chauffeur," Remo said, indicating the smaller prints. His breath clouded the cold air.

"You are certain?"

"Absolutely. I saw his heels close up. They were aiming for my face every two seconds."

"Perhaps we should erase those prints," Smith suggested.

"Why?"

"Occam's razor. Pare away the extraneous facts in order to see the problem more clearly."

Remo fetched a broom from the kitchen. He swept the chauffeur's footprints clean. He was feeling more limber. He was also preoccupied with this latest mystery and wanted to solve it more than he cared for the racking pain in his muscles.

"Now, these are Chiun's sandal prints," he said when he was done. "See? They leave, but don't return."

"Erase them."

That finished, Remo said, "I think these are the Chinese student's tracks."

"Are you sure?"

"He was wearing sneakers. These are the only sneaker tracks."

"Do it."

Remo scoured those prints away, careful not to obscure any remaining footprints.

"Now we have two sets of tracks left," he said confidently.

"The tall man in the fur hat," Smith offered.

"That's what I say. He goes in and he comes out, right?"

"Obviously."

"But look," Remo said, kneeling beside one set of prints. "These are stamped over the other set, so they were made last. Right?"

"Obviously."

"He was in the house when I arrived; therefore, he had to be the first one to go in—before me, before the chauffuer, but after Chiun and Zingzong left."

"I see what you are getting at," Smith said, his face tightening.

"The footprints going into the house were made after the ones going out."

"That's impossible," Smith snapped. "He had to enter the house before he could exit it."

"That's usually the way it works, yeah," Remo admitted.

"Perhaps there are prints in back, or he entered through a window."

"That's what I wondered back at the safe house, where he left only one set of prints, but no go."

"We cannot eliminate any possibility without verifying it ourselves."

"Let's go."

But there were no footprints in the rear of the house—unless bird tracks counted—and there were none near the back door, which was partially blocked by a steep drift.

They returned to the front of the house in dejected silence.

Standing over the confusion of footprints, they stared at them in a lengthening silence as the brittle wind blew snow off nearby roofs.

"You say there was only one set at the safe house?" Smith ventured.

"Yes," Remo said distantly, still looking down at the snow. "Going in. Not coming out. They had to belong to the tall guy in the fur hat. I saw him enter the limo."

"What did he look like?"

"I only caught a glimpse. He kept to the shadows. But I'm sure he was the guy in purple I caught rifling Chiun's trunk."

"How could there be only one set going in if he had come out?"

Remo gave Smith a frank look. "That's what I want you to explain."

"I cannot," Smith admitted. "In fact, I fail to understand how there would be only one set of his prints, no matter in which direction they ran."

"That part I can explain," Remo said. "He must have gone in before yesterday's snowstorm. They got covered up."

"But you claim the tracks going in were visible after the storm."

"During it, actually. It had to be the other set that was covered up."

"Which would have been the tracks leaving the car. But

you saw this man enter the limousine during the storm. What you describe, Remo, is a physical impossibility."

"So are these," Remo pointed out in a dull voice. "The freshest tracks lead into the house, but he's not in there."

They regarded the tracks in another pained silence.

"I cannot explain it," Smith said at last.

"Well, here's another one for you," Remo put in. "When I entered the house, I didn't sense him until he spoke. It was as if he had no heartbeat, no respiration, no physical presence. But I could see him."

"You are not claiming to have seen a ghost?" Smith wondered.

"I'm not claiming anything," Remo said quietly. "But you see the same tracks in the snow I do."

"I give up," Smith said. He started off to his car.

"Where are you going?" Remo asked, following.

"To Folcroft. Our only lead is Chiun."

"But he disappeared."

Smith turned. "Have you ever known the Master of Sinanju to go anywhere without creating a disturbance?"

"I've never known him to stay in one place and not create a disturbance," Remo said truthfully.

"Then we will find him," Smith said confidently.

Remo limped to the car and climbed into the back.

His ribs hurt as Smith pulled away from the curb. He ignored the pain. It was the worry in his heart, the sick hot pain of loss, that bothered him most.

10

The entrance to Folcroft Sanitarium was a wrought-iron gate set into stone posts. Each post was topped by a lion's head. The lions looked as forbidding as props from an old Frankenstein movie.

"Sit up," Smith called back.

Remo had been scrunched down in the back seat because the bumps hurt less than if he sat up.

"Why?"

"The guard," Smith said, slowing down as he approached the gate. "I don't want him to become suspicious."

"Screw him. You run Folcroft, not him."

"Please," Smith said edgily.

Groaning, Remo pulled himself up by the coat hook.

"Anyone ever tell you you're a pill, Smitty?"

"Don't call me that, Smitty."

"I've been calling you Smitty since day one," Remo reminded him.

"And I have been objecting since that day," Smith muttered, braking carefully. "Just don't let the guard hear you."

"Good morning, Dr. Smith," the guard said. He looked to Remo. "Nice afternoon, isn't it?"

"Peachy," Remo said bitterly.

"I have some paperwork to catch up on," Smith told the guard apologetically. "Unimportant paperwork," he added quickly.

"Then I won't keep you, sir," the guard said, tipping his cap.

"Smart move," Remo said as they slid into Smith's private parking slot. "You really stressed how suspicious this is."

Smith got out and opened the door for Remo.

"Will you need assistance?" he asked Remo.

"I'm ambulatory," Remo snapped back.

Remo stepped out, surprised at how much it hurt to walk. He let Smith close the door.

Together the two men walked into the Folcroft lobby.

A lobby guard took note of them and said nothing. They went to the elevator and up to Smith's second-floor office.

Leaving the elevator, Remo fell in behind Smith and noticed Smith walked with the suggestion of a limp in his right leg. Remo keyed his breathing down and brought up the creak of cartilage against bone that told him Smith's right knee was the problem.

"Have that knee checked lately, Smitty?" Remo asked as Smith unlocked his office and ushered him in.

"My semiannual physical is not for another seven weeks."

"Wasn't what I asked," Remo said.

Smith said nothing. He went directly to the oak desk and eased himself into the cracked leather executive chair.

Feeling under the worn desk edge, Smith hit a concealed stud. There came a click, and a concealed panel rolled back on the desktop.

The familiar computer terminal hummed up as if on command. A keyboard unfolded, offering itself to Smith's age-gnarled fingers. They set to work.

Remo tried sitting on the edge of the desk. It hurt, so he settled for standing. He watched from over Smith's shoulder.

"What are you doing, Smitty?" he asked, watching a series of texts flash on the screen. To Remo's eyes, the glowing letters were visible as clusters of bright green pixels. He had to step back to see them for what they were—words and sentences.

"I am doing a key search," Smith told him.

"Forget keys. Find Chiun."

"I am not literally searching for a key," Smith explained. "A key search is a global data search keyed off specific data parameters. I am inputting Chiun's physical description and certain behavior patterns unique to the Master of Sinanju."

"Don't forget his fourteen steamer trunks," Remo said.

"Thank you." Smith typed in "large steamer trunks" under the rubric PHYSICAL ATTRIBUTES.

When he was done, Smith tapped a control key.

The screen winked out and the terminal hummed. Lines of text flashed on the screen faster than the human eye could register them. Remo caught momentary sentences. "Asian drug suspect gunned down in Newark." "Bruce Lee and Elvis spotted in San Francisco airport." "Vietnamese boat survivor killed by drunk driver."

"The system is running through all news feeds," Smith explained, "seeking any Chiun-configuration pattern."

"What if he hasn't made the news?"

"The key search will run until he does," Smith said flatly.

"Then why are we waiting like we expect an instant answer?"

"Because we may get one."

The screen stopped flashing. The message SORT COMPLETE appeared. Under that was a blinking BUBBLE SEARCH Y/N?

"What's a bubble search?" Remo wanted to know, as Smith tapped the Y-for-yes key.

"A brute-force search. The key search has isolated over six hundred possible Chiun sightings."

"That many?" Remo said in surprise.

"I did say 'possible,' " Smith returned coolly. "I've assigned probability numbers to each sighting. The bubble search will cause the high-probability sightings to bubble to the surface and the low-probability ones to sink back into memory for later retrieval."

Remo watched. He saw no bubbles. Instead, there was a SEARCH COMPLETED message, and in numerical order, text digests of various sightings appeared.

They read them together.

Twenty minutes later, they reluctantly concluded that none of the high-probability sightings were of the missing Master of Sinanju.

"Where could they have gone?" Remo wondered.

"Anywhere. That is the problem."

"No, I mean where could he have gone that he didn't dismember a stubborn cabdriver, annoy a waitress, or nearly kill a bellboy for dropping one of those damn trunks of his?"

"I do not know," Smith admitted glumly.

"Then I guess we wait until he causes the inevitable ruckus," Remo said, folding his lean bare arms.

Smith returned to the key search.

"No time. I will attempt to locate Zhang or the masked chauffeur."

"Don't forget the tall guy in back."

"Description?" Smith asked, fingers poised to input.

"Oh, about six foot, maybe taller. He was bending to get in when I first saw him. Wore a long coat, and later, a purple silk gown."

"Knee- or ankle-length?"

"Lower," Remo said thoughtfully. "Almost like one of Chiun's kimonos. I don't remember seeing his feet."

"You mentioned a fur cap," Smith prompted as they keyed.

"Hat. One of those Russian-style things. What do they call them?"

Smith thought a moment. "Ah, astrakhan," he said, inputting the word. His fingers stopped in mid-word.

Remo leaned closer. "Yeah?"

"Odd. You've described a person very familiar to me, but I cannot recall who it is."

"He didn't look familiar to me. The chauffeur, yes. Zingzong, too, but only from the back—if that makes any sense."

"I am not surprised. No one in the West knows what Zhang looks like from the front, but he may have the most famous back in modern history."

"Care to clue in an intrigued assassin?" Remo wondered.

"One moment. Would you assume the tall man in the astrakhan hat was Asian?"

"I assume so, yeah, but I don't know that I can cite you any reason to think that. Come to think of it, he's pretty tall for an Asian, if he is one."

"Hair and eye color?"

"Got me. Didn't catch either."

Frowning, Smith completed the sparse description and initiated another key search.

"So who is he?" Remo asked as Smith leaned back, watching the search.

"We won't know until the search is completed," Smith said.

"I mean Zingzong."

"Zhang Zingzong is—or was—a student at the Beijing School of Iron and Steel."

"Sounds charming. I'll bet finals are pretty noisy."

"He escaped to the West only a few weeks ago, after months of being sheltered by Chinese citizens sympathetic to the pro-democracy forces over there."

"One of the student leaders?"

"No. In fact, his role in Tiananmen was insignificant. Do you recall, Remo, the Chinese man who stopped that line of T-55 tanks a few days after the massacre?"

Remo blinked. "Him! That was Zingzong?"

"Yes. He escaped China to Hong Kong and from there to the West."

"Are you sure? I mean, I hate to say this, but I wasn't impressed by the guy at all. He reminded me of a scared rabbit. How do you know it's the same guy?"

"Our intelligence resources within China identified him early on. We facilitated his escape from the mainland. He is very brave. It was a dangerous escape."

"I'll take your word for it," Remo said vaguely. "So why are we so interested in him?"

"He is a global symbol of Chinese resistance. One who, if the old-guard regime falls, may be in a position to be inserted into the leadership vacuum. We are keeping him safe until that time."

Remo grunted. "Great job you did."

"Word must have leaked. There were several attempts to abduct Zhang, which I find very odd."

"Not to me," Remo shot back. "Chinese leaders who would crush their own with tanks wouldn't exactly hesitate to kidnap a defector."

"That is the odd part. This has not their stamp on it. I would have expected an execution or assassination, not abduction. Ah."

Smith leaned forward, seeing the SEARCH ENDED message.

The subsequent bubble search assigned a number-one priority to an obituary for a Chinese restaurant owner.

"Dead end," Remo grunted.

"No, we have another avenue. The owner of the New Rochelle house. But that will have to wait until tomorrow."

"Why tomorrow?"

"Because the registrar of deeds for Westchester County is not open on Sunday," Smith said crisply.

"You don't have that stuff in your computer?" Remo asked in surprise.

"The Folcroft data banks are massive, but they do not contain data not accessible through computer hookups," Smith said with more than a trace of regret.

"This doesn't make sense," Remo said. "How did those guys know Zingzong was stashed in my house?"

"No doubt the same sources that betrayed the three previous safe houses. You have to understand, Remo, that the Chinese have the largest espionage apparatus in the world. Their eyes are everywhere. The FBI has been unable to trace their leak."

"You're giving up too soon."

"The key search is running. Something will turn up."

"Chiun can't cross the street without attracting attention."

Smith frowned. "I agree, but . . ."

"What is it?" Remo asked.

"That boat of his," Smith asked. "Where is it moored?"

"The junk?" Remo said. "I asked him about it once, and he said he'd gotten rid of it."

Smith's face fell. "Too bad."

"I didn't believe him, though."

Smith reached for a blue telephone.

"What are you doing?" Remo demanded.

"I am about to call every marina on the eastern seaboard, until I locate that junk. What is its name?"

"*Jonah Ark*. That was the name when we got it. Someone told Chiun it was bad luck to change a boat's name, so he kept it."

It took four calls until Smith found a lead.

"The *Jonah Ark*?" the Port Chester harbormaster asked him. "Yeah, sure. She set out this morning."

"Did the captain say where he was going?"

"No. But they couldn't go far. Had only a crew of two. One an old fella. Asian. That ship needs a six-man crew, minimum."

"Thank you," Smith said, hanging up. He returned to his computers, saying, "The ship left this morning. I'm ordering a satellite search."

"Through this cloud cover?" Remo said, nodding to the picture window behind Smith. The clouds were like a lead blanket hanging in the sky.

"No choice."

It took an hour for the transmission from the orbiting KH-11 recon satellites to travel from space to a relay point on the continental US and, by a circuitous route, to Harold Smith's computer screen. The results were not encouraging.

"Nice overhead shot of these clouds," Remo said bitterly. "Oh, look! There's a break. Is that Cuba?"

Smith said nothing. His lemony face was dour and disappointed.

Remo started to pace the floor, his face worried.

After a moment, keys began clicking. Remo came back to the desk. Smith sensed his unspoken question and answered it.

"I am alerting the Coast Guard, Air Force, and all law-enforcement agencies to watch for any sign of our quarry."

"How do you do that without it pointing back to you?"

"Through surrogates," Smith said simply, as if Remo had asked how Smith balanced his checkbook instead of for an explanation of how one man, unknown and possessing nothing more than a sophisticated computer system, could simultaneously set in motion the vast security resources of the United States simply by inputting clicking computer commands.

When Smith was through, he leaned back again.

"So we wait?" Remo asked.

"We wait."

"This is driving me crazy," Remo said in frustration. "Tell you what, I'm going to Chinatown."

"Why?"

"An unimpeachable authority once told me it was the thing to do in situations like this," Remo said.

11

The junk *Jonah Ark* was discovered becalmed off Key West three days later.

Word was flashed to Harold W. Smith at Folcroft Sanitarium that a Coast Guard vessel had located and boarded the junk, finding her deserted.

Dr. Smith reached for the telephone to inform Remo Williams. It was another in a long series of dead ends. The house in New Rochelle had been a rental. The owner, located in Denver, had explained he had rented it through an agent. The agent's address proved to be a mail drop.

More puzzling had been the owner's response to Smith's query about the strange garage with the revolving floor.

"What garage?" the owner had said.

Smith discovered a variance for the garage. The builder— Blue Bee Construction of Hong Kong—proved to be a blind.

As Smith waited for Remo to answer his phone, he reflected that a massive effort had been undertaken to trap Zhang Zingzong. It involved vast resources and support personnel. According to the FBI, known Chinese security operatives were not especially active. But who else could have managed all this?

Remo's voice came on the line. "Yeah?" He sounded tired.

"The Coast Guard found the junk," Smith reported.

Remo's voice brightened. "Great."

"Not great. It was abandoned. I think deliberately, to throw off pursuit."

"Us?"

"Anyone."

"Smith, we gotta find them," Remo said urgently. "I've been hanging around Chinatown so much I've got a monosodium-glutamate headache just from breathing the air."

"I have reason to believe we shall have a lead within a day, perhaps sooner."

"How?"

"I'll keep you posted," Smith said, hanging up.

He returned to his terminal, his lemony face unhappy.

Harold Smith could not very well tell Remo Williams that even as they hunted desperately for clues to Chiun's whereabouts, down in Virginia, National Security Agency linguists were painstakingly translating an audio recording of an argument between the Master of Sinanju and Zhang Zingzong, which had been picked up by a microphone concealed in Remo's television set.

The bug had been planted by Harold Smith to monitor the unpredictable Remo and Chiun. It was the latest in a string of such eavesdropping devices. Most had been found by Chiun. This one had managed to escape his notice.

Smith called up the still-running key search.

There were no concrete Chiun sightings anywhere in his news-gathering outreach area. Smith was surprised by two new Bruce Lee sightings, one in Honolulu and the other in Hong Kong. He had noticed quite a few of them over the last several days. Almost as many as Elvis sightings.

Smith dismissed the reports. He wished that it were feasible to put out a global watch for Zhang Zingzong, but to do so would alert the Chinese government that Zhang was abroad. Smith dared not assume Beijing was not already aware of this. And to put out the watch notice would jeopardize the defector, wherever he was.

He consoled himself with the knowledge that if Zhang

were in Chiun's company, he was safer than if he were in the brig of a US submarine lurking under a polar icecap.

A *bapping* red light ignited a control key.

Smith stabbed it. The NSA emblem came up. It was a Code Gray—the code for Smith's translation request. The NSA linguists never realized they were not responding to an emergency Defense Department interagency request.

Smith hit the scroll key. Text began to unfold.

It was a very raw transcript. The translation team had been stymied by Chiun's Korean pronunciation of Mandarin Chinese words. Chiun had evidently been speaking in the rapid, squeaky tone he used when excited. There were numerous bracketed notations denoting untranslatable passages.

One unmistakable fact emerged from the wreckage of the translation.

The Master of Sinanju had departed for Beijing, China, in the middle of the night, long before Remo's encounter with the mysterious occupants of the black limousine. The hectoring Chiun subjected the hapless Chinese student to as he was forced to carry Chiun's steamer trunks to a waiting string of taxis went on for twenty minutes. The last sounds on the tape were the click of the light switch and the closing of the door.

There had been other aspects of the tape that came through, but they offered Smith no more of a clue as to the Master of Sinanju's motivations than that final click. A bargain had been struck between Chiun and Zhang. And a certain name had been repeated several times.

Smith put in a call to Remo.

"What have you got?" Remo demanded, his voice tense.

"A note in a bottle," Smith told him.

"Where?"

"I do not have physical possession," Smith said evasively. "It was discovered washed up in the Gulf of Mexico. It said, 'Please help me. He is taking me back to Beijing. I do not want to return to China.' "

"Zingzong?"

"Yes. Are you up to going to Beijing?"

"Wait a minute," Remo said sharply. "How do you know this isn't a wild-goose chase to throw us off?"

"You said Chiun and Zhang argued before they disappeared."

"Yeah, but—"

"Do you happen to recall a certain name repeatedly mentioned?"

"It was all Chinese," Remo pointed out. "I wouldn't know a name from a dame."

"Did you hear the name Temujin?"

"Yeah," Remo admitted. "Several times. I thought it was some Chinese swearword Chiun was using on the other guy."

"The Chinese seldom curse," Smith said. "It is a Khalkha Mongol word meaning 'ironworker.' It is the given name of Genghis Khan. Have you ever heard Chiun mention him?"

"You mean sweet Genghis?"

"Sweet?"

"He gave the House of Sinanju a lot of work in the old days." Remo's voice darkened. "How did you know Chiun mentioned him?"

"We'll discuss this later," Smith said quickly. "We must find Chiun and recover Zhang. You are going to Beijing."

"Okay," Remo said. "I'm going to Beijing. Last time I was there, they were calling it Peking."

"And the last time I was in the Chinese capital," Smith said, working his computer keyboard, "it was known as Peiping."

"I have the feeling I'm not going to like it, whatever they call it," Remo growled.

"I'll make the arrangements. But there is something you must appreciate, Remo."

"What's that?"

"We are in a strained state of relations with the People's Republic. The current President has placed a high price on maintaining those relations."

"Maybe too high," Remo growled.

"Not our responsibility," Smith returned. "The Chinese government has known since your last visit there that the Master of Sinanju works for America and that he has an American pupil."

"So what?"

"So this. While you are in China, you must avoid any

incident in which you betray your Sinanju training. It could lead to an international incident."

"Too bad no one clued Chiun in on that."

"I cannot do anything about Chiun," Smith said, brittle-voiced. "If and when you find the Master of Sinanju, get him out of the country as quietly and circumspectly as humanly possible."

Remo's snort of derision was like a burst of static over the phone line. "It would be easier to overthrow the Old Guard in Pek . . . I mean Beijing," he said.

"Please, Remo."

Remo sighed. "Just tell me where to go," he muttered.

"By the time you reach Hong Kong, I will have your travel documents processed. Check in at the Beijing Hotel. You will be contacted by an operative friendly to the West. The code name is Ivory Fang."

"Sounds like a regular welcome wagon. What's his Chinese name?"

"I do not know. Ivory Fang will be expecting you."

"All right, I'm on my way."

The phone went dead. Smith returned to the computer. He returned the NSA transcript to memory and input the name Temujin.

Perhaps if he refreshed his knowledge of the reign of Genghis Khan, this would begin to make sense.

He wished he had not been forced to tell Remo that falsehood about a note in a bottle. A more plausible story would have allowed him to bring up that other name the translation had repeatedly mentioned, Wu Ming Shi.

According to the translators, Wu Ming Shi was Mandarin for "nameless." Yet it seemed to appear in the context as a name.

A Military Airlift Command C-130 ferried Remo to San Francisco. There he transferred to a civilian flight to Hong Kong.

There was some problem at the Hong Kong offices of LUXINGSHE, the Chinese International Travel Service. Remo had to resist the urge to turn the blank-faced main-land Chinese officials on their heads and kick-step on their clucking tongues. But he remembered Smith's admonishment not to betray his Sinanju affiliation to anyone, including his pro-Western contact.

So Remo waited patiently for the customs agent to affix the all-important red stamp to his false visa, which was in the name of Remo Loggia. Under "Object of Journey to China," Remo had written, "To get out as fast as possible."

His humor was not appreciated.

Finally he was allowed to board the CAAC flight, finding the seats too narrow for even his lean-by-Western-standards build.

The 727 lifted off, flying so close to a Hong Kong high-rise that Remo could see into the top-floor windows. He caught a brief glimpse of a *Wiseguy* episode, thinking that it would probably be the last sight of American culture he would see for a long time.

Perhaps a very long time. China was a big place. And the Master of Sinanju was an expert at not being found.

12

The ticket agent insisted in a bored, impassive voice that there were no soft-seat tickets left.

"I insist upon soft-seat tickets," said the Master of Sinanju in a low voice.

The Chinese ticket agent was contrite.

"The train is nearly full," he said in polite Mandarin. "Foreign tourists have all soft-seat tickets."

"I am a foreign tourist," Chiun retorted haughtily. "I am a Korean."

The ticket agent shrugged, as if to say that while Koreans might possibly be deemed foreign, they are not otherwise significant.

The Master of Sinanju whirled on the student, Zhang Zingzong.

Zhang was standing apart, his eyes worried and glancing often toward the green-uniformed People's Armed Police officers who moved through the human swarms circulating through Beijing's Xizhimen train station. His pockets were stuffed with cigarette packs purchased at a local concession.

"You!" Chiun hissed. "Speak to this stubborn man."

Zhang pretended not to hear Chiun's rising voice while he lit a Blue Swallow cigarette. Waiting passengers in the crowded station were staring at the Master of Sinanju's colorful purple-and-red kimono.

A man had fallen asleep on his luggage. People were stepping over him as if it were a common thing to find a man asleep on the floor, which in congested Beijing, it was. He woke up to the sound of Chiun's voice, snuffled sleepily, and turned over.

Zhang Zingzong kept his face averted. Perhaps the police would not notice him. He feared being recognized more than he feared the Master of Sinanju's wrath. But only by a small margin.

"If you do not assist me, Zhang, I will shout your name to the very heavens," Chiun warned.

Zhang's eyes went wide. He reached out for the Master of Sinanju's brilliant robes. It was like grasping fire that did not burn. The silk retreated from at the approach of his fingers, as if sensing them.

"Please do not do that," Zhang begged. "I will do as you say."

"Who is this man?" the ticket agent asked suddenly.

Over Zhang's protests, the Master of Sinanju whispered into the agent's bent receptive ear.

The ticket agent looked to Zhang sharply. His eyes flew open.

"You!" he hissed. "You tank man!"

"The very same," Chiun said firmly.

"No!" Zhang said. "Not me. Not me!"

"He is very modest," Chiun confided to the ticket agent in the manner of one old friend speaking to another.

"Can you prove this?" the ticket agent said to Chiun.

The Master of Sinanju responded by spinning Zhang Zingzong around, presenting his trembling back to the ticket agent.

That satisfied the ticket agent. He said, "Ahhh," and with great ceremony produced two soft-seat tickets.

"These being held for foreign diplomats," he explained, low-voiced. "They can ride hard seats. Go, now."

To Zhang Zingzong's astonishment, he was whisked to the waiting train.

They found their seats, which were soft and for a crowded Chinese excursion train, relatively comfortable. In contrast to the rest of the train, their car was occupied by Western tourists and a few local cadres in gray Mao suits.

Presently the train began huffing out of the station. It was a steam engine, painted black with red piping. It cleared the station and picked up speed, heading northwest to the town of Badaling.

Chiun sat by the window. He watched the communes and market towns flash by. The clicking of the train wheels over the rail links became monotonous.

Beside him, Zhang Zingzong said nothing, which pleased the Master of Sinanju. He did not enjoy Zhang's company, but he dared not let him out of his sight. The Chinese man had already tried to escape twice. Once by leaping from the junk in the Gulf of Mexico, and again in Cuba, from which they were able to obtain a direct flight to Beijing.

Chiun looked over to the Chinese. He had placed his knapsack on the seat divider between them and laid his head on it. He was already asleep.

Chiun sniffed in disgust at the foul cigarette smell on his breath, but at least it kept the man's face turned away from the ever-passing PLA soldiers who went up and down the aisles, examining the train passengers with hard unflinching eyes. Not even the tourists were spared their basilisk glares.

A frumpy European woman looked over the back of her seat and caught Chiun's eye.

"*Dui-bu-qi, waigong,*" she began, reading from a Chinese phrasebook. "What town are we passing?"

"Why ask me?" Chiun replied stiffly. "I am no Chinese tour guide. And I am *not* your grandfather."

The woman blinked. "You speak English?"

"Obviously," Chiun said, turning his face to the rock quarries outside the sooty windows.

The woman persisted.

"Isn't China amazing? There are so many people!"

"The same is said of rabbits," Chiun muttered.

Zhang Zingzong stirred. His shaggy head brushed the

Master of Sinanju's kimono. With a look of distaste on his parchment countenance, Chiun pushed him away.

Zhang twisted about, his head ending up on the outside seat rest.

The Master of Sinanju was so relieved not to be subjected to the Chinese man's nicotine breath that he thought no more of it until a PLA soldier, swaggering down the aisle, stopped at their seats. He loomed over the unsuspecting Zhang.

The PLA soldier turned his butterball face this way and that, trying to discern Zhang's face clearly.

The Master of Sinanju pretended not to notice, but the reflection of the soldier in his window held his cold hazel eyes.

"You!" the soldier grunted at Chiun. "You know this man?"

"*Bu*," Chiun said flatly, and returned to his window.

The soldier looked at Zhang again, his face tightening in concentration. Then, removing a rubber truncheon from his belt, he smacked Zhang Zingzong over the head without preamble or warning.

"Dog's eyes!" he shouted in Mandarin. "I know your face!"

Zhang recoiled in his seat, his eyes blinking.

"I am only a worker," Zhang protested meekly.

"Show identification!"

Zhang hung his head. "I have none," he admitted. "It was stolen."

The truncheon went under Zhang's chin, forcing his face up to the light. "Liar!" the PLA soldier hissed.

Zhang said nothing. His hand groped for his knapsack, wedged between the seat divider and his side.

The Master of Sinanju surreptitiously stabbed the hand with a single sharp fingernail. Zhang winced and his hand withdrew.

The PLA soldier saw none of this. He took Zhang by the shoulder and pulled him to his feet.

"You will come with me, man without identity."

The commotion attracted a great deal of attention in the tourist-class car. There were a few muttered protests.

"How can they do that?" a middle-aged man said to his wife. "Just take a person away like that?"

"What I don't understand is, why doesn't he stand up for his rights?" the wife returned.

"Someone should do something," another person added.

Everyone agreed that the man's rights were being trampled upon and someone should do something.

But no one did. The train rolled on.

While the passengers' attention was on the poor figure of Zhang Zingzong, the Master of Sinanju took up the abandoned knapsack and placed it under his seat.

Then he floated out of his seat and up the aisle, after the PLA soldier.

Two cars forward, he came to the hard-seat section, crowded with Chinese passengers. The seats were narrower and without cushions. People sat on one another's laps and on luggage in the aisle, eating from cardboard food containers and drinking warm tea from plaid-design vacuum bottles.

They scrunched out of the way as the PLA soldier marched the silent and teary-eyed Zhang Zingzong toward the engine car.

The Master of Sinanju negotiated the aisle with silent deftness. Few saw him approach, for their eyes were on the unfortunate captive. Chiun breezed past them like a ghost in fiery raiment.

After he had passed, no one could help but notice him, however. For his costume was alien even to China.

Behind the engine was a car dominated by a curtained booth where a khaki-uniformed woman sat behind a microphone and tape-deck system, broadcasting a mix of native folk songs and foreign music to the hard-seat section of the train.

A knot of soldiers was loitering by the booth, laughing and joking with the woman.

Zhang Zingzong was ushered into the official car and slammed down on a rude wooden bench.

He sat there, head downcast, hands folded between his knees, submissive under the hard, accusing glare of his captors.

The other soldiers gathered around. Angrily they began hectoring Zhang Zingzong in high, truculent voices.

Then the Master of Sinanju appeared in the rattling car. One soldier noticed him only because he turned away to light a cigarette. His eyes narrowed at the sight of the aged Korean.

Face placid, the Master of Sinanju beckoned to the soldier.

The soldier hesitated briefly. He pocketed his unlit cigarette and strode up to the Master of Sinanju.

"What you do here, old tortoise?" he demanded.

"Please," Chiun said in flowery Mandarin, "do not shout at this unworthy one, for my ears are very old and sensitive. I have something of importance to impart to you concerning that murderer." Chiun indicated Zhang with a fluttery fingernail.

"He is a murderer?"

"There is a body in the car behind us," Chiun hissed.

"Show me!" the soldier said, tight-voiced.

The Master of Sinanju swirled his skirts turning around. He floated down the aisle, the soldier stepping on feet and knocking over luggage as he stumbled after him.

Chiun stopped before a luggage alcove.

"In here," he said, drawing the curtain aside.

The soldier looked in, holding on to the edge of the alcove as the train rattled along.

"I see no body," the soldier said.

A shiny knuckle connected with the base of the soldier's skull. He collapsed without a sound.

The Master of Sinanju folded the soldier's legs so that they did not stick out. He let the curtain fall.

Then, his face innocent, he padded back to the official car.

There, they were still haranguing Zhang Zingzong.

The Master of Sinanju selected a soldier and tugged on his green sleeve. The soldier bent down and accepted the Master of Sinanju's breathily urgent words whispered in his ear.

He followed him back to look at the body promised to be there. It was the last sight he beheld before his brain died.

He had short legs. Chiun hooked the PLA-issue boots to restraining straps, so they stayed out of sight.

At first, the next soldier did not believe that there were two bodies in the next car. He turned to his comrades and repeated the old Korean's claim.

"This old one says there are dead passengers in the next car."

The soldiers gathered around the Master of Sinanju.

"How could this be?" one said skeptically. "Someone would have complained before this."

"I am sorry," said the Master of Sinanju, spreading his vermilion-and-lavender kimono sleeves. "Did you think I said the next car? I meant the last car. My Mandarin is poor."

"The last car is empty, but for luggage," he was told.

"There are two bodies there."

"I do not believe you."

"PLA bodies," Chiun added blandly.

That did it.

After a hasty exchange of words, they decided to follow the old Asian to the last car. One man—the one who had arrested Zhang in the first place—agreed to stay with the prisoner. He was not happy about it. He wanted to see the bodies too.

The Master of Sinanju allowed the PLA soldiers to go ahead of him. They stampeded through the rattling, swaying cars like a caterpillar of many unsmiling heads.

The train began rounding a sharp turn, forcing the chain of stumbling soldiers to grab at seat backs and overhead racks.

Eventually they made it to the rear car, carefully negotiating the bumping steel platforms which joined the caboose to the rest of the train.

The soldiers burst in. Seeing nothing in the gloomy caboose, they proceeded to toss luggage around and upend packages, looking for the bodies.

One turned an angry face in the direction of the Master of Sinanju, who stood serene on the bouncing platform between the cars.

"Where are the bodies!" he demanded.

"I am looking at them," intoned the Master of Sinanju. And he stamped his foot once. The coupling below cracked with a clank, separating the caboose from the train.

The soldiers were abruptly thrown off their feet as the last car lost momentum and slowed.

Then the caboose rolled backward. It gathered speed until it hit the sharp turn the train had just negotiated.

It jumped the rails and turned over twice, throwing off bits of iron and wood and luggage. And broken green bodies.

Pleased, the Master of Sinanju began to work his way back to the front of the train, where the final soldier's body lay, ripe for the harvesting.

13

The moment Remo Williams stepped off the jetway ramp and into the congested Beijing airport, it all came back to him.

A sea of Chinese faces swam before him like biscuits with eyes and mouths. It wasn't, as the old expression went, that they all looked alike. It was that the Chinese people, used to centuries of obedience, presented similar inoffensive masks to the world, their expressions uniformly bland.

Styles of dress were looser than the last time Remo had been to Beijing. The ubiquitous Mao jacket was obviously passé. Remo spotted only six upon arrival—all on older men. And the women wore dresses, not baggy khaki pants. Remo was surprised how Western they looked.

Remo eased into the crowd. People gave way, smiling the identical smile of the East. One that was brought up like a shield in the face of trouble as well as pleasure.

Remo towered over the Chinese throng, even the ever-present baby-faced soldiers. Eyes followed him curiously. He moved past the ticket counters, searching for an exit sign.

Every sign was in Chinese. He frowned. He couldn't read Chinese.

Remo stopped, uncertain what to do. Between the lack of visual clues of the faces surrounding him and the alien calligraphy of the language, it was like being on another planet.

Even in countries where Remo couldn't read the language, there were clues. A Spanish word similar to an English one. A half-remembered French phrase. Here, Remo couldn't even connect with the letters.

While he was puzzling out what to do next, a slim Chinese woman in a blue brocade jacket and slacks came up to him and bowed with her head.

"Fang Yu," she said in a breathy voice.

"Uh, you're welcome," Remo returned. "Speakee English?"

The Chinese woman straightened, smiling broadly. It made her eyes light up like those of a child.

"Fang Yu is my name, and I speak excellent English—or so I am told by other American tourists I have encountered."

"Great," said Remo in genuine relief. "I need to get to the Beijing Hotel."

"I will be happy to escort you," said Fang Yu.

"That's kind of you," Remo said. "But if you'll just dump me into a taxi, I'll manage from there."

"Not at all, Mr. Loggia."

Remo blinked. She knew his cover identity.

"Okay, let's go," he said suddenly.

They found a modern moving walkway and stepped aboard. Remo looked Fang Yu over. She was short, small-boned, and delicate without seeming fragile. She wore her glossy black hair in a modern shag cut. Her makeup was tasteful and yet alluring, her small lips very red.

She wore round tortoiseshell eyeglasses. They made her resemble a delectable almond-eyed owl.

"You said your name is Fang Yu," Remo said casually.

"Do you like it?" she asked, giving him a shy smile.

"Not bad. Yu. Would that by an chance mean 'ivory'?"

"No," she answered without skipping a beat. "It means 'jade'. It is my personal name. My family name is Fang. In my country, unlike yours, we place our last names—what you call surnames—first."

"Oh," Remo said. His sudden change of expression alarmed Fang Yu.

"Is there something wrong?" she asked, touching his bare arm suddenly.

"No," Remo said quickly. "Do people call you Yu?"

Her returning smile was eager. "You may call me Yu if that will please you."

"I'll bet you hear a lot of 'Hey, Yu' jokes."

"A few."

They stepped off at the end of the moving walkway and Remo saw his first English—a multilingual sign in which CUSTOMS was the third word from the bottom.

"I will take you to your luggage," Fang Yu said.

"Didn't bring any," Remo told her.

It was Fang Yu's turn to look perturbed.

"No luggage?"

"Hate the stuff."

Fang Yu stared at Remo curiously. Then she shrugged and together they went down the corridor to Customs.

"Wait here," she told Remo. She went to a counter and filled out a form in Chinese. She returned and handed it to Remo.

"Present this with your visa and passport to the man in the last station," she told him. "I will meet you on the other side."

Remo went to the last station. The customs inspector had the sleepy eyes of a melting Buddha. He looked at Remo for a long time after examining his documents. He stamped Remo's passport with such sudden violence that Remo had to suppress his Sinanju reflexes. He almost neutralized the man.

Joining Fang Yu, Remo asked, "What did you write on that form?"

"That the stupid Hong Kong airline people lost your luggage and you were very upset."

"Oh."

Outside, the Beijing air was snappy and cold, the sky gray. Coal smoke and diesel exhaust mixed in an unappealing bouquet. Snow clotted the ground in dirty gray patches that had been pounded into submission by uncountable Chinese feet.

A cab whisked them into Beijing traffic, which consisted of trucks, pedicabs, the rare automobile, and moving flocks of the stripped-down Flying Pigeon bicycles which were as common on Chinese streets as the Volkswagen Beetle used to be in America.

Fang Yu was issuing sharp directions to the driver. Her Chinese was quick and guttural, not at all like her breathy, polished English.

As they moved through a rickety residential neighborhood, Remo could smell cabbage, although the cab windows were closed. The scent brought back half-buried memories of Remo's last visit, when he and Chiun had recovered the Sword of Sinanju from a Chinese museum.

Remo pushed all thought of the Master of Sinanju from his mind. A truck trundled by, its flatbed overflowing with piled cabbage.

Cabbage lay stacked in the tiny alleyways. Apartment-house balconies had become cabbage sheds. Bicycles flew by, cloth sacks heavy with hard spherical burdens hanging off handlebars.

"Cabbage must be on sale this week," Remo remarked.

"It is winter," Fang Yu remarked quietly. "In winter, we eat cabbage for breakfast and dinner."

"Rice for lunch?"

She shook her glossy hair. "Cabbage."

"Chinese people must love the stuff."

"No one loves cabbage," Fang Yu answered. "It is for winter eating, not for pleasure. It is December now. By February the price of cabbage will be five times what it is now, three times what it was in October. Only the foolish buy winter cabbage in winter." She shrugged. "But there are many poor fools in China these days."

Eventually they reached the Beijing Hotel. Remo waited with folded arms while Fang Yu haggled with the front desk. Many strange glances were cast in his direction. Since he wasn't the only American in the lobby—the Beijing was popular with Western tourists—Remo waited until they were in the ascending elevator before asking Fang Yu a question.

"What was the problem?"

"No luggage," Fang Yu said aridly. "It is very suspicious. You may be reported to the local cadre. Please inform your superiors that the next time they send an agent, he must bring luggage—even if it is filled only with towels."

"Wait a minute. Are you Ivory Fang?"

Fang Yu said nothing. She led Remo to a simple white-painted hotel-room door and opened it with her key. They entered.

It was not much different from a Western hotel. The decor was subdued. The rug was peach, the bedspread yellow.

"I asked you a question," Remo said as Fang Yu pulled the draperies open. She pushed aside the sliding glass door and stepped out onto a balcony. Remo joined her out in the cold.

Down below, the vast expanse of Tiananmen Square lay open to their eyes. The square was only sparsely populated. Most of the walking figures looked like tiny Gumbys. PLA soldiers.

"Yes, I am," Fang Yu said quietly.

Remo started to speak. Fang Yu silenced him with a slim finger on his lips. Her scent was in his nostrils suddenly. It was very, very faint. Possibly even a natural scent. Remo liked it. She smelled of dying roses.

"What are you looking at?" Remo wondered.

"I have never seen it from such a vantage point," Fang Yu said in a dreamy voice.

"The Kentucky Fried Chicken fits in real well," Remo remarked dryly.

When there was no reply, Remo said, "Were you there? When it happened?"

Fang Yu looked down at the square, saying nothing for a long time. Presently she whispered a low question.

"Do you know the sound a human head makes when it is crushed under the treads of a tank?"

"No," Remo said truthfully.

"Pong," Fang Yu said distantly. "Pong. A hollow kind of sound—as hollow as the souls of those who drive the tanks and the butchers who give the orders." She spat out the word "butchers" with sibilant vehemence. She turned suddenly.

"We have to assume this room is bugged. We will speak of important matters later. Where do you wish to go?"

"I don't know yet. I have to find a man. A Korean."

Fang Yu's eyebrows lifted like commas.

"He's on his way to Beijing, if he's not already here," Remo continued. "He may be with a Chinese, a young man."

"How will we know these two?"

"The Korean is over eighty, and he will wear a kimono. Probably of silk, and travel with several steamer trunks. Where he goes, he will cause great commotion. He's very excitable. His voice squeals."

A notch appeared between Fang Yu's slim eyebrows. "You make this Korean sound like Old Duck Tang."

"Who's that?"

"You know him as Donald the Duck."

"I think you've zeroed in on his personality," Remo said dryly. "Exactly."

"I will look into this," she murmured at last. "You will wait here. Are you hungry?"

"I will be."

The notch disappeared. "Then I will take you to a most excellent Chinese restaurant," she said, smiling again. "You will savor it very much. The food is what you Americans would call scrumptious."

Remo closed the sliding door after her, shutting off the clattery hum of Beijing traffic. He hadn't even noticed the sound until it was gone.

"I will return at eight," Fang Yu called over her shoulder.

"I'll be here," Remo said. He watched Fang Yu slip out the door, enjoying the undulant sway of her slim hips.

Suddenly, locating the Master of Sinanju didn't seem as urgent as it had been.

14

There was a great commotion at the Badaling train station when the excursion train from Beijing pulled in, minus its red caboose.

In the soft-seat cars, the commotion manifested itself as a repeated forlorn cry.

"What about my luggage?"

"We search for passenger luggage," the unhappy Head of the Train said in his stilted English. He looked worried.

The Master of Sinanju arose from his nap and hectored Zhang Zingzong to take down his lacquered trunk from the overhead rack.

Zhang struggled with the heavy trunk, but in his heart he was grateful. There had been fourteen such trunks when they set forth. The others had remained in Havana, to be called for when they reached their unknowable ultimate destination.

Zhang Zingzong had no idea what their ultimate destination was, but he knew that what he carried in the teak box in his knapsack whispered of a thousand footsteps to come.

The Master of Sinanju following like a silken votary, Zhang carried the trunk out to the platform. He signaled for a rickshaw and loaded the trunk aboard. It filled the entire rickshaw seat.

"No room for us," he told the Master of Sinanju.

Chiun lifted a spidery hand. Another rickshaw rattled up, pulled by a heavily bundled man who might have been a young fifty or an old thirty. Beijing winters took a lot out of the men.

Chiun gathered up his skirts and settled into the open seat. Zhang started to climb in. The Master of Sinanju stopped him with a warning nail to his sunken chest.

"You will stay with my trunk," he said firmly, "and see that it is not stolen."

"We have few thieves in China," he protested indignantly. "Thieves are beheaded here."

The Master of Sinanju looked around him haughtily. "I see many heads," he said, "but I also see many thieves."

"No thieves," Zhang repeated.

"All Chinese are thieves," said the Master of Sinanju, staring straight ahead, his cold hazel eyes unwavering.

Zhang climbed onto the steamer trunk, wincing at Chiun's sharp admonishment not to scuff the lacquer.

"*Wo-men yao qu Wan-Li-Chang-Cheng,*" he spat at the driver.

The rickshaws started up through the cabbage stink of the city street, leaving the excursion train behind. PLA soldiers swarmed over it like green mites over the corpse of a fire-blackened centipede.

They were passed by lines of tour buses on the way to the Great Wall of China.

The hilly terrain all around them resembled a bleak snowswept lunar landscape. Here and there sections of apparently flexible stone battlements undulated into view.

The eyes of the Master of Sinanju grew bright as he
recognized sinuous sections of the Great Wall of China.

"Faster!" he called to his driver.

The lazy Chinese drivers, of course, did not move faster,
he noted. If anything, the obdurate ones slowed their lacka-
daisical pace.

The Master of Sinanju arranged his kimono skirts impatiently. Soon, he thought, soon.

The rickshaw pulled up to the tourist parking area in the
lee of the Great Wall.

It towered twenty feet high, and was broad enough for
horsemen to ride its stone-paved road—for the wall was as
much an elevated road as it was a barrier—five horses
abreast.

It dwarfed the people milling under it, as well as the many
tourist buses.

The Master of Sinanju stood up in the rickshaw, his hands
grasping the opposite wrists in the concealment of his joined
kimono sleeves, and surveyed the Great Wall's lines.

This was the section that was open to tourists. The inner
wall was despoiled by a modern brick parapet and handrail.
Chiun wrinkled his nose. Was this what the Chinese had
come to? Offering up their mightiest monument for the
edification of big-nosed foreigners? Were US dollars so
bright that they would allow even their supposed enemies to
walk along its dragonlike spine?

Chiun cast his eyes east, where the wall had been dese-
crated by vandals. It lay in ruins. To the west, the wall was a
vanishing small thing coiling through the Yanshan Mountains.

"Come," said the Master of Sinanju.

Zhang Zingzong dropped from his perch. Without waiting
for word, he heaved the big trunk off the rickshaw seat and
set it on the cold stone ground.

The Master of Sinanju bestowed a single dollar bill upon
the eager Chinese drivers. He was astonished that they
accepted the paper money without first holding out for gold.

Even their avariciousness had fallen on evil times.

"What will we do with this?" Zhang demanded, pointing
to the trunk. The rickshaws were being turned around, their
drivers seeking new customers.

The Master of Sinanju looked around.

"It will be safe on top of that bus." He was pointing to an empty tourist bus with an overhead wire luggage rack.

Zhang Zingzong laboriously carried the trunk over to the bus and clambered atop. He knew from recent experience what the Master of Sinanju would do next.

No sooner had he gotten to the top and leaned over than the old Korean reached down and took up the trunk by one brass handle. He jerked upward. Under this slight manipulation, the trunk seemed to become weightless. It rose floatingly, and Zhang had to scramble to grab the brass handle that was suddenly before his nose.

He wrestled the trunk onto the luggage rack and then clambered back to Chiun's side.

"What happen if bus goes away before we return?" he asked, looking around in case PLA soldiers had seen them.

The Master of Sinanju said nothing. He went to a rear tire and one sandal swept out. The tire expelled air with a firecracker report. The bus listed to one side. The Korean disappeared to the other side. Another report, and the bus settled further.

The Master of Sinanju returned, saying, "Show me the way, Chinese."

Zhang Zingzong started for the wall, going up the steep railed parapet to the top.

The tourists were a mixture of Chinese and foreign nationals. Chattering of Young Pioneers, wearing identical red kerchiefs, they strolled by under the watchful eyes of a woman with her hair pulled back into a tight bun.

They walked calmly, Chiun ignoring the looks he received from Chinese and foreigners alike. They stepped over a thin break in the wall to one of the unrestored sections.

"I think it was here," Zhang Zingzong told him, looking back with furtive glances. "This section is off-limits."

"Then you should not be attracting attention by looking about guiltily," Chiun told him firmly. "You must be as the quiet winds from the north."

"The winds from the north are cruel. They are Mongo winds."

"Mongol."

"That what I said. Mongo wind." His L never quite made it off his tongue.

The Master of Sinanju looked north to the steppes. These

were the so-called Mongol Plains. The mountains stopped here. A winter haze obscured the far distance like a convocation of low-lying phantoms. Just under the Wall lay a sea of pagoda-style roofs.

Here on the northern side of the Wall, the stone facing had been carried off, exposing its earthen-and-rubble core.

"It was down there that I found the box," Zhang Zingzong said quietly. "I was being persuaded by PLA men. I ran down here, and like a fish burrowing into the mud of a pond, I burrowed into the dirt and rocks. I breathed through one nostril, which I left uncovered."

The Master of Sinanju began walking down the steep rubble-and-earth side. His feet held the ground like a fly's, his spine remaining perpendicular to the wall.

Zhang had to climb down using all four limbs. Even so, he stumbled once and rolled the rest of the way down.

He was astonished when he landed at the Master of Sinanju's feet. He thought he had passed him.

"Get up, lazy one," Chiun said coldly. "And show me the spot where you found the box of Temujin."

Zhang dusted himself off with his bare hands. He looked around the exposed Wall. Creeping forward, he came to a spot where two irregular stones abutted one another.

"It was here," he said, pointing.

Chiun looked at the joined stones and then north. His eyes narrowed.

"The box," he said, putting out one yellowed claw of a hand.

Zhang pulled the now-frayed knapsack off his back and set it on the ground. He knelt as he undid the straps and extracted the ornate teak box.

The Master of Sinanju accepted the box from the straightening Chinese student. His fingers sought the secret catch. It sprang. The lid exposed three of its edges.

Carefully the Master of Sinanju removed its contents, revealing a human skull. It gleamed from every point, for it had been preserved by a covering of beaten silver. Here and there, yellow-brown bone showed through the metal.

But the Master of Sinanju had no eyes for the skull's natural imperfections. He was looking at the flowing script hammered into the skull's silver brow.

He read silently, his papery lips thinning in thought.

"What does it say?" Zhang asked eagerly. "A scholar told me what the words said, but we do not understand their meaning."

"That is because it is a riddle," Chiun whispered. " 'I am the wrath of Temujin,' " he recited. " 'If you dare, seek my power in this wise. Where you find me, stand and look true north through the Blind One's eyes. Follow the horizon until you come to the broken dragon.' "

"This makes no sense," Zhang murmured. "How can one look through the eyes of another—especially one who cannot see?"

Chiun faced north. He held the skull before him. Then, raising it, he brought the hollow of the skull up to his face.

Zhang Zingzong watched him curiously, all fear gone from his face. In truth, the fear departed after the strange Korean had lured the soldiers from his interrogation car. When the Master of Sinanju had returned to confront the lone PLA man who had Zhang in custody, there had been a brief argument and the PLA soldier had decided to arrest the uncooperative Korean too.

He had taken a single step toward the Master of Sinanju.

A flashing upward kick had sent the PLA soldier's chin snapping back with such force it broke his jawbone and spine with a single spiteful crack. The soldier had fallen to the floor, his head hanging from his neck like that of a harvested chicken.

After that, the woman in the broadcast booth had been rendered unconscious by a pinching of her neck nerves.

They were not molested after returning to their cushioned seats. It had not escaped Zhang Zingzong's notice that the PLA soldiers ceased prowling the train.

The Master of Sinanju held the skull up to his wrinkled mummy face. He looked into the bare bone bowl, turning the skull until he was satisfied.

"What you do?" Zhang asked.

"I am looking north," Chiun replied.

"How you know it is true north?" Zhang asked.

"I know," the Master of Sinanju intoned as he peered through the empty bone sockets of the skull.

"What you see?"

"I see emptiness," answered the Master of Sinanju as he lowered the skull. "We will go now," he said.

"Back to Beijing?"

"No," said the Master of Sinanju as he returned the skull to the teak box. "To emptiness."

Zhang looked toward the distant mists.

"Not wish to follow you there," he muttered.

"If you are willing to renounce your portion of that which we seek, you may remain here."

"No," Zhang said quickly. "My half belong to me, to China."

"Then come," said the Master of Sinanju.

They climbed up the steep wall, Chiun floating, Zhang scrambling over the bulwark of half-frozen earth.

They were met by a trio of PLA soldiers at the top.

"What you do here?" one demanded. Their hands were on their sidearms. One slapped a rubber truncheon against his legs. Their dark eyes had hardened into identical black jewels of hate. Their breaths steamed.

"We are simple tourists," said the Master of Sinanju unconcernedly.

"Where from?"

"I am from North Korea. And this man is from—"

"Luo Yang!" Zhang said quickly. "I am a worker there. In Number One Tractor Plant. Make Iron Plow machine parts."

They spoke in the clipped Mandarin dialect, wasting no words, all except Chiun, who employed the flowery Chinese once spoken in the courts of the Shang dynasty.

The soldiers looked them over with sullen contempt.

"You may go," one said to Chiun. "But this man is under arrest for vandalizing the Great Wall."

Zhang stiffened.

"As you wish," said Chiun, bestowing a short bow in their direction.

The soldiers took Zhang by his biceps and marched him away.

Chiun padded after them, as silent and undetectable as a winter breeze filtering through the bare ginkgo trees.

He extended one forefinger to the green-tunic back of the soldier on the left. The other floated before the identical spot over the right-hand soldier's spine. The play of cloth made selecting the correct spot a matter of momentary concentration.

Then the Master of Sinanju struck. Needle-sharp finger-nails drove in as one. They pierced the thick skin over the spine, slipping between the vertebrae.

The soldiers never felt the sting of Sinanju, never knew that their spinal cords had been instantaneously severed.

They walked three more paces. Then their legs stopped receiving signals from their brains. They collapsed.

Sandaled toes crushed their falling skulls.

Zhang felt himself pulled aside; at the same time, the third PLA soldier noticed the absence of his comrades' footsteps.

He turned. His hard mask of a face broke into surprise.

Then it broke. Period. Shattered by a tiny yellow fist that came up and took away the world.

"Come," Chiun said, gesturing impatiently toward Zhang Zingzong.

Zhang flew after him. They ran back to the restored section of the Great Wall and mingled with a line of tourists returning to their buses.

Chiun pulled Zhang out of the line when they reached the bottom, leading him to the bus, where an angry driver was finishing changing the second of two deflated rear tires.

"Can you drive a bus?" Chiun demanded of Zhang.

"No," said Zhang. "I have never driven anything."

"Then I will teach you," the Master of Sinanju said.

He hustled Zhang into the crowd of foreign tourists who were waiting for the driver to restore their bus to running order.

Chiun separated the folding doors and pushed a hesitant Zhang in. No one thought there was anything unusual in this, and so no one protested.

Zhang found himself pushed into the driver's seat. He looked around the steering wheel nervously.

"What I do?" he muttered.

"Wait," Chiun hissed. He drifted to the back and saw that the driver had finished tightening the lugs. He began cranking the hand jack. The bus was slowly ratcheted back to its normal pitch.

Chiun flew back to Zhang. "Turn the key!" he hissed.

Zhang turned the ignition. The engine grumbled into life just as the rear wheels touched the ground.

"Now push that pedal with your foot," Chiun commanded, pointing to the gas pedal.

Zhang hesitated. Then the driver jumped in front of the bus, screaming and waving frantic arms.

Zhang hit the accelerator. The bus surged ahead. The driver jumped out of the way.

"Turn the wheel!" Chiun cried as they barreled toward a fear-frozen gaggle of Young Pioneers.

"Where?" Zhang said, panic-stricken.

Chiun seized the wheel. He sent the bus veering away from the children, who scattered like white pigeons.

A group of PLA soldiers rushed out of nowhere to see what was going on.

They ran directly into the path of the bus.

"How stop?" Zhang cried, eyes so wide they looked like they would fall out from between their pulled-back lids.

"For soldiers," Chiun said firmly, "you do not stop."

The People's Liberation Army were used to being obeyed. They stood their ground, and waved their arms to signal a stop, believing that the Chinese driver would obey without thinking.

They realized their miscalculation four feet too late.

The bus began chewing up limbs and breaking bones.

Bodies bounced off the grille. They were all the same lime-green color, so the Master of Sinanju did not interfere with Zhang Zingzong's driving.

He was getting the hang of it. And so quickly. Perhaps the modern Chinese were not so backward after all.

The bus rumbled away. They lost a few rear windows to PLA bullets, but none threatened them. The Chinese may have invented gunpowder, Chiun thought smugly, but they had never mastered the art of aiming.

15

The Green Lantern Restaurant was near Purple Bamboo Park. Remo was surprised, as Fang Yu led him inside, to find it not at all like the ostentatious Chinese restaurants of America, but a simple room with square tables out of a 1940's movie.

The waitresses hovered by the kitchen, regarding Remo with giggling girlish glances.

"Are they going to wait on us or wait us out, hoping we'll die of starvation?" Remo asked after they had endured a ten-minute wait.

"This is not a tourist restaurant," Fang Yu told him. "They have probably never served a Westerner."

"Think they ever will?" Remo said hopefully.

Fang Yu beckoned toward the gaggle of waitresses. Her command was short and pungent.

One waitress lost her giggly face and approached.

Her Chinese question came so rapidly Remo couldn't even distinguish between syllables.

Fang Yu spoke quickly in reply, making hand gestures that somehow conveyed to Remo a sense of many exotic dishes.

The waitress padded off into the kitchen. The others followed her shyly, with furtive backward glances.

Fang Yu turned to Remo, putting a hand on his.

"You will love the crap here," she said, smiling brightly.

"Crap? It's that bad?"

Fang Yu's eyes flew wide, her face going red. "I mean carp. It is fish. Crap is a different American word. I get mixed up sometimes."

Remo frowned. "I don't remember ordering carp."

"Carp is all they serve in this restaurant. It's a specialty."

Remo's frown deepened. "No rice?"

111

"Of course. What is a meal without rice?"

The food came in less than a minute. And kept coming. They served spicy dishes and bland dishes and intermediate dishes.

"I thought you said they only served carp here," Remo said as he pushed some spicy tidbit into his mouth with chopsticks.

"What you think you have been eating?" Fang Yu said.

Remo looked up in surprise. "All this is carp?"

"Good carp, huh?"

Remo nodded. So far it was. He had never been a fan of the tiny orange fish, but some of it actually melted in his mouth. A few dishes he had to push aside. The smells told him they contained ingredients that would act as toxins to his refined metabolism.

He wished he had put aside the boiled carp. It was the only dish that didn't taste good.

On the other hand, he liked the carp soup so much he asked for seconds.

Remo finished the meal with a bowl of steaming rice. It was the kind that clumped together because cooked grains were sticky.

"Japonica," he pronounced. "Grown, I'd say, on the island of Honshu."

Fang Yu stopped, a mouthful of Fragrant Carp on its way to her red mouth.

"How you know that?" she asked, startled.

"I know rice," Remo replied, tweezering another clump to his mouth with an expert flick of his chopsticks.

Fang Yu shrugged and resumed her eating. But her bright eyes glanced toward Remo oftener, and her smile came more easily.

Two hours later, they stepped out into the cold Beijing night, full.

"How hard is it to get a cab in this neighborhood?" Remo wondered, looking up and down the nearly deserted street.

"Nearly impossible," Fang Yu assured him. "I am surprised with you, Remo," she added.

"You mean *at* me," Remo corrected.

"No, I do not think so. You use your chopsticks like one born in China. And you can tell where the rice comes from by its taste."

"I've been around," Remo said evasively.

They began walking. The wind was cold and Fang Yu impulsively took his arm. Remo did not resist. He had become used to the familiar touch of her hand.

Here in China, he felt different. Back in America, he had learned to watch himself in public, careful not to make new friends or fall into relationships. It had been especially difficult these last few months, after an artist's conception of his face had been plastered on several consecutive editions of the *National Enquirer*, which claimed he was an evolutionary superman. For over a year, Remo couldn't move openly through the US. Lately Smith had agreed that memories of his face had faded. But only after Remo had pointed out that the *National Enquirer* wasn't like the *National Geographic*. People didn't stockpile their copies. They filled them full of coffee grounds and threw them away.

Here, in China, cut off from Chiun, he stuck out like a sore thumb, but strangely, Remo felt more comfortable. Maybe it was the company, he thought, glancing at Fang Yu.

"What are you thinking, Remo?" Fang Yu asked as they crossed a snow-slick street.

"I'm thinking that I'm having a pretty good time," he said truthfully.

"And I am too," Fang Yu said, squeezing his arm slightly.

"But I have a mission. I gotta find that Korean."

"I have told you, there is no word of him yet. What can you do without word?"

"I don't know," Remo admitted. "Guess I'll just hang around Beijing until he shows up."

"Beijing is the nerve center of China. If Old Duck Tang comes to Beijing, or any other place in China, I will hear of it. For no one can move unseen through China for long. China has a billion eyes. He will be seen, his presence will be reported. And I will hear of it."

"How?"

"We have a word. *Guanxi.* It means 'connections.' I have these connections. If there is word," she repeated firmly, "I will hear of it."

As they walked along, Fang Yu led Remo into a narrow alley.

"What's this?" Remo asked.

"You will see."

They came to a red door in a blank wall. Fang Yu took a
key from her purse and opened the lock. She pushed open
the door and Remo stepped in carefully.

Sensing no presence inside, he reached out for a light
switch. A finger brushed one.

Light flooded a cramped, feminine, but Spartan living
room.

"Where are we?" Remo asked as Fang Yu secured the
door behind her.

"This is my place," she said shyly. "I have three rooms. I
am very lucky to have them."

Except for the Asian-style decoration, the apartment looked
like one of the smaller New York City apartments. There
was a portable Silver Mudan TV set on a wheeled cart. A
beaded curtain made a poor substitute for a divider between
living room and bedroom. Beyond the first beaded curtain
was a second, and the sound of a refrigerator motor straining.

"Nice," Remo said.

"Is your apartment in America as nice?"

"Not as well-furnished as this," Remo said with a straight
face.

"Perhaps I will see it someday," Fang Yu said, going to a
tabletop cassette deck. It looked like a fifteen-dollar Times
Square special, but it occupied a place of honor on the table
and looked as if it was religiously washed clean every day.

"You like disco?" Fang Yu asked, inserting a cassette.

"No," Remo said quickly. Polite was one thing, but disco
another.

Fang Yu turned. "No?" she asked. "I was hoping you
would show me the latest disco dance."

"It's called the lambada and it's not at all like disco. You
dance close together."

"You show me how to do it?"

"Really, really close," Remo added. "I don't think I
know you well enough for the lambada yet."

Fang Yu looked confused. "You do not want to dance
with me?" she asked unhappily.

"Actually, I'm a terrible dancer," Remo said. "Honest."

"You not dance at all?"

"Never."

"Oh," said Fang Yu. "When you take American girl out

on date, what do you usually do with her after you have eaten in an excellent restaurant as we have?"

Remo had to think about that one.

"Actually," he admitted, "I don't date much these days. My work usually gets in the way of my social life."

"How about your sex life?"

"My what?"

"Is that not what they call it in America, or is there new phrase? I wish to know the most modern American phrases so that when I go to America, I will not sound foolish."

" 'Sex life' is still in vogue," Remo said. "Except maybe for me," he added wistfully.

Fang Yu came over and took one of Remo hands in both of hers. Her hands were warm to the touch and Remo inhaled her delicate rose-petal scent once more.

"My work for Chinese tourist bureau too gets in the way of my sex life," she said sadly. "For I have none."

"I have an idea," Remo said suddenly. "Let's take a break from work."

"But I do not know what to do next," Fang Yu said, coloring modestly.

"Leave everything to me," Remo returned.

He drew her through the beaded curtain and to the bed.

16

Remo Williams awoke to an empty bed.

He missed Fang Yu immediately.

Remo shot bolt upright, taking in all sounds around him like a human sensory sponge.

"Yu?" he said, even though he knew she was not in the modest apartment. There was no other heartbeat. Beyond the walls, yes. Other heartbeats, other sounds of sleeping apartment occupants. But not Fang Yu.

Remo threw back the thin covers. He felt great. He had

not had sex like that in a long, long time. It made him feel refreshed, cleansed of subtle poisons.

Their lovemaking had started the way it usually began for Remo with a woman.

Fang Yu had been shy at first. Remo liked that. That, too, was refreshing. He wondered if the Chinese woman were a virgin. He decided not to ask. Better to be surprised. It had been a long time since sex had held any surprises for him.

Fang Yu had looked upward when she asked, "How does it begin with you and American women?"

"Like this," Remo had replied, taking up her left hand. He held it with one of his, aware of a faint trembling in her wrist. Remo began tapping with his right index finger, in the prescribed way of Sinanju. Step one.

It was designed to bring a woman to watery-kneed climax just standing there. This facilitated two ultimate Sinanju purposes—to bind a woman to a man by brute sexuality. Whether she wanted to or not, she would lie open to him within moments.

Or, when applied to a female enemy, it was an excellent interrogation technique. Simply stop tapping at a crucial moment, and the subject would beg, plead, even grovel for the withheld finger. Remo had known American women subjected to step one to become sexually aroused at the sight of male index fingers forever after.

"What is this?" Fang Yu had asked uncertainly.

"Step one," Remo replied. "Collect them all."

Fang Yu's eyebrows drew together in pretty perplexity as Remo continued tapping. Her trembling quickened. She looked up, and her ivory-hued face in the dimness was so appealing Remo said, "The hell with step one. Let's go directly to thirty-seven. Maybe we'll get lucky and land on Boardwalk."

He withdrew his finger and began undressing her.

They fell into bed together, naked and tentative. Soon there was nothing tentative in the work they plunged into or the sounds they made.

It was not Sinanju. It was something even older and more powerful.

Remo enjoyed Fang Yu's responsive thrusts and matched them with his own. They climaxed together, shivering and passionate, and after a few tasty butterfly kisses, returned to the fray.

Remo remembered that they had fallen asleep in one another's arms, sweating, spent but satisfied.

Now he was alone. So where was Fang Yu?

As the delicious memories faded, Remo's training reasserted itself. Was this a trap? Remo went to the door. Locked. He flicked on the light and began going through the apartment, looking for something, anything, that would tell him if this really was Fang Yu's apartment.

Unfortunately, except for a cassette of the *Saturday Night Fever* soundtrack, several Madonna tapes, and a dog-eared copy of *Jonathan Livingston Seagull*, every bit of writing in the apartment was in Chinese.

"Damn!" Remo said. He wished Chiun were here. Chiun could read Chinese. He returned to the bed and drew on his clothes.

"When in doubt," he muttered to himself, "seek escape. So spake Chiun the Wise."

Remo slipped out into the night. The cold made the flesh of his bare forearms tighten, the hair lifting. He sucked in the cold distasteful air and blew it into every cell of his body. It was like firing up a zillion tiny subcutaneous heaters.

Remo walked, feeling warmer than if he were swathed in an electric blanket.

Having no idea where he was, Remo simply oriented himself by his inner compass. Tiananmen Square and his hotel lay to the southeast, he remembered, so he walked southeast.

The only foot traffic he encountered were stooped workmen shoveling waste from public lavatories into wheelbarrows. Remo remembered that they called it "night soil," and used it to fertilize their fields during the warm months. Probably it went into storage during the winter.

Beijing was honeycombed with narrow alleys called *hutongs*, so it was simple enough to avoid the nearly identical PLA soldiers and People's Armed Police. They walked the streets like an occupying army, always in pairs. Occasionally one would fly by astride a bicycle, bundled up against the cold and pumping the pedals like mad. They made Remo think of the Wicked Witch of the West in greatcoats and fur-trimmed hats.

As Remo approached Tiananmen Square, they became as numerous as bluebottle flies around a horse.

Remo tried to avoid the square itself, but the walls of the old Forbidden City blocked him. He doubled back and took a chance on the most direct route, East Changan Avenue, which formed the north boundary of the square.

Changan went through the vast stone-paved square itself. In his black T-shirt and chinos, Remo was as well-dressed as The Shadow for moving around unseen. But Tiananmen Square was well-lit by ornate standards to expose all hiding places. Remo flitted from clots of darkness, moving with ninjalike stealth behind the unsuspecting backs of sentry guards.

He paused in the shadow of the Great Hall of the People and its giant portrait of Mao, whose Buddhalike serenity belied his bloody reign. The Beijing rose up on the other side.

The square was so vast, Remo's best chance was to run.

He started off, keeping his elbows tight to his sides, not pumping because wild motions could be read by peripheral vision.

He was more like the shadow of a passing cloud than a man as he moved through the square right under the noses of PLA sentries.

Remo would have made it all the way to East Changan had it not been for the limousine coming toward him.

It ghosted up East Changan like a dreadnought, turning into the square.

The sudden appearance of the black limousine caught Remo by surprise. He stopped dead, watching it go by.

In every detail—from the square grille to the absence of bumpers—it resembled the predatory black limousine from America!

Remo switched directions and went after it.

The limo disappeared through an iron gate in front of the Great Hall of the People, on the western side of the square, facing the Monument to the People's Heroes, an obelisk which resembled a Chinese version of the Washington Monument with a kind of Iwo Jima bas-relief running around its base.

PLA soldiers shut the gate after the car with a ringing clang.

Remo stopped, hesitant. He was in the middle of the square, exposed on every side. He knew the Great Hall of the People was a meeting place used by the upper leadership of Red China. If he crashed it, he would have to use his Sinanju abilities, and Smith had warned against that. To say nothing of the international incident he would cause.

Remo decided on the subtle approach. He sauntered up to the guards at the gate. He was so artfully inconspicuous that they jumped at his friendly, "Hi, fellas!"

The PLA men looked at him angrily. Like many Asian soldiers, they looked younger than their years, like Boy Scouts with automatic weapons.

There was nothing playful about the way they brought those weapons off their shoulders and pointed them at Remo.

"Oops!" Remo said, putting up his loose-fingered hands. "Didn't mean to spook you guys. Anyone speak English here?"

"You not be'ong here."

"I'll settle for Pidgin English." Remo grinned. "Relax. I was just wondering about that limousine that just scooted through that gate behind you."

The soldiers looked blank.

"The car," Remo prompted. "The one you just let in."

"No car pass through here all night," he was told.

They looked nervous. Remo detected their respiration quickening. Their heart rates picked up. His innocent questions about the limo were upsetting them.

Remo pressed on. "I was just wondering if it was some kind of special Chinese model. Nice workmanship. Love the bold, uncompromising lines. Kinda like a Stalin Continental."

"You ask too many question," the other solder announced. "We must detain you."

"Hey, aren't we overreacting to a little window-shopping?" Remo said. He lowered his arms as the pair approached.

One man shouldered his AK-47, which made it easier to take out the other. Remo did that with a high kick that sent the muzzle flashing up into the guard's startled face.

Unfortunately, the guard's trigger finger was tight on the trigger. A hot burst of automatic-weapons fire flared like a Roman candle in the night.

The other guard decided to unshoulder his rifle again. Remo reached out and pulled it off his shoulder for him so fast the strap broke. The guard's shoulder also broke. Remo slapped him on top of the head, and his face actually bounced when it hit the hard stone cobbles of Tiananmen Square.

The short burst of automatic-weapons fire galvanized the patrolling soldiers. They began shouting unintelligible questions at one another. They converged on the gate where Remo was.

Remo decided that going over the gate worked best for him. He might find the limo too.

But he changed his mind halfway up. Guards were coming from within, unshipping their AK-47's.

Remo jumped down with alacrity. No point in getting trapped behind the gates. He'd take his chances out in the open.

PLA soldiers clopped over the square, their weapons up. They looked ready to use them.

Remo elected to throw up his hands and walk into the middle of the square. Mao's tomb lay to his right. Too far away to make a break for it. The People's Monument looked inviting, however.

They formed a circle around him, dropping their muzzles in line with his stomach and back.

"American tourist!" Remo warned. "You shoot me and all the Yankee bucks will dry up. Got that?"

"Who are you?" an older soldier demanded truculently.

"My ID's in my pants pocket. I'll take it out, okay?"

The soldier used his weapon to gesture to Remo's pockets.

Remo clapped his hands suddenly. The unexpected report was like invisible lightning. Everyone blinked.

Except Remo. He executed a Sinanju leap called the Twisting Dragon. He went up, arched his back sideways, and landed twenty feet short of the People's Monument—close enough to sprint the remaining distance as the soldiers reacted to the impossible disappearance of their prisoner.

Remo lay flat on the monument's flat summit, and amid a confusion of shouts and curses, the circle of PLA broke apart. The soldiers charged around the square aimlessly, blowing whistles and adding to their own confusion.

Remo stayed on the statue, hugging it like a patch of shadow. Every time a soldier approached from one side, Remo slipped over to the other. No one saw him.

Eventually the search pattern widened further, leaving Tiananmen Square all but deserted.

Carefully Remo floated down from the statue and calmly walked toward his hotel.

He figured the lobby was probably crawling with PLA, so he went up the side of the Beijing Hotel like a human spider and reached his balcony without incident.

Remo stripped to his shorts and waited for the inevitable knocking on the door. He imagined the People's Army would turn the hotel inside out looking for any Westerner matching his description.

Remo rumpled his hair when he heard pounding on the door next to his. The pounding continued. When no one answered, Remo's acute hearing told him that the next room was empty.

That gave him an idea.

He hurried to his door and slipped out. Two green-clad soldiers were shaking the next door with their banging.

"He's escaping to the balcony!" Remo called, hoping that they understood English.

One did. He pounded the lock into submission with the butt of his rifle and jumped in.

Unfortunately, the other one came for Remo.

"Where have you been all night?" he demanded.

"Here," Remo said. "Honest."

The guard looked past Remo's naked shoulder into the hotel room.

"What you do all night?" he demanded.

"I was playing pong," Remo told him.

"I do not know pong."

"It's kind of war game played with people's heads and T-55 tanks," Remo explained in a serious voice.

"You have tank in room?"

"I like to improvise," Remo told him, bringing his hands up and together with enough force to crack a girder.

The PLA soldier's head happened to sit exactly at the point of impact.

It went *pong!*

Jumping back in case the jugular started spurting from flying bone chips, Remo was amazed that the sound was exactly like Fang Yu had described.

The jugular hadn't been severed, so Remo caught the man on his way down to the rug. He dragged the jerking body to the other room, his head like a collapsed balloon on his red-stained shoulder.

Remo laid him on the floor. He noticed the other soldier fighting to open the balcony door, and slipped up behind him.

The guard whirled.

"Your friend fainted," Remo explained, jerking a thumb back.

Startled, the guard hurried around Remo. "What happen?" he asked as Remo followed him.

"I don't know. He was playing pong and just keeled over for no reason."

"What is—"

Pong!

Remo eased the second PLA corpse to the rug and beat a hasty retreat for the door.

On his way out, he noticed the first soldier was missing an eye. A gray string of eye-controlling muscle hung out of his empty socket, along with a squish of oozing gray brain matter.

"Oh-oh, can't leave anything lying around," Remo said cheerfully. "Might cause problems later."

He went in search of the eye. It wasn't in the room, by the door, or out in the corridor.

Remo snapped his fingers. "Ergo, it's in my room," he said aloud. He was in a happy mood. Not only had he gotten laid, but he was getting other frustrations out of his system.

It turned out the lost eye had rolled under his dresser. Remo had to get down on one knee to get at it. It jumped out of his reach the first time he touched it. It was slippery slick.

Finally Remo got it between thumb and forefinger. He was straightening up when he heard the *ding* of the elevator.

Remo rushed out of his room and made for the next room.

Too late, he saw Fang Yu coming up the corridor.

He slipped one hand behind his back and put on a disingenuous smile. As she approached, he made a pretense of leaning against the doorframe.

"Well, well, look who's dropped by," he said, toeing the door closed on the bodies of the dead soldiers. "Here to test the mattress, are you?"

"Is something wrong, Remo?" Fang Yu asked, her face worried.

"Why do you ask, Cinderella?"

"Lobby filled with PLA men," she said anxiously, slipping into clipped Pidgin English. "They very angry. I had to sneak upstairs and take elevator to this floor. Why you leave?"

"You weren't there when I woke up."

"Ah," she said taking him by the elbow. "Soldiers come. We must speak quickly." They closed the door to Remo's room behind them.

Since Remo was in his shorts, he couldn't palm the late PLA soldier's eyeball into his pants pocket, so he folded his arms. The eye felt like a hard grape against his concealing forearm.

"I woke up and you were gone," he told Fang Yu in a brittle tone. "I didn't know what was up, so I came back here. What happened?"

"I went out," Fang Yu said simply.

"Glad it was good for you too," Remo said thinly.

"I did it to please you," she said quickly, her voice filling with hurt and resentment.

"Funny way to show it."

"No, listen," Fang Yu said urgently. "I woke up, very excited. You were asleep. I knew you wished to find this Korean, Old Duck Tang. I know many people in high places, so I went to see one of them. From this man I learn that there was an incident at the Long Wall of Ten Thousand Li, you know, our Great Wall. Many soldiers die."

Remo's stiff expression softened. "I'm listening."

Fang Yu sat on the edge of the bed. Remo looked down at her, trying to gauge her truthfulness by her expression. He found it impossible.

"A bus was stolen at the Great Wall," she said. "Soldiers were crushed under its wheels. Then it was discovered that a caboose had come loose from a tourist train going to Badaling. It was found in a ravine, filled with more PLA men. All dead."

"What happened to it?"

"The coupling had been shattered. Such a thing is not known to happen. There is talk of sabotage and hooligans."

"Might not be him," Remo said half to himself.

"When the train arrive, a woman was found to be uncon- scious. She was train propaganda broadcaster, like Ameri- can JD, you know? "

"DJ. JD is 'juvenile delinquent.' Close, but not exactly the same thing."

"She spoke of a Chinese man the guards took into cus- tody and an older man in a kimono who lured the guards from the train. These were the same ones who were found dead."

"That's Chiun!" Remo said. "Definitely Chiun."

Fang Yu's eyes turned to wary slits.

"Thought you did not know his name," she accused.

"Chiun is his code name," Remo said quickly. "You know, like Ivory Fang is yours."

"Ah. So you are pleased?" Fang Yu said slowly.

"Yeah, this is great."

"Have soldiers come to this floor yet?"

"Yeah, they didn't find anything."

Fang Yu's sigh of relief was like a breeze through poplars.

"Good. Then we have time to make love again."

Remo joined her on the bed without hesitation.

Fang Yu was moaning like a midnight sigh when he sud- denly realized his left fist still clutched the elusive eyeball. He slipped it under the pillow and finished what he was doing.

"You like me again?" Fang Yu wondered.

"I only have eyes for you," Remo said sincerely.

17

Remo had wanted to leave as soon as they were done, but Fang Yu had insisted it was too dangerous to do so.

"In morning, we will simply walk out, like any other tourist and guide," she had promised.

And so they waited for dawn to break, catching sleep in fitful breaks, like entwined cats.

"Ever think of going to America?" Remo asked as Fang Yu nestled in his arms.

"All the time," she said dreamily. "First thing I will do is dye my hair like Madonna."

Remo groaned.

"You not think Madonna pretty?"

"Like a plucked chicken," Remo spat. "I can get you out of the country," he suggested softly.

Fang Yu looked up, suddenly interested.

"You mean to come back with you?" she asked.

Remo smiled. "I can be habit-forming."

"My soul belongs to China," Fang Yu said distantly.

"China's a mess. How can you stand it?"

"We have had many emperors in China's past," she told him quietly. "Some were kind and some cruel. Now the Communists are our emperors and their cruelty is without measure. But all emperors die in their time. Even Communists, which are like dogs who sink their fangs into their own tails. I wish to be here when China awakens."

"Oh," Remo said. He was surprised at how disappointed he felt. He had known Fang Yu less than a day.

"But I could come to visit you," she added quickly. "Stay long time. Maybe you will return to China after the Communists are crushed."

"We gotta get through the night first," Remo pointed out.

"Why PLA want you, Remo?"

"What makes you think they want me?"

"I hear one giving your description to front-desk man."

"And what'd he tell them?"

"You will be insulted."

"Try me."

"Front-desk man, he say all Westerners look alike to him. Big noses and round eyes stick out. All rest of face lost."

Remo grunted a laugh.

"I think front-desk man spoofing PLA," Fang Yu said. "No one cooperates with PLA if they can help it."

Remo looked down at her, cradled in his arms. "Spoofing?"

"Is that not the correct word? A tourist from Missouri say it once for me. I like that word. Spoofing. Sound sexy."

"Spoofing works for me."

"Excellent," Fang Yu said, snuggling closer. "If PLA return, we will spoof them together."

They were not disturbed by the PLA, however. The whir and ching-a-ling of bicycles of Changan Avenue roused them from sleep. After dressing, they walked leisurely through the lobby and out into the Beijing morning.

"Guess they widened the search for that guy, whoever he was," Remo said airily.

Fang Yu looked up quizzically. Then she led Remo to a waiting taxi. The morning air smelled of cabbage and coal smoke. Fang Yu smelled of rose petals. Remo stayed close to her scent, enjoying it.

At the bustling Beijiao market they took a local bus to the Great Wall.

"This better than tourist bus," Fang Yu explained. "Tourist bus stay only ninety minutes. Have to come back on same bus. This way we can stay as long as necessary."

The bus was crowded. One woman held a squawking chicken on her lap all the way. Once out of the city, the terrain became almost instantly rural. The driver stopped by the roadside when hailed by an old man who was prodding a fat sow with a stick applied to her buttocks.

The man and the sow were allowed to board.

"Equality," Remo muttered. "It's wonderful. Even the pigs ride the bus."

"Pig must pay too," Fang Yu said without humor.

Remo grunted absently. He was watching the mountains.

The switchbacks of the Great Wall of China became visible in the distance, coming in and out of view as the bus rumbled along.

"Do you know about Great Wall?" Fang Yu asked suddenly. "It is mightiest Chinese achievement."

"Not really," Remo said. His thoughts were on Chiun now. Why had he come to Beijing and what was he doing?

"Americans are very proud because they have gone to the moon," Fang Yu told him. "But if an American stands on the moon and looks to China, he could see the Great Wall, so magnificent is it."

"Is that true?" Remo asked in surprise.

"I am told it is. But I have never been to the moon."

"I have," Remo said suddenly.

Fang Yu became excited. "You, Remo? You have been to the moon?"

"Yep. Last night. Several times."

Fang Yu actually flushed and looked away. She gave Remo a playful nudge to the ribs.

"Now I know how to shut you up when I need to." Another nudge. Remo grinned. He couldn't believe how good he felt.

After two hours on the road, the bus trundled onto a parking·area. The driver let them off at the Great Wall. Fang Yu took Remo's hands and practically pulled him up the parapet to the top of the Wall itself.

Walking along the undulating Wall was like traveling along a stone bridge laid out by architects who had never heard of level ground. They found a deserted spot in the shadow of a crenellated battlement on the far side and looked northward through one of the narrow slots cut in the wall.

"This section was built during Ming dynasty, many years ago," Fang Yu explained. Pride was strong in her voice and it made Remo a little sad. It told him she would never leave China.

"At first, the Wall was not one wall, but many walls," she was saying. "Then Mongos come."

"Who?"

"Mongos. Surely you know of them. Everyone know of Mongos." Her English was slipping again, reverting to native Chinese speech patterns.

"Oh, Mongols," Remo said. A thought struck him. "Genghis Khan was their leader at one time, wasn't he?"

Fang Yu made a face. "Mongos dwell in north. Very
harsh people, and cruel. Not like Chinese. Not cultured. In
the old days, the Mongos would come down from steppes
on their horses. Nothing could stop them. In the winter,
horse and men die on way, but Mongos like locusts. Crush
all in their path. Kill men and children. Ravish women.
Some days they ride for days, never resting. Mongos do not
plant, so they eat whenever they find. If they find no food, a
Mongo will stab wound in his horse and drink the blood.
Live longer."

"Nice guys," Remo remarked.

Fang Yu shook her head. "Not nice at all. These walls
were built to keep out Mongos. Then Mongos grow too
strong. They conquer China. That was our Yuan dynasty. It
was a cruel time." Her voice dropped. "This is a cruel time
too. No more Mongos vex us. People's Army become China's own Mongos. Perhaps Mongo blood has poisoned us, I
do not know."

Remo took her in his arms.

"Never mind," he said firmly. "Look, I've got to follow
this Korean."

"The bus went north, into Mongo land."

"What's up there?"

"Nothing. No rocks, no trees, just snow and steppe and
wolves. There is nothing up there in Mongo land. That is
why Mongos capture China. They have nothing. Want something. Everyone want something. What do you want, Remo?"

"I want you," he said simply. "But first I want to find
that old Korean."

"Then I will go with you into Mongo land."

"That's the answer I was hoping for," Remo said, looking
into her dark, frightened eyes.

They kissed under the shadow of the battlement with the
knifelike wind sweeping down from the steppes.

Fang Yu continued shivering even after the wind dropped
off.

Riding the Iron Rooster train, Remo looked as inconspicuous as feathers on a cat.

They had what Remo learned were soft-seat tickets. Even
surrounded by tourists, Remo stuck out in his black T-shirt
and chinos. Not a PLA soldier who passed through the car
failed to cast an accusing glance in Remo's direction.

One stopped and began hassling Fang Yu in Mandarin, while Remo pretended to look unconcerned.

Their exchange was tight and contentious. The soldier kept repeating whatever it was he was saying. After answering several queries, Fang Yu lost her patience and practically spat her replies back.

Grudgingly she produced some documentation and personal ID.

The soldier looked these documents over and unhappily returned them. Then he stormed from the car. They were not bothered by PLA men after that.

"What was that all about?" Remo asked.

"*Deel lae loe moe,*" Fang Yu muttered, watching the soldier bull past an old woman attempting to negotiate the bouncing aisle.

"What's a *deel lae loe moe*?" Remo wondered.

Fang Yu's fingertips flew to Remo's lips, silencing him.

"Shhh! Do not say those words aloud! It very embarrassing."

"So what is it?"

"Chinese curse. That man was what we call *dai*—stupid. Very stupid. He ask me if I accompanied you as guide. I tell him yes. Still he ask questions. Demand to see your travel permit."

"What'd you do?"

"I show it to him, of course. Here."

Remo accepted the passportlike document and looked it over. Inside there were a red stamp and in English a list of cities which Remo was officially entitled to visit.

"Where are we going, by the way?" Remo said.

"Our ticket say Baotou, but we get off one stop early, at Hohhot."

"Hohhot isn't on my list," Remo pointed out.

"That is why we get off there. If they look for you, you will not be where they expect."

"What do we do in Hohhot?" Remo asked, pocketing the document.

"We disappear," Fang Yu said simply.

The train rattled on. Fang Yu dropped off to sleep, leaving Remo to stare out the window in bored silence.

China rolled by, vast, gray, and mountainous. Remo felt as helpless as he'd ever felt in his life. Cut off from Chiun, unable to get around China without help, and forbidden to use his Sinanju powers, he might as well be an ordinary CIA agent on a wild-goose chase. He didn't like the feeling. He was used to fast results, shaking information out of people when necessary and wisecracking his way through situations. No one understood his humor in China. Worst of all, they stared at him like he was a freak.

He mentally damned the political restrictions that kept him from doing his job the most direct way possible. If he had had his way, he would have crashed into the Great Hall of the People and taken the Chinese leadership hostage until Chiun was located and brought to him.

That would have worked. Hell, he'd have been home by now.

"Politics," Remo muttered half-aloud. He hated politics.

Thinking of the Great Hall of the People reminded him of the black limousine. He had meant to ask Fang Yu about it. He looked over. She was asleep, a pillow under her spilling black hair, her glasses still on. She looked like a wise lady owl.

Remo let her sleep. He hoped he'd remember to bring it up again. It was bothering him.

Then, as if some invisible genie had decided to grant his wish, Remo saw the black limousine scoot up the road that ran parallel to the railroad bed.

Remo started. It came up from behind like a silent ghost. It looked exactly like the Tiananmen Square limousine, and the one he'd encountered back in the US—right down to its snoutlike grille and double set of headlights.

Remo looked down, but the train's height prevented him from seeing directly into the car interior. No telling who was behind the wheel.

Remo nudged Fang Yu awake. She resisted his prodding.

"Fang Yu!" he hissed urgently.

"Mmmmm?"

"Fang Yu," he repeated, shaking her.

"What?" She blinked, looking around drowsily.

"Take a look and tell me if this is a Chinese limousine."

Fang Yu peered past Remo, sending fragrant rose-petal billows into Remo's nose.

"What you talking about?" she asked poutingly. "I see nothing."

Remo's head snapped around. The limo was gone.

"It was just there," he said doubtfully. Craning his neck, he spotted its rear deck about a hundred yards ahead. It was picking up speed.

"Look," Remo said, pulling her close to the window.

Fang Yu put her hands and cheek to the glass and tried to see past the curving forward cars of the train.

"I do not see car," she said unhappily.

"It's gone now," Remo said. "It was a long black limousine. I saw it go into the Great Hall of the People last night."

Fang Yu resumed her seat. "So what? Official limousine go in and out of Great Hall all the time. They are called *Hong Qi*—Red Flag limousines."

"I saw one of these in America just a few days ago," Remo told her.

Fang Yu's eyebrows shot up. "Oh?"

"Yeah. It looked nothing like anything I'd ever seen. The chauffeur was Chinese."

"Red Flag limousine," Fang Yu said simply. "Big shot drive them in China. High cadres. People like that."

"What was one doing in America?"

"I do not know," Fang Yu said in a voice that implied bored disinterest.

"Do Red Flag limos have a square grille?" Remo asked intently.

"What is a grille?"

"The front part."

"I suppose so," Fang Yu said vaguely. She was rapidly losing interest in the conversation. "I am going to nap again. Do not wake me again just to look at Chinese limousine, okay?"

She drifted off almost instantly.

Remo put his chin in his hand and looked unhappy. The sudden appearance of the limousine bothered him, but it must have been what Fang Yu had said—an official vehicle. Probably lots of them in China. It didn't explain the one prowling the streets of New Rochelle, but it made more sense than the theory that it was the same one. No way it could be following him, he thought. Only he and Fang Yu knew where they were. Not even Smith had that information.

18

Boldbator the Mongol galloped across the barren steppe.

He bounced in his padded trousers on the high wooden saddle, feeling the magnificent muscles of his short-legged horse surge and release with every lunging step and the wind flapping his long brown *del* caught at the waist with an orange sash.

The blazing sky overheard was like a brilliant blue dome protecting the world. The steppes were an endless plate of dun and old snow extending to every point on the compass.

"Ai yah!" cried Boldbator, the cold air hot in his lungs. He loved the steppe, its vastness and wild freedom. To ride from horizon to horizon was to live.

The trouble was, there were no adventures beyond either horizon for Boldbator the horse Mongol, descended from a long line of free-riding nomads. Once, his kind had ranged from south China to the far lands of Europe, conqueror-kings in the saddle.

No more. Not even Mongolia lay united under the Mongols. Here, in Inner Mongolia, Boldbator was a Chinese serf. And his brothers to the north in Outer Mongolia held firm in an oval of land, allied to Russia, but warily friendly with China, like a lump of cold mutton caught in the mouths of two ravening wolves.

The thought made Boldbator whip his fine cream horse harder. The steed responded, as is the way with a good Mongol horse. Nostrils flaring, he pounded the steppe like the drumming beats of a thousand demons.

Boldbator rode with ghosts this day—the spirits of his mighty ancestors. He wished they were with him now. They would be khans of both Mongolias, as well as the Russias and the soulless Chinese to the south.

One day, he thought, huddled in his bouncing saddle. One day the Next Khan will come . . .

The red dreams of Boldbator the horse Mongol were cast from his active mind by the sight of a long object against the horizon.

His keen eyes, sitting sharp in the crinkles that wind and sun had cut around them, grew steely with interest.

Here was the Great Mongol Road. No vehicle would attempt to pass it in the dead of winter, for there were few villages and no sanctuary to be found on the way.

Boldbator lashed his responsive pony around and veered toward that dim shape.

As he galloped toward it, his eyes saw it for what it was. A bus.

He trotted up to it slowly, for the windows were shattered and its painted sides were riddled with the shiny pits of bullet strikes.

The north wind carried the metallic taste of blood to Boldbator's broad nose.

Boldbator came to a halt only a few yards from the bus. It lay askew the road. There were bodies around it. Green bodies. Soldiers of Beijing.

Boldbator dismounted, and reassured his snorting pony with a firm slap.

Clutching his reins tightly, ready at an instant to remount or, if the worst happened, to slap his pony to safety, he padded forward.

The soldiers were all dead, but one. They lay in sprawled positions. No visible wounds on them. But they were dead nonetheless.

The one who groaned did have a bullet wound, Boldbator discovered. It let the blood bubble up from his heaving chest like a pot coming to a slow boil. With each exhaled breath, more bubbles appeared. A lung wound. Such wounds were invariably fatal.

Boldbator knelt beside the dying soldier.

"What did this to you, dog of Beijing?" he asked quietly.

The soldier turned glazed eyes to Boldbator and said simply, "A *guaihu* in the form of a man."

"By what name is this devil known?"

The soldier inhaled. His chest wound swallowed the newly formed bubbles. He gasped two words, "Finish me."

Boldbator nodded. He unsheathed his knife and with a soft caressing glance of its edge across the soldier's exposed throat, sent him into eternity.

Then Boldbator led his nervous pony around the bus. There were no other living ones—no hint of what had befallen the soldiers.

Boldbator did find tracks. Jeep tracks. They led north.

Boldbator remounted and rode after them. He did not ride hard. Who knew but that he rode toward his death, and why should a man hurry toward his appointed hour—even a brave Mongol?

Many *li* along, Boldbator came to an abandoned jeep. A soldier sat at the wheel, back stiff, eyes staring ahead as if waiting for the world to end.

He did not stir as Boldbator approached, and the Mongol realized he was frozen. Dismounting, he passed a hand over the man's sightless eyes. Dead. The wolves would get him. Good for the wolves, thought Boldbator.

He saw that the jeep's gas gauge was on empty, and two sets of footprints, one heavy, one very light, led north.

Boldbator stared north a very long time. What manner of men could lay waste to Chinese soldiers?

"Mongol men!" he cried in answer. Grinning fiercely, he leapt atop his mount and charged in the direction the footprints led him.

He knew not how many *li* he would have to ride, but it mattered not. He was a man among men. So, too, would these two be.

In his wild heart, Boldbator rejoiced at the thought of encountering them.

Night had fallen and the moon was high and full, a lighter blue than the afternoon sky, but blue nonetheless. It was a good moon. Strong, giving much light.

The wind from the north chopped at Boldbator's weathered bronze face and padded sheepskin *del*. He had pulled his earflaps under his chin to protect his ears. In this wind, they might freeze and have to be cut off. It was a terrible thing to have to cut a man's frozen ears off to save the rest of the man, for Boldbator had done this once, years ago. A worse thing still, to cut off one's own ear.

Boldbator rode on. Clouds came. They swallowed the strong moon with a darkening power beyond appeal.

Enough silver-blue light bled through to show Boldbator his horse's shaggy mane, but that was all.

He lost the footprints in the darkness, which he cursed.

The smell of a cooking fire came from the west. Boldbator rode toward that. He must find hospitality, for if he lay down on the steppe with his horse, the wolves would get them both.

Boldbator had seen a single steppe wolf bring down a fully grown horse. The whinnying was terrible, even to a Mongol.

There were four circular *gers*, their painted-wood doors facing south, where the bitter north wind could not insinuate itself into the felt-covered Mongol tents.

Food smells mingled with the dung-smoke aroma like a warm welcome.

Boldbator rode up to the *ger* from which smoke rose from a slim black stovepipe. He nudged his horse to give a warning whinny so that the inhabitant of the circular tent would not be startled by his approach.

"*Sain Baina!*" Boldbator called out.

A man pushed open the door and eyed him stolidly. His face was unseeable, for the strong light behind threw it into darkness.

"*Sain Baino,*" he rumbled, adding grumpily, "Another visitor. And on such a night. Why come you here, man?"

"I am Boldbator, son of Gongonching," Boldbator said, dismounting. "I seek two great warriors who slew Chinese soldiers like true Mongols. I smell by your smoke that you eat late."

"We do have visitors, loud one. But warriors they are not."

Boldbator tethered his horse to a rack and carried his wooden saddle into the *ger*.

Gathered around the black stove were an old woman and three Mongol sons. And with them a scrawny shivering Chinese youth and a very old man in a sheepskin cloak who looked more Mongol than Chinese, but seemed to be neither.

"I am Boldbator," he proclaimed loudly. "Mongol among Mongols."

To his surprise, the old one returned his greeting in perfect Khalkha Mongol.

"I am but a traveler from a distant land," he said, "so-
journing in the Land of Eternal Blue."

"And this shivering one?" Boldbator asked.

"He is a Chinese. My servant."

"A hardier servant would be advised for one who jour-
neys through this harsh land."

"Join us, friend," the head of the household said. Boldbator
saw that he too was an old man, but sturdy. He had the
wind-blasted face of a lifelong horseman.

Smiling, Boldbator took his place on the Oriental rug,
where the rest of the party was pulling bits of meat off a
roasted sheep—all but the old man in the sheepskin cloak,
who ate cold rice from a wooden bowl with his fingers.

Boldbator pulled off a greasy glob of mutton with his
fingers and shoved it into his mouth. As he chewed, he
spoke.

"I rode far this night, after seeing a sight I never before
thought I would see."

No one said anything. They continued their eating.

"I came upon a bus," Boldbator continued, "deserted on
the steppe, and all around it dead Chinese soldiers, as if
whelmed by a tremendous wind."

"Perhaps it is the sweet wind that has blown through
history," suggested the old man without looking up from his
rice.

Boldbator caught a flash of his clear eyes. They were like
agates in the slits of his lids. He was very old, much older
than Boldbator had first thought.

"I know of no such wind," said Boldbator.

"Nor I," said the head of the household. "And I, Darum,
have lived on the steppe all these fifty years."

"Fifty years is young," the other old man said.

Boldbator grunted through his mutton. Grease dribbled
down his chin. He caught some of it in his blunt fingers and
sucked them clean with lip-smacking relish.

"The men who did this were Mongols," he said. "True
Mongols of the old days. I followed their tracks all night,
not caring if I died on the frozen steppe if my last sight was
of such warriors."

"You speak like a true son of Genghis," the old one said.

"We are all sons of *Ssutu-Bodgo*, the Heaven-Sent."

"I have yet to meet any warriors," the old man said flatly.

"What name do you go by, old one?" Boldbator asked suddenly.

"It is not a man's name which speaks loudest, but his deeds."

"Well-spoken, and truly spoken," returned Boldbator, dropping the subject.

The conversation took other directions. The restiveness in Beijing, the wolf problem, which was severe this hungry winter, and the long months until lambing season. Eventually it came around to the destination of the old man and his Chinese serf.

"I will go to the Gobi next," he said, putting aside his bowl.

"And then?" Boldbator wondered.

"I will know when I have reached the Gobi."

"I see no alien horse tethered outside."

"Horses can be bought, even on the steppe—if one offers enough gold."

Boldbator roared his amusement. The others joined in.

"There is not enough gold in the world to induce a true Mongol to part with his horse in winter!" Darum scoffed.

The old man was silent for a long time.

"I seek the treasure of Temujin," he said in a firm but quiet voice.

Silence greeted his pronouncement.

"It has never been found," Boldbator said eventually. "Even the Khan's true burial site has remained a mystery through the ages."

"I will give ten percent of what I find to any Mongol who rides with me to the place of the treasure and enables me to bear it safely away."

"I would ride with any Mongol who would dare, but not with an old man and a shivering Chinese," Boldbator countered. "Otherwise I would be a fool who throws his life away."

"What else are you doing with your life, Mongol who was prepared to die for a glimpse of courage?"

Boldbator pounded his chest. "I ride. That is life itself."

"And when you are old?"

"I will watch my sons ride if I still walk the earth. Perhaps

I will live long enough to witness the coming of the next khan. For that is what I truly live for."

"A man who shares in the treasure of Temujin need not settle for waiting."

Boldbator paused. His almond eyes narrowed.

"He could be the Next Khan," the old man said pointedly.

Boldbator toyed with a stringy flap of mutton that hung off the burnt carcass, as if considering whether or not it would be good eating.

At length he spoke. "What are you, old man?"

"I am a Korean."

"I could not follow a Korean, even if you were the Master of Sinanju himself, striding out of the mists of history to stand by the side of the Khan to Come."

"You know of the Master of Sinanju, Mongol?" the Korean asked, interest silvering in his voice.

General laughter greeted the old Korean's question. Even the old woman laughed, exposing strong shovel-shaped teeth in which strands of mutton were caught.

"All Mongols know what the Master of Sinanju was to the khans of the old days. Woe to Mongolia that those days perished," Boldbator muttered darkly.

Darum lifted up a cup of fermented mare's milk and offered a toast.

"May they return again one day," he said solemnly.

"They may be closer than you think," said the old Korean, who declined to join in the toast, offering his cup instead to his Chinese servant. The Chinese spat out his milk and began coughing. Everyone roared anew—all but the coughing Chinese and the pensive old Korean.

"Why say you that, old one?" Boldbator wondered, after the laughter had died.

"What would you say if I said the Master of Sinanju was abroad in Mongolia on this very eve?"

"I would say, where is your proof?"

"And I would say that you saw the very proof in the Chinese corpses freezing on the steppe."

Boldbator's eyes shifted to the old Korean.

"I would agree with you, then," he muttered.

"Would you follow the Master of Sinanju if he asked it of you, horse Mongol?"

Boldbator raised his cup. The others followed his gesture.

"I would follow the Master of Sinanju to the ends of the earth as his slave," Boldbator announced proudly.

"Think carefully on your words, horse Mongol. For what if I said I could make the Master of Sinanju appear before your eyes, tonight, on this very eve, in this very *ger*?"

"I would speak them to his face," asserted Boldbator. "But first I would ask you how you could work such magic."

"Words," intoned the old Korean. "Six in number."

"They would have to be powerful words," Boldbator said carefully, his milk forgotten.

"They are."

"Then speak them."

The old Korean stood up suddenly, flinging off his sheep-skin cloak, to stand revealed in silken robes the color of a royal phoenix.

"I am the Master of Sinanju!" cried the old Korean.

Whereupon Boldbator the Mongol touched his head to the Oriental rug in the prescribed full bow.

"My horse is yours," he said simply. And he wept with joy.

19

The Iron Rooster pulled into Hohhot after darkness had fallen.

Fang Yu had to tell Remo they had arrived. He had no way of knowing otherwise. He had become a little irritable having to depend on her to find his way around. In a nearly thirteen-hour ride he had seen no English signs at any of the train stops.

Fang Yu led the way to a forward car.

Suddenly she turned and pushed Remo back.

"Go back," she hissed. "Go back."

Remo looked past her and saw the soldier who had earlier confronted them over Remo's documents.

"He know this not your stop," Fang Yu said bitterly.

"Damn," Remo muttered. He led the way back, punching the square button that made the automatic doors between the cars roll aside. Most had to be encouraged with a hard sideways shove.

They passed through the cars. Remo could tell the nosy soldier was still following them. His heavy boots made a distinctive clopping.

"What we do?" Fang Yu whispered.

"Step ahead of me," Remo urged.

Fang Yu hurried by. She hit the square button and the door rolled aside.

Remo followed her. The door slid shut behind him.

He stopped. Fang Yu hesitated. He urged her to keep going with an angry shake of his head.

Fang Yu picked up her pace.

Behind Remo, the steel door rolled aside. The soldier walked right into Remo's open-handed blow. His skull made a melon-imploding sound in the sudden sac his head became. Remo was disappointed. It didn't go *pong*. It was more of a *hong* sound.

Quickly Remo stuffed the body under the platforms between the cars. Then he went after Fang Yu.

"Come on," he said, pulling her by the hand.

"What happen?" she demanded excitedly. "Where soldier?"

Fang Yu's question was answered as they passed between cars and she spotted a patch of green under her feet.

She gasped like a stepped-on cat.

"What you do? Why you do that?" she said angrily.

"What else was I supposed to do?" Remo hurled back.

"He was Chinese soldier. You think you can just kill Chinese soldier like this is Western movie? He will be found. Questions raised."

"So?"

"They behead criminals in China. You not know that?"

"I don't care," Remo said, squeezing her hand tightly.

Fang Yu went silent as they passed through several softseat cars, where their English might be understood. They found an exit car and stepped into the darkness of the Hohhot station.

Fang Yu waited until they had departed the station on foot before she resumed her argument.

"You crazy?" she spat. "There will be a search when that man is found."

"Let them search," Remo growled. "We had to get off the train."

"We could have got off at Baotou. Stayed few days. Come back. Get off at Hohhot then. Why you in such a big rush?"

"My mission is important."

"Your mission matter a lot if we end up on courtyard with our heads in baskets!" she hissed.

Remo stopped. He looked down at her, his eyes angry.

"Look, get off my back! I can handle it. What's the big deal?"

"You want to know big deal?" she said, shaking an ivory fist in his face. "Big deal is that government very anxious since Tiananmen. Soldiers find body, they make example of innocent peasants and workers. People punished for your crime. Suffer very much. Never see family again."

Remo opened his mouth to vent a retort. But Fang Yu's point started sinking in. "Sorry," he said.

"You not the one who will be sorry," she said excitedly. "If you want Fang Yu's help, you do as Fang Yu say. Not make trouble for poor oppressed Chinese people. We have enough trouble without big-nosed foreign devil causing more."

"You're right," Remo said earnestly. "I apologize."

Fang Yu frowned. "You promise you behave?"

"Scout's honor," Remo said. Her expression didn't change, so he said it again in plain English. "I promise. Are we friends again?"

"When we stop?" Fang Yu asked unhappily.

"I think it was when you called me a big-nosed foreign devil," Remo said seriously. Then he added, "Never."

And he looked both ways in the Hohhot alley before he took her up in his arms and kissed her under the Mongolian moon.

"Okay, what's next?" Remo asked as they walked along.

"Can you ride horse?"

"I went on a pony ride once," he admitted. "But that was back in my orphanage days."

"You orphan?"

"Yes."

"Remo! I orphan too! Cultural Revolution orphan. My

parents sent into countryside because they came from bad family."

"Bad?"

"Intellectual. In those days intellectuals were considered bad people by Mao. Peasants and workers were always good—even when they steal and lie. Mao say they good. Everyone go along, because we Chinese. What choice have we? Crazy times. These times are not so crazy, just terrible."

Hohhot proved to be a fairly modern city, Remo found. The main difference between it and what Remo had seen in China so far was the preponderance of Mongolian-script signs instead of Chinese calligraphy. Its value was lost on Remo, who could read neither.

Dress was different in Hohhot, Remo saw as they wended their way through twisting side streets. Native Mongolians went about in colorful long cloth coats girdled at the waist by a sash. They looked as Asian as the passing Chinese, but their features were broader, complexions rawer, their noses more buttonlike.

The Chinese on the street were dressed in identical unisex blue work uniforms. Fang Yu explained that they helped the backward nomadic Mongols manage their capital city.

At one point they passed a mosque with a clock painted on its face. According to the immobile hands, it was 12:45 and would be for eternity.

Fang Yu found a small hotel that didn't ask questions, although Remo got a thorough looking-over by the broad-faced woman at the front desk. She looked more Cheyenne than Mongolian.

Fang Yu handed Remo a key and lifted one for herself.

"Separate rooms?" he said in surprise.

Fang Yu blushed. "What will Mongolians think—a civilized Chinese woman in same room with foreign devil?"

Remo couldn't tell if she was joking until she punched him in the ribs playfully. He gave her a sheepish smile.

They went up the stairs together and parted at Remo's door with a quick kiss.

"Stay in room," Fang Yu whispered. "I make all arrangements."

"You sure you'll be okay alone?"

"Not worry. Chinese women can take care of selves."

Remo found the room cramped and filled with overbuilt

furniture. The bed was so high it looked as if it would float to the ceiling, taking the white damask bedspread with it.

What appeared to be a spittoon stood at the foot of the bed.

There was also a phone, and Remo went to it eagerly.

Unfortunately, the instructions were limited to Mongolian and Chinese.

Remo whirled the rotary dial several times, hoping to hit the outside-access number. An assortment of pops and hisses assailed his ears. Finally he got an excited voice speaking Mongolian—or possibly Chinese—but not English, as he found after a ten-minute attempt to get the operator to summon someone̅who spoke or even had heard of English to the phone.

Remo hung up in disgust.

"So much for calling Smith," he grumbled.

He threw himself on the bed and practically hit the ceiling on the rebound.

Angrily he folded his bare arms and wished he had brought a change of clothes. There was no shower in the room. In fact, there wasn't a bathroom. The thing that stood at the foot of his bed was not a spittoon, he realized, but a chamber pot.

The spittoon was the narrow-necked vessel by the telephone.

Remo decided to ignore both conveniences.

So he closed his eyes and went instantly to sleep. It was easier than dealing with the complexities of Inner Mongolia.

20

Dawn warmed the frost-rimed grasslands of the Mongolian steppes.

Huddled on the communal bed, nestled with the entire Darum family and the single Chinese, Boldbator woke as if struck by lightning.

He crawled out from the snoring cat-pile of family members.

Chiun, reigning Master of Sinanju, was awake and rolling up his sleeping mat, which he placed in his great steamer trunk. He had slept apart from the others.

"Command me," said Boldbator.

"I crave tea," Chiun said blandly.

Boldbator blinked. "A woman could do that for you," he protested.

"But I have asked you," said the Master of Sinanju, locking the trunk. "Tea. And none of your Mongolian *tsai* with yak butter and salt. *Lurn jiin* would be excellent, for we have a long journey before us."

Boldbator set the brass pot to boiling. He made the tea in silence. The scent aroused the others. They climbed off the heated *kang* that kept them alive in the insufferable cold, stretching and blinking like contented cats.

Cold mutton filled their bellies. The Chinese looked as if he had not slept at all. He lighted a cigarette from the stove.

"What will you require for the journey?" asked Boldbator, pouring the tea into a delicate porcelain cup the Master held in both hands. He sat by the stove. He wore a green *del* with a white sash. The skirted coat fitted him perfectly.

"All the Mongols you can muster," Chiun replied at length.

Boldbator's hard eyes sought the sons of Darum. "You, you, and you—are you with me?"

"Aye," they said without hesitation.

"And I too," said Darum. "I tire of winter inactivity. My blood runs sluggish from stove heat and dung-smoke. I yearn for free air."

"So be it," Boldbator said sharply. "We are five. Are five Mongols enough for you, O Master?"

The Master of Sinanju shook his aged head. "I will need fifty times five for what I contemplate. For I expect trouble from the Chinese."

"The Chinese do not give trouble to horse Mongols," Boldbator boasted. "They are troubled by horse Mongols!"

And the *ger* reverberated with laughter once more.

Within an hour, they were a dozen—all the men who could ride from the four clustered yurts. The women waved them off with stoic pride.

The Master of Sinanju rode Boldbator's fine cream horse.

He had exchanged his sandals for felt boots, completing the traditional costume of a Mongol horseman.

"You honor us," said Darum.

"I wish to pass unrecognized for who I am," Chiun said simply.

"What do we seek in the Gobi wastes?"

"A broken dragon."

"I have trekked the length and breadth of Mongolia," Boldbator said, "and I have heard no tales of any dragon, broken or otherwise."

"It is there," Chiun said simply.

"If one dwells in the Gobi," Boldbator vowed, "we will find it."

They rode all day, the Chinese on a pony, the Master of Sinanju's trunk balanced on a spitting, complaining double-humped camel. It was no weather for camels, but even a stubborn dromedary knew better than to refuse a Mongol.

They rode north, over the relentlessly flat steppe. At each cluster of yurts and every outpost town they encountered, Boldbator shouted greetings at the top of his mighty lungs.

"Ho, Mongols! I am Boldbator, ally of the Master of Sinanju. We seek the treasure of Temujin. Who will ride with us?"

At Baiyinnar, the first town they reached, they collected thirty Mongols. Only five joined the caravan at the next *ail*. But by the noon hour, the unsentimental winter sun looked down on over a hundred Mongols riding proud. At each stop, Boldbator bartered for white horsetails.

In the end, nine white horsetails hung from a makeshift standard top. Only then did Boldbator carry it high and proud.

The Master of Sinanju, riding beside him, nodded his appreciation to see the honored standard of Genghis Khan blowing in the north wind after so many barren centuries.

"Who will ride behind this standard?" Boldbator cried when they reached the next town.

And this time, no Mongol of riding age refused him.

But in every town there are unfriendly eyes and ears, and soon the word had spread throughout Inner Mongolia that the Master of Sinanju had returned to the land of Temujin, and that he had gathered behind him a mighty army.

Word reached Beijing about the time they came to the

undulant edge of the Gobi, marked by a patchwork of straw designed to keep the dunes from eating into the steppe. Beyond this crisscross bulwark, the dunes rose high and purple in the dying sunlight.

The Master of Sinanju called for the caravan to come to a halt. The sun was low in the sky now, bronzing the dunes, which as the horses kneaded them with their tireless hooves, made whispering sounds of welcome—or warning.

The Master of Sinanju cast his eyes to true north. Then he spat words at his servant, Zhang Zingzong, who went to fetch a teak box from the camel-borne traveling trunk.

Boldbator watched in silent interest as a silver skull was removed from the box. The Master of Sinanju brought its hollow side to his face and stared into its bone emptiness.

Boldbator leaned closer in his saddle. His chin lifted. He could see that the Master of Sinanju stared through the sockets.

"We go on," Chiun said at last, handing the skull back to the waiting Zhang Zingzong with a careless toss.

Boldbator looked back upon his ranks of Mongols. His heart swelled with pride.

"We ride!" he proclaimed.

And the horde moved on, their hooves on the gravelly sand like the constant drone of invisible insects.

They rode another hour. They would have ridden all night, since darkness had fallen upon them, and missed the dragon, but for the Chinese rider, Zhang.

He rode as if every bone was arthritic, and was the butt of constant joking among the Mongols—banter that was not lost on him even if he did not understand the language.

Hunched over the pommel of his saddle, he shivered in mute misery, a constant cigarette bobbling off his loose lips.

They were riding at a steady mechanical pace that kept the horses fresh when Zhang Zingzong's pony gave a sudden whinny and stumbled.

In the near-dark the cry "Wolf!" ran the length of the mass of horsemen.

But it was no wolf, they saw as the pony picked itself up, the Chinese clinging to the saddle.

They laughed at Zhang Zingzong and called him a clumsy food grower.

Laughing, Boldbator ordered the group to press on.

"Hold," said the Master of Sinanju suddenly. He angled his horse—Boldbator's horse, really—over to the spot where the pony had stumbled. His hazel eyes narrowed as he raked the stiff sands with his cold gaze.

Boldbator joined him. "What do you know?" he asked anxiously.

"No horse stumbles on mere sand."

"Perhaps hot ash from his cigarette caused the pony to falter." But Boldbator saw that Zhang Zingzong's lips still clung to a half-smoked butt.

The Master of Sinanju dismounted. He knelt in the Gobi gravel, which cracked under his feet like a thin layer of ice.

His clawlike hand went into the sand and rooted around. He inhaled sharply, a gasp, half-surprise and half-joy.

"What do you feel?" demanded Boldbator as the Mongols drew their horses into a protective circle.

Chiun shrugged. "Gather the horses," he said suddenly. "Have them form four lines, like the spokes of a mighty wheel."

It took some lusty shouting and shoving on Boldbator's part, but the horsemen were finally mustered into position.

"Now have them walk in a circle," Chiun commanded.

The horsemen obeyed Boldbator's lung-splitting order. They guided their steeds—mares and stallions alike—around and around like satellites orbiting an unknowable world.

The horses wore down the crust of frozen sand until it no longer made its whispery complaint. Soon the gentle rise and fall became a pocked flatness, and still the horses promenaded.

Boldbator stood off from the equine wheel with Chiun, Zhang, and the camel. He held the reins of their mounts.

"We will have to camp soon," he muttered, casting an eye to the sun-gored western horizon.

"We will camp here," Chiun replied. "The dragon lies here."

"Where?" Boldbator asked, looking over the growing circle in the gravellike sand.

"The next horse to stumble will show us."

Two horses stumbled, actually. One, and in quick succession, the other.

"Stop!" Chiun cried. "All of you. Dismount!"

The Mongols stopped in place, retaining their perfect wheellike formations.

Boldbator followed the Master of Sinanju into the perfectly arrayed lines of horsemen. He lit a yak-butter tallow to provide light as Chiun knelt in the sand.

A hump of dirty brown bone stood up from a pock of sand. Boldbator touched it carefully.

"It feels like stone," he announced. "Truly, these are the bones of a fierce dragon."

"Order your Mongols to uncover every last rib," the Master of Sinanju commanded.

And with pride in his voice, Boldbator did as he was told. Gladly he did this, for a mere day ago he had been a young Mongol pounding the steppe in frustration and loneliness, but tonight he was a leader of warriors, the next khan.

They uncovered the dragon with their bare hands. Its thick ribs were cracked and broken. No shred of flesh or hide clung to them. The dragon had died an impossibly long time ago. It had a very long neck and a long tail. Its midsection was unusually stout.

"This dragon is strangely formed," Darum remarked as it lay naked under scores of raised tallows. The light was fitful and haunting.

"No doubt it is Chinese," Boldbator grunted. "No Mongol dragon would let itself grow fat like this one."

Oblivious of this, the Master of Sinanju ranged around the exposed skeleton, his mouth compressed in thought, his eyes like slits of steel, cold and implacable.

He stopped at the skull of the dragon. It was blunt-toothed for a dragon, Boldbator noted. Others remarked on this too.

But the Master of Sinanju paid them no heed. He knelt before the dragon's skull and with delicate fingers brushed the remnants of sand from the narrow stone brow.

His whisking nails exposed incised markings on the petrified bone. In silence he regarded them.

No one disturbed him.

At length the Master of Sinanju stood up and turned to face the expectant Mongol cavalrymen.

"Hear me, descendants of the Golden Horde!" he proclaimed. "Take to your mounts, for we ride to Karakorum!"

And giving a lusty shout of triumph, the descendants of Genghis Khan roared their approval with one voice.

All save Boldbator. Upon hearing the name of the ancient seat of Mongol power, he began weeping with joy.

They were riding into history. All this in a mere day.

21

Remo snapped awake at the tentative rapping on his hotel door.

He eased off the bed and floated to the rough-hewn panel, feeling refreshed and alert, asking, "Who is it?"

"Fang Yu."

He opened the door and the Chinese girl slipped in, shutting it quickly after her.

"Trouble?" Remo asked.

"The dead man has caused it," she whispered. "We cannot wait. We must ride north tonight."

"Lead the way," Remo said.

They went out, sneaking from the hotel the back way.

It was snowing, and snowing hard.

Fang Yu led Remo to what he took to be a Mongolian tavern.

Inside the solid oak door, it was exactly that—a saloon.

Wide bronze faces regarded them with a kind of curious indifference. Fang Yu looked around, then nodded. She strode boldly over to a corner table, Remo following, his eyes swiveling around the room. If there was going to be trouble, he wanted to be ready.

Fang Yu presented Remo to a thick-necked Mongolian man who sat nursing a cup of steaming-hot wine. He wore a black leather vest and quiltlike pants. His face had all the color and expression of a bronze gong.

Fang Yu rattled off a quick burst of Chinese.

"Speak English," the Mongol said brusquely. "I do not

wish our conversation to be overheard. There are many ears here, three times as many as there are heads to carry them."

"This is the man," Fang Yu repeated in English.

"Can he not speak for himself?" the Mongol grunted thickly.

"Call me Remo."

"I am called Kula. Can you ride, one called Remo?"

"Yes."

"You lie!" Kula the Mongol spat. "This Chinese girl tells me you cannot."

"I can learn," Remo said confidently.

Kula grunted. "The price is double."

"What?" Fang Yu demanded hotly. "We agreed on price!"

Kula took a sip from his cup, never taking his eyes off Remo. "He cannot ride, so he must be taught. It will slow us."

"I told you he cannot ride!" Fang Yu spat.

"But he lied to me. Lying adds to the risk. If he lies about one thing, why not another? The price is double," Kula repeated, draining his cup.

Remo drew Fang Yu out of earshot of the sullen-eyed Mongol. "Forget it," he said. "We don't need this guy."

"We do," Fang Yu said. "He is Kula—the bandit chief of this province. Without him, there is no safe passage."

"We'll make our own safe passage," Remo said loudly enough to be overheard.

The Mongol laughed at that. "I like him," Kula burst out. "But the price is still double."

"Very well," Fang Yu said reluctantly. "We pay. Five hundred *yuan*."

"Done!" said Kula the Mongol, slapping his cup on the age-stained table. "We ride now. Come."

The Mongol stood up, hitching up his leather belt. A short dagger dangled from it by a silver chain. Gesturing, he led them to a rear door and into an adjoining stable. Horses neighed at their approach.

"Have you no better clothes, white foreigner?" Kula demanded. "The steppe winds will lift the skin off your meat in sheets and split the muscles from your bones."

"I lost my luggage in Hong Kong," Remo said sourly.

"The Chinese are looking for a murderer," Kula rumbled

throatily. "Since you will ride a Mongol horse, you must dress like a Mongol."

"No chance," Remo said.

"Please," Fang Yu said, her hand going to Remo's bare arm.

Noticing the contact, Kula grunted. "What one hears of the prowess of Westerners must be untrue. Of course, she is Chinese. No Mongol woman would have you."

Remo and Fang Yu ignored the crude remark.

"Please Remo," Fang Yu implored. "Do not be stubborn now. Our lives are in danger."

Remo relented with a mute nodding of his head. He accepted a stack of padded clothes that resembled a rolled-up sleeping bag.

He went behind a stall and changed. He returned looking like an overgrown child who had been bundled up by a parent.

"That better," Fang Yu said.

"I'm not wearing this hat," Remo muttered, raising a cap with long floppy earflaps.

"Your ears will fall off," Kula said curtly.

"So my ears fall off," Remo said, looking around for a place to dump the cap.

Kula shrugged. "They are your ears," he said.

Remo stuffed the hat in a pocket, just in case.

The Mongol led a snow-white horse out of a stable bay.

"This is a good horse," Kula grunted, throwing a silver-filigreed wood saddle over the horse's back. "You will ride him. He is good for a new rider."

"If you say so," Remo said dubiously. The horse shook its long head nervously.

When Kula had finished tying the saddle, Remo climbed onto the horse. His felt boots found the iron stirrups. The high pommel and flared back of the saddle made him ride high, as if on a camel's hump. He hoped it wouldn't tip over.

The others saddled up and led their horses outside.

Kula the Mongol looked back. "Why you wait?" he grunted.

"How do you start this thing?" Remo asked sheepishly.

"You never see cowboy movies?" Fang Yu demanded.

"Refresh my memory."

"Shake reins."

Remo found the reins and gave them a shake. Desultorily the horse ambled on.

Outside the stable, the others mounted their steeds, and together the three clopped up the street.

"This isn't so bad," Remo said as he got used to the muscular rhythms of his horse. "What's his name?"

"Mongol horses do not have names," Kula spat.

"Shhh," Fang Yu hissed. A trio of PLA soldiers wearing drab greatcoats sauntered around a corner.

"Cover for me," Remo said. He pulled his cap out and hastily donned it. He snapped the earflaps together under his chin and pretended to discover a loose bit of silver filigree on his saddle. This kept his face averted from the soldiers.

The PLA soldiers cast wary eyes in Kula's direction. He returned their suspicious glares with a bold, challenging look.

The soldiers trudged on through the gathering snow.

They cantered beyond the city limits, where clusters of felt-covered circular tents dotted the flat white plains. Kula steered them clear of these, saying, "Mongol *gers*. Outsiders call them yurts. Many *gers* make an *ail*."

"How you people keep from freezing to death in this cold?" Remo asked.

"You will see," Kula grunted. "For we will pass the night in a *ger* if we are lucky enough to find one this night."

"And if we don't?" Remo asked.

Kula shrugged fatalistically. "Then our dead flesh will feed the wolves of the steppes."

Remo looked to Fang Yu. The Chinese woman looked stolidly ahead, controlling her fear. Remo felt no fear. Instead, he felt apart and alone in the great endless steppe.

They had cleared the outer perimeter of yurts when suddenly Remo felt his horse sink under him. His feet touched the ground on either side of the saddle. Hastily he stepped free, one foot tangled in an iron stirrup.

"What the hell is going on?" Remo yelled as he jerked his foot free of the remaining stirrup. Just in time, because with a whinnying and a kicking of his legs, the horse rolled onto his back and started to squirm in the dirt like a dog scratching his back.

Which, as Remo found his feet, was exactly what the horse was doing. It rolled and flung its mighty legs at the falling snow, struggling with its ungainly weight.

Kula and Fang Yu brought their mounts around and watched. Fang Yu covered her mouth with one mittened hand. Her eyes squeezed tight with repressed humor. Kula, less conscientious, roared deep throaty laughter.

Feeling foolish, Remo growled, "How do you get a horse to stop doing that?"

"You do not," Kula rumbled. "A Mongol would not let a horse do this in the first place."

"I'm no Mongol."

"That is evident," Kula said with dry impassivity. But there was humor in his twinkling eyes.

Remo turned to Fang Yu. "How about you? Any helpful hints?"

Fang Yu tittered into her hand and looked away.

Finally the horse clambered up to its feet. It waited patiently, flicking snow off its tail.

Remo approached carefully, touching the saddle. It was still cinched tight, so he remounted.

They got under way again.

Several hundred yards further along, the familiar sinking sensation returned.

This time Remo threw himself clear. He hit the steppe and jumped back angrily.

"What is your problem?" he yelled at the squirming horse.

The laughter of the others burned his ears. Remo reached out and grabbed the bit.

"This is getting old fast!" Remo said tightly. And with a quick heave, he pulled the horse to his feet.

To his surprise, the pony responded. Remo mounted again. He nudged the horse's flanks with his heels. It stepped smartly.

"You are learning," Kula said soberly.

"I'm a quick study," Remo said smugly.

"But so is the pony," Kula added.

A little further along, they came to a tussock of yellow grass. Remo's horse paused and, lowering its head, sank its teeth into a tuft.

Angrily Remo pulled up on the reins. The horse snorted, but straightened its muscular neck. He tried again. Remo pulled him back. After several minutes of pulling and nudging its flanks, the horse gave up on the tempting grass.

Remo urged him along, and soon caught up with the others, who had not waited this time.

As he drew alongside the other horses, Kula nodded in silent approval.

"Mongol horse or not," Remo said, "I'm calling him Smitty."

They rode on for hours. The darkness was relieved only by the moon. Clouds obscured it. And still they rode. Remo had gotten tired of his earflaps slapping his neck with each bouncing step of his horse and discovered they could be snapped at the top. This left his ears exposed to the cold dry air, but it also enabled him to hear sounds the others could not.

Distantly a wolf bayed. The wind made constant background sound. With nothing to inhibit its sweep down from the cold north, it blew cold and constant, like a wall pushing a million slim glittering blades before it.

The world was a barren desolation in every direction.

It seemed to Remo that if the Master of Sinanju was anywhere on the steppe, finding him would be more luck that anything else.

He felt very sad, and lonely. Lonelier than he'd felt in a long time. He angled his steed closer to Fang Yu, but other than a sidelong glance cast in his direction, he got nothing from her, not warmth, not comfort, and barely recognition.

"I smell blood," Remo said after a long silence broken only by their mounts' restless snorting.

"*Ai yah!*" barked Kula. "A Westerner whose nose is keener than a horse's! If there was blood in the air, the horses would know it first. My horse is not nervous. Nor is yours."

"To the northeast," Remo said stubbornly. He pointed in the direction from which the smell came.

"It is the smell of dung fires we seek, not blood," Kula said with finality.

"I'm looking for a man," Remo persisted. "And where he goes, blood sometimes spills." He noticed he was talking like a Mongol. He hoped that was all that would rub off.

Kula looked to Fang Yu. Fang Yu shrugged. Her look said all Westerners are mad.

"Look, I know what I'm talking about," Remo snapped.

"If you are so certain of your nose, foreigner," Kula said, "why do you not ride in the direction it tells you?"

"Good idea," said Remo, forking his mount away with a rightward twist of the reins. He spanked Smitty's cream flank. The horse broke into a gallop.

Kula and Fang Yu exchanged looks.

"Ai yah!" Kula cried, taking off after Remo. Fang Yu brought up the rear, muttering, "Crazy foreign devil."

They galloped in a loose pattern. Overhead, the moon ghosted in and out of the clouds.

During one period of exposed moonlight, they spied a brushed-silver hump in the distance. Light snow swirled around it.

A wolf bayed, very close.

Kula reached over to Fang Yu's reins and drew her horse closer to his.

"Wolves," he said ominously. "We must be careful."

"What about him?" Fang Yu asked.

"He is either mad or foolish. I cannot stop a madman and would not bother with the other."

As they watched, Remo pulled up at an abandoned bus and dismounted.

"He has sense enough to hold on to his horse, at least," Kula muttered.

"He is an American," Fang Yu said. "Cowboy blood runs in them all."

Kula nodded at this undeniable morsel of wisdom. There must be some skill in the American, for he himself smelled the cold tang of blood now.

They watched Remo move among humps of snow surrounding the bus. Patches of green showed here and there when Remo brushed at them with an uncovered hand.

"PLA men," Fang Yu said.

"This must be the bus they hijacked," Remo called back. "These guys are all dead."

Kula let his horse approach, Fang Yu trailing, her eyes searching every direction.

"What killed them?" Kula demanded from afar. He would

approach this place of sudden death no closer than necessary to carry on conversation.

"I think my Korean did it," Remo admitted, kicking loose snow back onto a gruesome dead face.

"Old Duck Tang?" Fang Yu asked doubtfully. "How he do that?"

"He just does it," Remo said, looking all around.

Kula dismounted, one hand tight on his reins. He examined several bodies. "I see no marks of death," he noted, low-voiced.

"That's how my Korean works."

"You say an old man did this?" Kula questioned.

"Yeah, and without this bus, he had to go on by foot."

"Then he would not survive, not without the warmth of a horse to keep him alive," Kula pronounced. "You might as well return to your own land. Unless you wish to carry his frozen carcass home."

"Hold this," Remo said, shoving Smitty's reins into Kula's hands. He climbed into the bus and looked around.

While Remo was preoccupied inside the shattered vehicle, Kula turned to Fang Yu, who had refused to dismount.

"It is not good to be found where Chinese soldiers have fallen," he rumbled. "Blame will be attached to us."

"Who would search the steppe in this weather?" Fang Yu remarked.

"True, but I do not like the look of these bodies."

Fang Yu looked toward the bus. "What is wrong with them?"

"There is no mark of wolves," Kula said flatly.

"Why is that bad?"

"Because I heard a wolf bay as we approached. If this white could catch the scent of blood from afar, so too will the wolves."

Fang Yu shuddered. Turning in her saddle, she tried to see in all directions at once. Then the moon was swallowed by a cloud.

The darkness was absolute. The horses whinnied nervously.

"Empty," Remo Williams' voice said in the darkness as he emerged from the bus. "They ran out of gas."

Then the snapping, slavering sounds of wolves ripped the comfortless darkness.

"Remo!" Fang Yu cried. Kula jumped to his horse. It reared up in fright, its forelegs kicking at nothing.

Only Remo Williams, his eyes trained to magnify ambient light, saw the wolves coming. They sprinted across the steppe like gray-furred comets. There were three. And they were tearing right for the horses.

Remo came off the bus running. He flashed to Fang Yu's side, smacking her mount on the rump. It bolted. Fang Yu held on. Remo wheeled and did the same for Kula's mount.

Carrying their riders, both horses galloped away from the racing wolves. Smitty followed Kula, who still clutched his reins.

Remo whirled to meet the oncoming wolves.

One leapt for his throat. He was the easy one. Remo grabbed his forepaws on the fly, spun and sent the wolf, legs kicking air, into one of the shattered bus windows. The wolf broke what was left of the glass and landed amid the seats. He didn't get up again.

"One down," Remo said tightly.

The moon came out again, igniting evil green wolf eyes like witch candles. One crouched to Remo's left. The other padded on from his right.

That one leapt with a sudden gathering of gray fur. Remo faded back, kicking high. His foot drove the wolf into a backward somersault. The snap of its neck told him it wouldn't rise again either.

"That's two."

The third skittered to a halt. His back arching, he slunk back three steps, eyeing Remo with furious intent.

"Come on, Lassie," Remo taunted, crooking one finger at the glowering beast. "Time to learn a new trick."

Warily it slipped to one side. Remo feinted with both hands. It dodged back. Remo advanced.

As Kula and Fang Yu watched from a safe distance, Remo did a slow dance around the last wolf, and he around Remo.

"We're not getting anywhere," Remo complained loudly. "Come on, stop wasting my time."

The wolf shifted one way, then another, sometimes advancing, other times retreating. It growled exactly like a dog.

"It is too smart for you," Kula shouted over. "It knows

you are a formidable enemy. Better that it think you are
weak."

"Appreciate the tip," Remo said. He retreated a few
paces. The wolf advanced warily.

Remo broke into a run, presenting his exposed back.

Emboldened by this show of cowardice, the wolf went
after him.

Remo reached the bus, broke off a shard of window glass,
and spun to meet the charging canine.

Snarling, the wolf jumped.

A glass fang whizzed through the Mongolian night.

It took the wolf full in the chest as its teeth snapped at
Remo's throat.

Remo's throat, along with the rest of Remo, ducked
under foam-flecked canine jaws. The wolf thudded against
the side of the bus and landed atop a frozen PLA corpse.

It leaked a little blood, and snow began collecting on its
gray-white fur. Its paws jerked briefly.

"And baby makes three," Remo muttered, picking himself up.

Casually Remo walked up to the others and accepted
Smitty's reins from a stupefied Kula.

"Shall we go?" Remo said lightly, feeling infinitely better.

They formed the horses into a line and pressed on.

"You learn to ride well in a short time," Kula ventured
after they had fallen into a rhythm.

"*Farhvergnugen*," Remo rejoined.

"Is that not German word?" Fang Yu asked in perplexity.

"Could be."

"You fight steppe wolf like you been fighting them all
your life," Kula said with newfound respect in his voice.

"One wolf is like another," Remo said airily.

"You fight like a tiger," Kula said. "Like white tiger.
Maybe I call you white tiger from now on."

"Call me what you want," Remo said. "Just don't call me
a quitter. I intend to find my friend."

"I believe you, white tiger," Kula said with simple sincerity.

Following the Great Mongolian Road, they came upon
the PLA jeep with its frozen driver next.

The snow had obliterated any further tracks. It made
Remo think of the mysterious footprints back in New
Rochelle—which seemed like another world removed from

this one. He cleared those thoughts from his mind. He had to find Chiun.

But all around him the steppe blended in a whirling world of snow. He felt like he was a tiny insect riding through one of those glass knickknacks that make snow when they're shaken.

Well into the night, they came upon a cluster of tiny brick houses from whose oilskin windows wan light glowed.

"We will sleep here," Kula announced brusquely.

"What if they don't want company?" Remo wondered.

"All Mongols know Kula. We will be welcome. Eat our fill of mutton and drink *airag*—fermented mare's milk."

"I'll pass," Remo said. But the warmth emanating from the house was welcome—even if it did smell like manure.

22

By the time it reached the border outpost at Koko Jebei, the New Golden Horde was five hundred strong.

Word had been flashed by shortwave from Beijing and the capital of the Inner Mongolian Autonomous Region to halt the movement of Mongol cavalry at all costs.

General Bo Wanding was prepared.

At the outpost, he had gathered the Fist Platoon, China's equivalent of a rapid deployment force, behind a wall of mechanized armor. They were the toughest, strongest, most politically unshakable soldiers in the Chinese Army. They feared nothing, not Russians, not Mongols.

They waited behind a line of T-55 tanks whose cannon pointed southward to the distant horizon line from where they knew the Mongol army must approach.

An impatient captain came up to the general.

"Should we not send spotter helicopters out over the desert to pinpoint their approach?" he suggested, eyeing the horizon uneasily.

"We are ready for them now," General Bo said. "We will be no more ready if we know the exact hour of their arrival."

"The men are tense."

"Good. Tension will keep their blood warm."

"Do you think the tales are true, General? That the New Khan has come into the world?"

"I do not know and I do not care," Bo spat. "I am a military man and I understand this much: that no legend can stand before the steel bite of tanks, or withstand the blast of cannon. What the counterrevolutionaries learned at Tiananmen, these barbarian Mongols will relearn on this very spot."

The captain nodded solemnly. He swallowed.

And so they waited. Eyes scanned the horizon through field glasses. Night fell. No Mongols came. No line of horsemen troubled the southern horizon.

Captain Shen Ching, shivering in the interminable wait, slunk off to relieve himself against the battle-gray fender of a T-55 tank.

His yellow urine turned red on the way to its destination as a long-nailed fist exploded his kidneys within his belly. His body was shoved under the tank.

A driver, tired of breathing the exhaust of his own body, popped the hatch on his tank, preferring to taste the bitter wind than suffer any longer.

A *swish-chuck* of a sound rang in his dead ears. His head rolled off his neck after the sword had sliced it away. Mongol boots kicked the glassy-eyed head under the tank. The body was pushed down. And so Boldbator entered the first tank undetected.

He slithered back through the driver's cockpit into the turret itself. Two men huddled there. They also died—one with a Mongol sword in his entrails, the other fighting to keep his neck from being snapped by the strong arm around it.

The arm proved stronger than his neck, which broke under a twisting wrench.

Casting the second limp body away, Boldbator reached up and undogged the turret by hand. He put on the broken-necked PLA soldier's helmet before he eased his upper body out into the bracing north wind.

He looked carefully to the left. Two helmeted heads

showed through the two turret hatches. He nodded toward them twice.

They nodded back, also twice.

To the right, there was but one shadowy helmeted head. It soon became two. Then three.

He cast his eyes about. In the darkness, a wispy form moved about, taking solitary pickets unawares, and conquering them with swift blows to head and body. Each conquered Chinese body was dragged under sheltering tanks or armored personnel carriers.

Boldbator grunted his appreciation. The Master of Sinanju sowed death wherever he walked.

They waited. Other turret lids clanged open. Other figures appeared. In the darkness, their padded jackets were indistinguishable from the heavy overcoats of the Chinese infantrymen.

An hour passed. The tension of the assembled Fist Platoon lessened as the men, massed behind the tanks, mistook the emerging tank crews as a signal to relax.

Then the first line of horses appeared.

General Bo spotted them. He barked a guttural order.

And in response, the occupants of the tanks fired up their engines. Boldbator slipped into his tank. He crawled toward the driver's pit, knowing that in the other tanks his comrades were doing the same.

He started his engine. The low, throaty rumble was matched by echoing surges on either side.

The order came to move out, to meet the oncoming Mongol charge head-on.

Boldbator grinned. And threw the engine into reverse.

General Bo at first thought it was the fault of a nervous tank driver. A tank backed up, crushing a jeep. The jeep's complement leapt to safety—all except the driver, who screamed incoherently at the remorseless steel treads chewing his frail flesh to rags.

Then other tanks backed up. And the foot soldiers of the vaunted Fist Platoon broke and ran in retreat from their own armor.

General Bo shouted over the din, demanding order.

Instead, he got a shock as a T-55 abruptly tractored around and came toward him. Its lights blazed in his face. And in the backglow, no longer shadowed by a helmet, was a wide bronze face. A Mongolian face, grinning with the lust of battle.

It was a ferocious expression that generation upon generation of Chinese soldiers had learned to fear.

And now it was coming at him, housed by a bulletproof monster of gray steel.

General Bo reached for his sidearm and brought it to bear on that taunting visage.

The bullet left the barrel with a spiteful crack.

The wide Mongol face disappeared. General Bo looked past the puff of gunsmoke his weapon had created.

The face came back up like a devil from a box.

The tank came on.

General Bo broke and ran. All around him his Fist Platoon scurried like chickens before a fox. They were dying like chickens, too. Treads gnashed and pulverized them.

And what the tanks didn't get, the horsemen did.

They came out of the south like thunder, joining with the PLA forces with flashing swords and the occasional cracking sidearm. But as Chinese soldiers fell, their AK-47's were scooped up by leaning horsemen, who never broke stride as they claimed the spoils of battle.

Soon the bursts of AK-47 fire were coming from horseback. The tanks were abandoned as the last clot of the ruptured Fist Platoon were thinned into sobbing men trying to escape with their lives.

Heads were liberated from running torsos. Arms fell from shoulders under clean downward strokes.

And like a dervish weaving a tapestry with threads of blood, among them moved the Master of Sinanju, his fingernails, like a thousand tiny daggers, seeking vital organs and arteries.

And then the roar of battle abated. The horsemen regrouped at the command of their leader.

General Bo crawled out from under a T-55, his arms raised in surrender.

"I am your prisoner," he said in shame.

A lone Mongol rode up to him. "Are you ignorant of your own history?" he demanded. "Mongols do not take prisoners," and he relieved General Bo Wanding of his head with an unexpected backhand sweep of his sword.

Then, their work done, the border of Outer Mongolia lay

open to them and they rode into it, masters of the everlasting horizon.

Boldbator carried the shaking nine-horsetail banner before them.

He turned to the Master of Sinanju, a wolfish grin splitting his pleasant visage.

"Like the old days, eh?"

"It is good to ride with Mongols," intoned the Master of Sinanju. "For too long I have been burdened by the soft ways of the West."

23

In the tan-colored desert home, Remo squatted on the floor, looking around. The interior of the house—which was built of mud brick—was surprisingly sumptuous. The floor was a profusion of Oriental rugs, and damask hangings covered the walls. There was no furniture to speak of—just ornate portable chests of drawers containing the household goods. They made Remo think of the missing Master of Sinanju.

They sat on a kind of low brick patio built into one inner wall because it was heated. The heat came from a brick stove nearby. A pipe carried smoke and heat to the shelf.

Remo accepted a cup of tea after first turning down mare's milk and a heated wine Kula called *kaoliang*. Fang Yu also took tea.

As they sat, Kula fell into long and earnest conversation with the only inhabitant of the house, a middle-aged woman named Udbal.

"What are they saying?" Remo asked Fang Yu between sips.

"Not understand Mongo talk," Fang Yu said. "Mongos not like us Chinese. Talk different, act different. During winter they do nothing except stay indoors and tend to their horses and sheep. They not grow food, believing meat is for men and grass for animals. They call Chinese people 'food-growers.' "

"I've heard worse said," Remo said dryly.

Finally the Mongol woman went to tend to a wok that sat in a hole atop the stove. Kula turned to Remo and Fang Yu.

"This is very strange," he muttered, low-voiced. "The woman says the men all have gone north, following a Mongol horseman known as Boldbator."

"Who is Boldbator?" Remo asked.

Kula shook his head. "I do not know him. But it is said he rides with a legend, who is called the Master of Sinanju."

Remo said nothing.

Fang Yu looked toward him. "The Master of Sinanju is a fable old men talk about in China, and Mongolia too," she explained for Remo's benefit.

"Is that so?" Remo said, tasting his tea. He had had to keep the woman from putting clotted milk and what looked like a lump of butter into it. It tasted salty, which was better for him than if there was sugar in it. Still, he'd never heard of salting tea.

"Did you not say the man you seek is a Korean?" Fang Yu asked suddenly.

"What of it?" Remo said guardedly.

"The Master of Sinanju of legend is supposed to be Korean, that's why."

"Coincidence," Remo said. "I'm looking for a different Korean entirely."

Fang Yu looked at him in owlish silence.

"It is said the Golden Horde rides again," Kula said, his eyes reflective as he stared into his steaming *kaoliang* wine. "They follow this Boldbator. Call him Khan."

"What!" Fang Yu exploded. She turned to Remo. "Remo, what you know of this?"

"Nothing. I'm looking for someone else entirely."

"The Masters of Sinanju were greatest assassins in history," Kula said. "For as long as they stood beside the throne of the khan, the khanates were safe. But Ogodai, son of Lord Genghis, made the mistake of invading Korea. And although the village of Sinanju was deemed sacred from conquest, this angered the Master of Sinanju at that time. He withdrew his support of the khan and so the empire began to decline."

"Nice fairy tale," Remo said.

"Do you tell the truth to me?" Fang Yu pressed.

"Why wouldn't I?" Remo said guiltily. He hated to lie, but he couldn't afford to tell the truth. US-Chinese relations were at stake.

"It is said that the Golden Horde rides toward Karakorum," Kula said thoughtfully, staring into his wine.

Fang Yu gasped.

"Where's that?" Remo asked.

"In what the Chinese call Outer Mongolia," Kula said proudly. "It was the imperial city in the days of Genghis Khan. Until that traitorous grandson of Lord Genghis, Kublai, swayed by its citified comforts, moved the seat of Mongol power to conquered Peking." He spat on the rug with great violence. "A fool's mistake," he added. "The food-growers took it back and razed Karakorum when they had the chance."

Fang Yu shifted closer to Remo. Remo put his arms around her protectively.

"It is said that in the days when the Master of Sinanju was a favorite of the khans," Kula went on, "they were attended by lesser warriors, who were called night tigers. These night tigers dressed in black and were fierce warriors, afraid of nothing."

Silence filled the house. Only the fussing of the Mongol woman as she fed yak chips into her stove disturbed it.

"Have you ever heard of this legend, white tiger?" Kula asked suddenly.

"No," Remo said quietly. Fang Yu studied his profile in the smoky light.

Kula grunted. "I yearn to ride with the Golden Horde, if these tales are true."

"You have bargain with us!" Fang Yu hissed.

"A bargain is a bargain, but blood is blood. My blood calls to me in the voices of my ancestors."

Fang Yu started to say something, but Remo quieted her with a squeeze of his hand.

"Is Karakorum in the direction we're going in?" Remo asked.

"It is," Kula admitted.

"We'll ride with you. Maybe we'll find my Korean on the way."

Silence.

"There is a better way," Fang Yu ventured.

"What's that?" Remo wondered.

"Ulan Bator. Kula can take train to Ulan Bator."

Kula snorted. "My horse cannot take a train."

"We ride to nearest city, which is Sayn Shanda," Fang Yu pressed, "then Kula take train to Ulan Bator, which is riding distance from Karakorum. Remo and I find other Mongol guide in Sayn Shanda. We go apart."

"If I have to leave my steed," Kula retorted, "I would not go. How could I join my people without a horse?"

"And what about my Korean?" Remo asked.

"Your Korean is going north," Fang Yu said. "Only city north of here is Sayn Shanda. He must go there. Else he die on steppe. This makes sense to you?"

"Some," Remo admitted.

"Then we go, all of us."

"Agreed," said Kula. "But first we eat. Then we sleep. Then we ride."

"Where *do* we sleep?" Remo asked, looking around the *ger*.

Kula spanked the stove-warmed platform.

"On *kang*," he said. "Mongol bed. Keep us warm at night."

"All of us?" Remo said. "Together?"

"Mongol tradition. Americans have no such tradition?" Kula demanded.

"Sure," Remo said. "It was called bundling and they stopped doing it around the time of the First Continental Congress."

"You will have to be tied with belt," Kula told Remo. "To protect Mongol woman from your lust."

The old woman smiled shyly in Remo's direction. "Well," he whispered to Fang Yu, "at least you and I will be together."

Fang Yu said nothing. Her gaze was distant.

24

The New Golden Horde rode unchallenged into the snow-dusted pastureland that was all that remained of ancient Karakorum.

The Mongols fell silent as they approached the ancient capital of the empire of the *Khagan*—the Khan of Khans. Not a Mongol spoke. They seemed not to breathe. The cadence of their ponies caused their earflaps to bounce like beating wings.

Before them lay a plain dotted by the clusters of *gers*. Black-spotted sheep and grunting yak ranged freely. Gaudy *ger* doors were flung open at their approach. No words were spoken and no replies given. The Mongol herdsmen took to their horses and joined the pilgrimage in silence. The women and children watched them go, weeping, although none could say what emotion caused the tears to come.

The sun hung low as they came to the place where Karakorum had once stood. They recognized it by the multitudinous white spire-tipped domes of the Erdeni Dzu lamasery that showed against low alpine hills.

The Master of Sinanju nodded to Boldbator. The Mongol lifted a hand to call a halt to the march.

Horses came to a stop, pawing the snow to expose tussocks of coarse brown nibbling grass.

Boldbator drew up alongside the Master of Sinanju.

"Speak your desire, O Master of Sinanju," he said quietly.

"Have your horse Mongols make camp, Boldbator Khan," said the Master of Sinanju.

Wheeling, Boldbator Khan lifted his voice.

"We camp here!" he shouted. "Let the word go to the last straggler. This night we sleep with the ghosts of our mightiest ancestors!"

And the answering cry shook the very heavens, it seemed to Boldbator Khan.

"And what of us?" asked Boldbator of the Master of Sinanju, whose sere visage, although buffeted by the freshening wind, refused to flinch.

"The skull of the dragon told me a riddle," intoned Chiun, Reigning Master of Sinanju, "and that riddle said that the man who overthrows the tortoise that moves naught but through time shall find the eggs of the tortoise if he digs far enough. We three shall ride to the tortoise."

Boldbator cast contemptuous eyes toward Zhang Zingzong, who understood nothing of their conversation.

"Him too?" spat Boldbator. "Why should a soft Chinese bear witness to the glory of the Lord Genghis Khan, the Heaven-Sent?"

"This man is a hero in his own land," Chiun said simply.

Boldbator snorted. "This food-grower? He can barely ride."

"He once stood up to the iron horses of the Chinese oppressors," intoned Chiun. "And the horses backed down."

"We have swept through the iron cavalry of the Chinese like locusts through wheat. I beheld no heroics from this man."

Chiun shrugged. "For a Chinese, it was feat enough. Besides, it was he who brought the silver skull from the Great Wall to me. I have promised him half of the treasure."

Boldbator spat.

"If it is the wish of the Master of Sinanju to do this thing," he growled, "I have no stomach to tell him otherwise."

"Well-spoken. Let us ride."

Chiun nodded for Zhang Zingzong to follow.

Their horses moved slowly, not because they were fatigued— although they were hardly fresh—but because they sensed that they neared their ultimate goal.

The tortoise was a great stone thing that sat in the center of the plain, brooding and inert, its gray stone shell a patchwork of Mongol designs. Its worn ancient head lifted skyward as if straining with its last ebbing strength.

"It has stood there thus for generations, to mark the spot where the Great Khans once ruled," Boldbator said reverently.

"Moving not," added the Master of Sinanju, "except through the years. Come."

They rode up to it, dismounting. The walled lamasery lay within sight, like an abandoned fortress.

Zhang Zingzong came off his steed like a man who had been nearly frozen. He slapped his sides with his padded arms. Digging into a pocket, he extracted a lighter and a crushed pack of Blue Swallow cigarettes. He was getting low again, he saw.

He watched in silence as the Master of Sinanju, looking like an old Chinese cavalryman in his padded riding costume, strode around the tortoise monument.

From the words Zhang Zingzong had overheard pass between the old Korean and the Mongol who dared to call himself khan, he knew that they were on the site of Karakorum, which had been razed by the Chinese Army in 1382, after the collapse of the Mongol-led Yuan dynasty that had ruled China.

He prayed they had reached the end of their quest. He was sick of eating rancid Mongol food.

The Master of Sinanju finished his inspection of the tortoise, which was less than a man high and longer than a full-grown horse. It weighed perhaps a ton.

So when the Master of Sinanju stepped behind the tortoise and slipped off his padded jacket to expose his spindly arms, Zhang Zingzong let the cigarette dangle from his slackening lips unsmoked.

The Master of Sinanju sucked in a lung-paralyzing quantity of cold Mongolian air, expelling it with sudden violence. More air came in, and was released. His old-ivory face reddened and then, eyes brighter than seemed possible for mere eyes to become, he put his shoulder to the tortoise's blunt backside.

The dirt protested. Then the tortoise began to move.

Boldbator the Mongol, seeing it lurch forward, fell in next to the Master of Sinanju, even though his strength made the tortoise move no faster.

Then, overcome by a sense of history, Zhang Zingzong joined them. He braced his shoulder and began pushing with his long legs. The tortoise kept sliding, pushing dirt ahead of its lifted throat.

Zhang felt the hard ground under his straining feet turn soft. They had exposed fresh ground, which had been disturbed by the undershell of the stone tortoise.

"It moves now," Boldbator grunted. "But not only through time, eh?"

The Master of Sinanju said nothing. His breathing came in surges. Each inhalation was a pause. Each exhalation seemed to inch the tortoise ahead another half-foot.

At length, ground that had not seen sunlight in generations lay in the dying red light of the Mongolian sun.

It looked like ordinary dirt.

Sweating in his fur-lined clothes, Boldbator Khan stepped around it, kicking tiny stones away with a boot.

Zhang, breathing hard, reached for a pack of cigarettes.

"The ground is hard," Boldbator told the Master of Sinanju without emotion.

"We are harder," Chiun said.

Boldbator retrieved his sword from his mount. On hands and knees, he crawled over the exposed ground, probing it with the point of his sword.

"Nothing," he said forlornly.

"Let me," said Chiun, taking the sword from him.

The Master of Sinanju took the sword in both hands and, holding it perpendicular to his body, walked back and forth the length of the patch of exposed earth.

The sword quivered each time he walked over a certain point, but nowhere else.

The Master of Sinanju raised the sword overhead and with a sudden cry brought it down.

It sank into the ground to its very hilt.

"Here!" cried the Master of Sinanju. "Dig here."

Boldbator Khan walked up to his sword and began to wrestle with it. It refused to budge at first, but by dint of main strength he got it to work back and forth, loosening the hard frozen ground.

As the sun set on them, he used his sword to excavate a deep hole as the Master of Sinanju stood watching, saying nothing, except to remark to Zhang Zingzong that if he intended to wither his lungs with tobacco stink, that was his business, but to burn them downwind.

Zhang wandered off, and like a peasant, squatted in the dust, smoking cigarette after cigarette, his eyes intent, his face without expression.

He felt useless. The Mongols despised him. Even the Master of Sinanju treated him ill. He wished he had never left China in the first place. He had been a hero there.

True, Zhang Zingzong never really believed himself a

hero. He had been a simple student who, in the white-hot aftermath of the Battle of Beijing, had stepped into the path of a T-55 tank column, unthinking, only hating. The shamed tank drivers had lost face and he had melted into the crowds. A tiny victory, nothing more. Everyone else called him hero. And the PLA branded him a counterrevolutionary.

Zhang Zingzong had lost his life, his wife, and his freedom. He had been hunted from Paris to New York. The West wanted to make of him a symbol of bravery, but Zhang had felt only fear after Tiananmen. Only the treasure of Temujin promised hope. He felt like a failure among these fearless Mongols. Sometimes he wished the tanks had ground him into dust with the true heroes, the martyrs.

It was two hours later that Boldbator Khan, while driving his sword deeper, felt the vibration of steel against something hard and resisting. It felt as if the blade were running through bone.

"I have struck something, O Master!" he called.

The Master of Sinanju padded forward unhurriedly. But his controlled movement bespoke his eagerness, as did his bright, avid eyes.

Boldbator withdrew his sword, offering it to the old Korean. Chiun disdained it with a wave and sank to his knees in the pit.

He drove one spindly arm into the cold disturbed soil and his fingers rooted around, his eyes shut.

At length he excavated a round dirt-caked object. His wrinkled visage was alight with a keen joy. His eyes became wide with anticipation, as his long nails dragged clods of dirt from the long-buried artifact.

The last crumb of dirt hit the ground. Chiun's eyes widened to their furthest. Then they squeezed with a sudden lid-tightening contraction.

"Aiieee!" he wailed, his mouth going round with despair.

Boldbator leaned down. Zhang ran up, losing his half-smoked cigarette.

"Another skull," Boldbator said bitterly.

"Another riddle!" Chiun spat. "Another stupid riddle. Had your ancestors nothing better to do than carve riddles in bone?"

Boldbator stiffened, but had no reply.

"What does this one say?" Zhang Zingzong asked in Mandarin.

The Master of Sinanju brushed the brow clean. The crown of the skull was broken, where Boldbator's sword cracked it. A jagged lightninglike fracture fissured the brow, but the ideographs were decipherable.

Chiun read them aloud.

" 'Now that you have beheld the seat of my mighty power, go to the lands that I have conquered. In Five-Dragon Cave you must walk the left path, or the false path will claim you.' "

He repeated the riddle in Mongolian for Boldbator's benefit.

"I have never heard of Five-Dragon Cave," Boldbator said.

"Five-Dragon Cave is unknown to me," Zhang Zingzong admitted.

"I know the place," Chiun said softly, so softly the others had to lean closer to understand him.

"Where is it?" Boldbator asked.

"In Chinese Mongolia." Chiun turned to Boldbator Khan. "Will you ride into China with me?"

"I would ride into hell with you," Boldbator proclaimed in a stricken voice.

"And your men?"

"They conquered China once before. Why not again?"

The Master of Sinanju put the same question to Zhang Zingzong in his native tongue.

Zhang's eyes went wide. His face shook. Tears started.

"Hah!" said Boldbator. "This Chinese is more afraid of his own people than of we Mongols. Some hero!"

Boldbator Khan's laughter shook the night. He felt more alive than at any point in his life before tonight. To feel this good, he thought, was worth dying for.

25

They set out for Sayn Shanda at the crack of dawn.

The snow blew in like a powdery wall. Suddenly Remo, Fang Yu, and Kula were trudging through a world of howling white noise.

Kula shouted over the howling wind for them to dismount.

"Grab the tails of your ponies," he barked after Remo and Fang Yu had found their feet.

Remo obliged. He felt foolish.

"Now what?" he called.

"Do not let go," Kula cried.

The horses pressed on by themselves. They pushed through the blinding snow like stubborn beasts of burden. They never stopped, never paused, not even to defecate. Remo learned to watch where he put his feet after he heard the telltale *plopping* sounds on the snow.

After the snow abated, they remounted and continued on.

"It is the Mongol way," Kula boasted, brushing snow off his leather vest. "A Mongol horse will seek his home, or the smell of other horses. It is important not to let go of the tail. He will not do this with a man astride him. For a horse knows who his master is."

The snow had tapered off and the wind dropped to an occasional puff of cold in their faces when they emerged from a snow-filled valley to behold a small city off the northern end of the Gobi.

A small airplane lifted off, to Remo's surprise.

"Is this it?" Remo demanded.

Kula nodded. "Sayn Shanda," he said proudly. "We have crossed the border into Outer Mongolia. Free Mongolia. Come."

They rode into town.

It was a curious mix of modern Asian metropolis and frontier town, Remo saw. Buses, trucks, and cars moved through the streets, and there were few bicycles, at least compared to Beijing. Horses were plentiful, though. He saw several hitched to Wild West-style hitching posts outside of otherwise modern high-rise apartment houses.

"We are safe here," Fang Yu told Remo. "PLA not cross border. Outer Mongolia no longer Communist."

"Does that mean I can call America?" Remo asked, noticing a man walk by wearing blue jeans and a T-shirt that said GENGHIS KHAN LIVES. Other passersby—both men and women—wore native *dels*. Many were Chinese in familiar blue work uniforms.

"We will find you hotel," Fang Yu said. "Rest up."

"You two do that if you wish," Kula rumbled. "I will find a warm *ger* and all the comfort I need therein."

They rode along. Remo noticed that the billboards and street signs were in Cyrillic, the Russian alphabet, not Chinese or Mongolian characters. He still couldn't read any of it, but he took comfort in being able to recognize certain letters.

They came to a hotel that looked no different from any Western hotel, except the statue standing out front was of a stout Mongol warrior in full battle dress. Unlike most of the Mongolians he had encountered, this one had a spray of beard on his chin.

"That is a good hotel," Kula said.

"How do you know?" Remo asked.

"It is the Genghis Khan Hotel," Kula explained. "That is his statue."

"Really?" Remo said. "They named a hotel after Genghis Khan?"

"It is chain," Kula said with a straight face. "The national chain of Mongolia. They are the best. Before, this was the Lenin Hotel and his statue stood in that very spot. No more. Mongolia get rid of Communists. Lenin out. Genghis back in. The old ways are returning. Our blood is the same color again. It makes me proud."

"Well, it takes a Mongol to know one," Remo remarked.

They dismounted. Remo looked around for a hitching post.

"I will take your steed around back," Kula offered. "There

will be a stable there. All Genghis Khan Hotels have full accommodations for horses too. I will call on you later to make arrangements for the return of these horses."

"You do that," Remo said, leading Fang Yu into the lobby.

"Bunk with a foreign devil?" Remo whispered to Fang Yu.

"Of course not," she said crisply.

Remo's face fell. He said nothing. Fang Yu had been distant all during the hard ride. He wondered if she regretted joining him.

They went up to the front desk, where a wide-faced Mongolian woman in a bright blue *del* beamed at them with the most dazzling teeth Remo had ever seen. She looked like an Asian angel, harmless and eager to please.

"*Sain Bainu*," she said.

"We don't speak Mongolian," Remo told her.

Her face brightened. "Ah, you English?"

"American," Remo corrected.

"But you speak English?"

"Yeah. How much for two rooms?"

"You pay in *yuan* or dollars?"

"Dollars."

"One dollar sixty-nine cents, please. In advance."

Remo looked at Fang Yu doubtfully.

"Mongolia just opening to the West," she explained. "Need hard currency very much. Good buy."

"At these prices, I could buy the whole freaking hotel," Remo said, digging out his wallet.

"Ah, freaking hotel not for sale," the Mongolian woman said, enjoying the taste of the new American word in her mouth.

A bellboy in a white *del* escorted them to their rooms after Remo explained for the fifth time that he had lost his luggage. Sympathy for him and clucking sounds of disapproval for the "freaking" Hong Kong baggage handlers greeted his remark.

"I'm going to make a call," Remo told Fang Yu as they parted at their doors. "Meet you later. For lunch?"

"After I shower. I will call on you."

"And maybe a get-reacquainted session?" he added hopefully.

Fang Yu looked away guiltily. "Perhaps."

"You'll feel better after you clean up," Remo said, trying his best to sound upbeat.

Once in his room, he grabbed the telephone. It had a rotary dial.

To his delight, the hotel operator spoke English. After inquiring how he liked his "freaking" room, she asked if he'd like to place a "freaking" call.

"What's the phone code for America?" Remo asked wearily.

Upon receiving the number, Remo punched it in, and then dialed one repeatedly. He was used to hitting a button and waiting, so he just kept dialing until the line rang and the sharp lemony New England consonants of Harold W. Smith pierced his ear.

"Remo, where are you?" Smith asked breathlessly.

"Believe it or not, Outer Mongolia. I've heard of Outer Mongolia all my life, but I never dreamed I'd wind up here. And I have you to thank for this."

Smith ignored the dry sarcasm of Remo's tone.

"Have you found Chiun and Zhang?" he asked.

"No, but I'm not far behind them, I think. Chiun's been cutting a swath through China and Mongolia. Did you know there were two Mongolias, by the way?"

"Yes, I did. What city are you calling from?"

"Sayn Shanda. It's in the non-Communist Mongolia. I guess that explains why the phones work."

"Remo, I am getting disturbing reports out of China. Troop movements. Concern in Beijing of a Mongolian uprising."

Remo sighed. "Chiun. Don't ask me how, but he's got half of Asia stirred up. From what I hear, he's raised an army. You know him. He never did like the Chinese much. Do you think he's out to conquer the whole place?"

"I do not know," Smith admitted. "It does not sound like him."

"None of this sounds like Chiun," Remo said, looking out the window. It was starting to snow again, not hard, just flurries. "What the hell is he up to?" Remo asked plaintively. "Why did he run out on us?"

"Remo, listen carefully to me," Smith said, low-voiced, even though he was speaking over a secure line. "Our reconnaissance satellites show a mass of cavalry moving south for the Mongolian joint border."

Remo brightened. "Great. Then I'll just wait for Chiun and his merry band to show up."

"We have reports out of China that the Twenty-seventh Army is being sent north by rail."

"So?"

"Those were the troops used to attack Tiananmen Square, after the local units refused. They're peasant soldiers, politically unsophisticated and therefore used to obeying their commanders. It is obvious to Washington that they are out to intercept the Mongol force."

"No problem," Remo said. "I'll stop Chiun before the Twenty-seventh reaches the China-Mongolia border."

"No," Smith said. "China has a deep-seated fear of a Mongol invasion, even to this day. The Twenty-seventh will not stop at the border. That rail line passes through the heart of the Gobi to the capital of Ulan Bator. They'll engage the enemy as deep into Outer Mongolian territory as they possibly can. The Twenty-seventh Army—which is politically unpopular—will probably be used for cannon fodder while other units are massed on the border as a mobile Great Wall of China. Your job, Remo, is to stop that troop train at all costs."

"Any suggestions?"

"That is up to you. But you must do it. A Chinese incursion into Mongolia will have grave political repercussions. Outer Mongolia, although friendly with China, is allied with Russia. The Russians would see an incursion as a prelude to an attack on the SU."

"SU?"

"Soviet Union. That's what we're calling it now."

"Oh. It's hard to keep up with a changing world."

"Remo, I'm counting on you," Smith went on. "The President is counting on you. Never mind Zhang Zingzong. Stop the Twenty-seventh Army first."

"And then?"

"Stop Chiun. Just as we cannot allow China to attack Outer Mongolia, a Mongolian attack on mainland China would precipitate an equal crisis. The Chinese are already embroiled in Moslem uprisings in the eastern provinces. It's a mess."

"Tell me about it," Remo said.

"Sometimes," Smith confided, "I think the cold war was a better time. All this nationalistic strife is making global strategy exceedingly difficult to manage."

"Global strategy is your problem," Remo said. "Mine is heading off this mess. But at least I have Fang Yu."

"Who?"

"Ivory Fang. My contact, remember? She's been a great help. Don't know how I'd've gotten this far without her."

There was silence on the line. Remo tapped the receiver hook.

"Hello? You there, Smitty?"

Smith's voice was arid. "Remo, Ivory Fang is not a woman. Ivory Fang is a male agent."

It was Remo's turn to be silent.

"You sure about this?" Remo asked in a small voice.

"Are *you* certain of *your* facts?"

"Believe me," Remo said ruefully. "I'm an authority on her femaleness. If she's not your contact, how come she met me at the airport and helped me this far?"

"I do not know, but you had better find out quickly. She could be an agent of the Chinese Security Bureau. Proceed under the assumption that you've been compromised."

" 'Compromised' is the word," Remo said. "I kinda like her."

"Do not let it cloud your judgment. You have a twofold mission. Every minute is crucial."

"Count on me," Remo said in a suddenly clear voice.

He hung up the phone, his features darkening. He stepped over to the window and looked out over the city of Sayn Shanda.

It was small by American standards, but surrounded by the vastness of barren Outer Mongolia, it seemed a miracle of civilization carved out of a forsaken wilderness.

The snow continued falling. Remo's sharp eyes picked up snowflakes as they swirled downward, memorizing their unique shapes. Someday, he thought, he'd spot two that were alike.

"But not today," he said aloud. He turned from the window. A second sooner and he would have missed it.

Down in the street, around a corner, came a long black limousine. It was identical to the one he had first encountered in New Rochelle. And it matched the one he'd seen from the train.

"This isn't China," Remo muttered under his breath. "No reason why a Chinese Red Flag limo should be way up here."

He decided Fang Yu could wait.

Remo flashed to the door. He moved along the corridor to the elevator. As fast as he went, he was able to catch himself as he turned the corner. Just in time.

Fang Yu stood by the elevator impatiently, her hair dry. As Remo hovered out of sight, the elevator came and took her away. Remo emerged from hiding. The indicator showed that the car was on its way to the lobby.

"That must be the quickest shower in history," Remo muttered. He plunged for the stairs.

At the bottom, he eased a fire door open and watched Fang Yu hurry through the lobby and out to the front door.

Remo followed, trying to be unsuspicious. He was still in his Mongolian riding costume.

Outside, the black limousine waited, engine purring.

A chauffeur popped from the front door and opened the rear for her. He wore black.

Fang Yu stepped inside. The door shut with quiet force. The chauffeur returned to his wheel.

Remo saw his black mask—not that he had any doubt who the man was. His pantherlike body language gave him away.

"Damn!" he said. Remo hesitated. The Twenty-seventh Army was on its way. Could he afford to follow the car?

The limousine pulled away from the curb.

"Damn it," Remo repeated. "What am I supposed to do?"

The limo slid down the street and around a corner, its rear lights red and resentful.

Under the stern gaze of the statue of Genghis Khan, Remo watched it go.

"Must get great mileage to go from New Rochelle to Outer Mongolia," he muttered. Then he walked around to the back of the hotel.

The stable was separate, of wood, but bore the same Cyrillic symbols as the hotel marquee. Remo went in and found a short Mongolian man in a gray *del*.

"Speak English?" he asked the shyly smiling man.

"Of course, English is a wonderful language," he said, adding, "Compared to Russian."

"Great. That cream horse is mine. A friend stabled him for me. His name is Kula."

"Ah, Kula. A horseman among horsemen. Everyone knows Kula."

"Glad he's so popular. Know where he went? I gotta find him—fast!"

"Come," the Mongol stablehand said, leading Remo back outside. He pointed west, saying, "See those freaking *gers?*"

"You mean yurts?"

"Only Russians call them yurts," the Mongol said contemptuously.

"The *gers*, sure," Remo said. "I see them."

"Go there. You will find Kula in one of those. That is a true Mongol hotel. Not like this ugly concrete thing."

"Well, what do you expect from the Genghis Khan Hotel?"

"Lord Genghis was a great man," the Mongol retorted seriously. "His was the greatest empire in history, and his memory was too long suppressed by the Russians. What do Russians know? They think Lenin was a hero—Lenin could not ride a camel, never mind a horse."

"I heard Genghis destroyed every city that stood up to him," Remo pointed out, "putting everyone to the sword."

The Mongol sighed happily. "Yes," he said wistfully. "That was our Lord Genghis. A fine role model for our children."

"Uh-huh," Remo said dryly. "Saddle my horse for me?"

"At once."

Remo gave the man a buck as his horse was brought out. He got on and galloped off.

The Mongol watched him with expert interest. He had never seen an American ride before. They rode better than Russians, but not so good as Mongols. But who could ride like a Mongol other than another Mongol?

Remo rode through the cluster of *gers*. He was in a rush, so he called out Kula's name as he picked his way along.

A wicker door spanked open and the Mongol came out, blinking sleep from his narrow eyes.

"Remo!" he exploded. "What are you doing here?"

"I need your help. The Chinese Army's coming this way by rail. They're out to stop that Mongol army. And they're moving south. I gotta stop that train."

"Wait. I will gather good riders."

"No time," Remo said. "Just point me toward the rail line."

"It goes through this very city. We are on the Trans-Mongolian Railway. We must ride south to meet these food-growers who think they are warriors."

"Then let's ride!" Remo said anxiously.

"One moment," Kula said. He ducked back into his *ger* and an excited Mongolian argument filtered out. Remo waited impatiently.

Kula soon returned, trailed by two Mongolians in padded *dels* carrying curved bows.

They looked at Remo and asked Kula several hot questions. Kula replied in kind. Remo said, "Shake a leg! Every minute counts!"

"I am coming," Kula said. He shot a final order to the others, who abruptly split in two directions.

Kula saddled up and joined Remo.

"We ride," he said. "Others will follow."

"What was that all about?" Remo asked after they had turned their horses around and started away.

"I tell them I follow you, the white tiger. They do not believe me when I speak of your mighty feats."

Their cantering horses put the *gers* behind them.

"Let's go!" Remo shouted.

They galloped across the plain. Remo rode like a man born in the saddle. He didn't notice. He was thinking of Chiun to the north, the troop train to the south, and Fang Yu, wherever she was, whatever she was doing.

He put her out of his thoughts. The desert stretched before him, endless and uncaring.

He had a job to do. Personal stuff could wait.

26

The railbed was half-buried in snow.

"Looks impassable," Remo remarked when Kula pointed out a section that the wind had blown clear of snow.

"In winter, it often is," Kula remarked. "But the Chinese will not let snow stop them. They are like ants. They will ride so far, and their soldiers will dig out each section of track. Then go on."

Kula dismounted, saying, "I will show you a trick." He went over to a section of track and took one rail between his strong teeth.

"Hear any popping?" Remo asked, looking down the line. It was hard to believe that under this snowscape lay a desert.

Kula released the rail. "You know this trick?" he asked in surprise.

"I've seen it in a million movies."

Kula nodded. "That is where we Mongolians learned of it too. And no," he said, straightening, "I hear nothing."

He remounted, and they rode on, following the tracks.

"We are only two," Kula pointed out. "How will two men stop a train loaded with Chinese soldiers?"

"Let me worry about that," Remo said grimly.

Kula noted the determination in the American's face.

They rode, every so often pausing to listen for vibrations on the rails. But they lay cold, devoid of vibration.

A white disturbance on the horizon that might have been rolling low-lying clouds caught Remo's attention.

"You have geysers in the desert?" he asked.

"No."

"Then it's train time."

It was a black troop train, they saw as it came around a long shallow bend in the railbed. A black steam engine pulled it along, sending billows of white steam into the clear blue.

Remo counted ten T-55 tanks on flatcars and a quartet of armored personnel carriers. The rest were passenger cars, loaded no doubt with PLA regulars.

Kula looked back over his shoulder. His gonglike face reflected metallic disappointment as it swiveled back to the train.

"They will not arrive in time," he said simply.

"Won't need them," Remo retorted, getting off his cream pony. Leading the horse, he went to the railbed.

Kula sauntered up. He took the reins from Remo. Then Remo sank to his knees.

He laid both hands on the nearest rail. It was cold to the touch. He warmed it with quick back-and-forth rubbing motions. Friction. Then he felt along the rail until he found a seam where the rails were welded together.

As Kula watched, his eyes often cast in the direction of the huffing steam engine, Remo made a spearhead with his right hand. He brought it up. Then sharply down.

The crack of cold metal separating made Kula, for all his Mongol poise, jump in his saddle.

Remo clambered over to the other rail. He repeated his chopping action. Another crack.

Then, quickly, because he could feel the vibration of the approaching train in the very air as well as from the rail, Remo moved down the track to the next set of weld seams.

Crack! Crack! The welds broke free. Remo touched the separated rails. The vibration was absent. The rails were no longer linked to the system.

Remo looked up. The train was bearing down. He expected a train whistle but there was none. The Twenty-seventh Army wasn't about to signal its encroachment into Outer Mongolia—or think twice about running over a lone man on the rails.

"Want to lend a hand?" Remo suggested calmly.

Kula jumped off his pony with alacrity. He got a grip on one rail while Remo pulled up each spike with his hands. Kula shouldered it off to one side while Remo attacked the other set of spikes. The other rail clanged as it found a new place in the snow.

Remo looked at the empty section of track and then to the train.

"Not enough," he decided. He moved ahead. Two more weld seams released under his chopping blows. Two more rails were shoved to one side.

Then, recovering their horses' reins, Remo and Kula walked as far away from the maimed section of track as they could.

Dong Gungwu clutched the throttle of the JS 2-8-2 Mikado steam engine tightly. He reluctantly put his head out the open window at times. It was harsh, this Mongolian wind. Also, he feared the legendary Mongol bowmen, the scourges of this barbarous land.

Dong Gungwu happened to poke his head out in time to see two Mongols on the railbed ahead. He left the whistle alone. He was under orders. He did not like the thought of driving troops—especially the despised Twenty-seventh Army—into foreign territory, but his job was good and he preferred this to the Beijing Lockup or a public beheading as a counterrevolutionary.

As he withdrew his wind-frozen face, he hoped the Mongols would have sense enough to get out of the way.

To his relief, he saw a few moments later that they did.

He also saw the bare section of rail.

Dong Gungwu grabbed for the airbrake. He threw it. The brake shoes clutched, driving wheels squealing in protest. But the rails were slick with fresh snow. The iron wheels locked, but could not obtain the necessary traction for a clean stop.

The black Mikado engine slid on toward that terrible gap. Dong Gungwu considered jumping from the cab. The snow looked uninviting. So instead he huddled under the furnace, arms shielding his head.

The train slid off the rails at nearly full speed. It kept going. Its iron cowcatcher abruptly snagged a cross tie.

The train folded like a tin pipe. The back of the engine went up and the coal car tried to climb it. The trailing cars slammed the lifting coal car. Coal flew like shrapnel. So did tiny figures in PLA green.

The first six cars piled up like a Los Angeles freeway accident. The bulk of the train had no place to go, so the cars simply tipped over, ripping up a good section of rail.

T-55 tanks snapped their restraining cables, dragging the anchoring flatbeds over the side.

The sounds of splintering timbers, squealing rails, and screaming men blended into a cacophony of ear-punishing sound.

All in all, Remo thought as he watched the commotion from a safe distance, it was a lovely train wreck.

The trouble was, there were a lot of survivors. And they had AK-47's and the temperament to use them.

Worried of face, Kula looked back over his shoulder.

Still no Mongols.

PLA soldiers pulled one another out of the shattered wooden passenger cars. They shouted and screamed. A few shots were fired, evidently at others whose injuries were so bad a bullet was the only remedy.

Then the bullets stormed toward Remo and Kula.

In response, they wheeled their ponies, just to be safe. They were out of rifle range. And automatic weapons were not rifles.

"This is not good," Kula rumbled. "Many of them live."

"I can fix that," Remo said. Handing Kula his reins, he said, "Take care of him, will you?"

And Remo started down, on foot, toward the smoking train wreck.

Kula the Mongol watched him go, his wide face a mask of incredulity.

"What manner of warriors are these Americans?" he muttered.

And because he was a Mongol, and would not be shown up by any foreigner, white tiger or not, he too dismounted. He slapped the ponies with a short whip. They galloped away to safety.

Grinning like a wolf, Kula unsheathed his ancestral dagger and ran after the brave American.

It was a good day to die, especially with the sky so blue. Kula loved a blue sky.

Remo felt the shockwave as the first bullet zipped by his head. He dodged it easily, even bundled in his padded Mongolian jacket. He smiled tightly, feeling more at home fighting human enemies and not the elements before him.

"Time to play pong," he called joyously.

Remo met the first advancing line of Chinese infantry with a handful of quickly made snowballs.

One by one, they smashed into the Chinese faces with unerring accuracy. It was enough to throw the trio off-balance while Remo moved in for the kill.

A chin came within range. Remo lashed out with a fist. He got an ear-splitting crack of sound as his fist struck the point of the man's chin with such violence that his jaw caved in, its hinges bursting out of either side of his face.

"That's for Tiananmen Square," Remo said. A high sideways kick staved in another's rib cage. A bayonet slashed for his face. Playfully Remo batted it away with his bare hands.

Finally he broke off the blade and yanked the rifle out of its owner's hands. The PLA soldier looked at his suddenly empty hands. Then he was trying to pull an AK-47 out of his mouth even after his spinal cord was severed.

Kula picked up a fallen rifle and emptied its clip in every direction. He got three. He also got a burst of return fire directed at him.

Remo turned at the sound. He frowned.

"I thought I told you to stay with the horses?" he complained as he distracted Kula's attackers with a flying PLA body. The hapless Chinese soldier landed atop two upraised bayonets lifted to ward off what was thought to be an overhead attack. The blades eviscerated him and the body knocked the others into oblivion.

"And miss out on all the fun?" Kula cried. "Too bad we are outnumbered, no, white tiger?"

"*You're* outnumbered," Remo growled. "To me, this is a fair fight. So stay out of it."

"Well-spoken, white tiger."

"And stop calling me that," Remo snapped, jamming desert gravel into a fallen Kalashnikov so that the blowback would kill or maim anyone who fired it.

Remo took off into a knot of soldiers just starting to organize themselves. They were breaking open metal cases of ammunition.

Remo said, "Excuse me," as he broke in on them. He scattered the near ones and took the case.

A snarling soldier pointed his weapon at Remo.

"Ting! Ting!"

"You win," Remo told him, throwing his hands up in the air. "I surrender."

The soldier advanced.

The descending ammo case clouted him in the shoulder. He fell backward. Remo stomped his head into bonemeal and blood, getting a satisfying *pong!* sound. He retrieved the case, bouncing it from hand to hand like a basketball.

"Anybody else want to play pong?" Remo called.

The answer split the air. Remo dropped the case and began weaving in and out of the furious bullet tracks, the air cold in his lungs, filling him with energy and power. He felt like a Master of Sinanju again, sowing death among his enemies.

Remo tried every variation—a knuckle punch to the knees. A knee to the small of the back. He cracked a neck with an elbow, jellied genitals with a booted toe, never repeating a blow and never missing.

But even as he thinned the first skirmishers, others crawled out of the wreckage. The air was warming with the spilled contents of the ruptured steam engine.

Then, from behind him, came a low drumming rumble.

Remo looked back, not sure what to expect.

Strung along a rise was a line of Mongol horsemen brandishing curved bows like American Indians. They raised them into the air with a high, nerve-chilling cry.

Then the arrows were nocked and the horses thundered down.

"I hope they know whose side I'm on," Remo yelled at Kula.

"They are Mongols," Kula called. "They are gentle people—to other Mongols. I would not want to be a Chinese soldier at this moment."

What followed next was a one-sided massacre. The air filled with the fluttery hiss of arrows. Remo, knowing that an arrow inflicted a more lethal wound than a bullet, took pains to stay out of the rain of shafts. And that was exactly what it was.

They fell in waves. Line upon line of arrows. They struck chests, arms, heads, and legs. One hapless PLA conscript sprouted quills like a porcupine. He screamed until a willow shaft impaled his throat.

Answering fire was ragged and without heart. Chinese

soldiers feared Mongol cavalry more than they feared death, and on this snowswept plain, the Mongol horsemen represented both.

A horseman galloped into view, and without stopping, pulled Kula onto his pony. They rode away, and Kula regained his steed.

That left Remo all alone under the next wave of arrows.

Remo had found shelter behind an overturned tank tangled with a splintered flatcar. Occasionally a PLA soldier would join him, seeking refuge from the endless fall of arrows.

Remo let them know they were not welcome by using them as shields. He caught dozens of arrows that way. When one human target was sufficiently punctured, Remo threw him contemptuously to one side and simply waited for another.

It took a while, but finally the PLA stopped trying to hide behind Remo's flatcar.

The PLA started to retreat, the Mongols hot on their heels.

The arrows had stopped, so Remo stepped out to meet the oncoming figures. He tore into the PLA with enthusiasm.

The sight of a lone Mongol—so Remo appeared from afar—single-handedly ripping PLA soldiers to shreds was enough to give the Mongol cavalry pause.

They came to a stunned stop and watched mute as statues. Kula's voice lifted over the screams of the dying, his words unintelligible to Remo's ears, but his tone unmistakable. It rang with pride.

Finally Remo had his fill of dismembering PLA soldiers and waved the Mongols on.

They came in like Apaches, whooping and using short daggers and swords to finish off the last stragglers.

The snow was pink and red when they were finished. The air was warm with rising steam and the heat that was escaping human bodies for the last time.

Kula cantered up to Remo, astride his own horse and leading Smitty. He offered Remo his reins in silence.

Remo mounted. "So much for phase one," he said. "There's time before the Mongol army gets this far south. Next we gotta find Fang Yu."

"She is lost?"

"She's not who I thought she was," Remo explained. "I gotta find out who she really works for."

"There are many ways to make a Chinese spy talk," Kula suggested, wiping his blade clean of blood with the shaggy mane of his pony.

Remo shook his head. "I'll handle Fang Yu on my own."

"We ride with you, white tiger." Before Remo could protest, Kula turned to the regathering horses and shouted in his native tongue.

The answering roar that filled Remo's ears meant nothing to him. But the intent was clear. Blades were lifted to the steely blue sky in salute.

"Looks like I have a following," Remo grunted.

Kula reached over and clapped his hands on Remo's shoulders.

"You and I, our blood is of the same color," he said with simple sincerity. "You lead and we will follow. No one will stand before us."

Remo glanced back to the wreckage of the Chinese troop train. Snow melted around the broken boiler.

"Let's hope this is the beginning of a streak," he muttered. But his voice lacked conviction. What would happen when he tangled with the Master of Sinanju?

He wheeled and spurred his pony back toward Sayn Shanda.

The Mongols fell in after him like the troubled wake of a great ship passing through white water.

27

They swept through the Middle Gobi, between the provincial capital of Mandal Gobi to the north and Holodo Suma to the south.

By this time, the New Golden Horde was three thousand strong. It was no longer a line of cavalry, but a caravan.

Collapsible *gers* were carried on camelback. Supplies burdened creaking yak-drawn carts. From each saddle hung a leather sack containing hardened milk curd and water, which after a day's bouncing would be churned into an edible porridge.

Heeding the call to horse, they had come from Ulan Goom to the west, from distant Tamsang Bulag, and even from the remote villages of the Delugun-Boldok Mountains, the fabled resting place of Genghis Khan himself.

"Praise Buddah that I lived to see this day," Boldbator Khan shouted lustily. "We are an army. We will soon know the joys that Lord Genghis spoke of—to conquer our enemies, to deprive them of their possessions, to make their beloved weep, to ride on their horses and embrace their wives and daughters. I look forward to that last joy with especial relish," Boldbator added with a low chuckle.

The Master of Sinanju's reply was sobering.

"We are too few to ensure victory," Chiun said, his squeaky voice pitched low so none of the other riders could hear.

"We have men, horses, supplies, and weapons. What more does a Mongol army require?"

"More Mongols," Chiun said simply.

"We have thousands of stout Mongols," Boldbator boasted.

"When one contemplates sacking China," Chiun returned, his voice like stone, "one can never have too many Mongols."

Boldbator strained to look behind him.

"I do not think there are better men in all of Mongolia," he remarked.

"Send detachments to the nearest towns," Chiun said. "Learn if they can what transpires in Beijing. Muster more horse Mongols. And no Uighurs, Kazaks, or Kirghiz!"

"At once," Boldbator said, turning his complaining horse around.

The sky overhead was too blue to be true. Boldbator's lifted voice seemed to bounce off its uppermost reaches.

"Bato! Jagatai! Take you twelve riders each to Mandal Gobi and Holodo Suma. Gather up all the riders you can. Shame them with words or beat them with your whips, but let no abled-bodied Mongol refuse the call! We will await you at Sayn Shanda! *Go!*"

The riders got organized. They split off from the main

body, which ranged in both directions as far as the eye could see.

"We can rest up at Sayn Shanda," Boldbator told Chiun after the thunder of hooves had died away. "Perhaps the latest news will have reached that place too."

Chiun nodded, his almond eyes never wavering from the horizon, beyond which lay Inner Mongolia and the prize he sought.

28

As they approached Sayn Shanda in the desert, Kula cantered his horse up to Remo's side.

"Shall we await you in our *gers*?" he asked.

"There's a long black limousine somewhere in town," Remo said, his eyes on the white fingerlike apartment houses that dominated the Sayn Shanda skyline. "Find it and I'll be happy."

"What is this machine to you?"

"I have a score to settle with the driver."

"I will bring you his head on the tip of my sword," Kula vowed.

"Just track it down," Remo said. "I'll handle the rest."

"It will be as you say," Kula promised.

Kula lifted his deep voice, and like a wave of many-legged centaurs, the horsemen charged down into the town, leaving Remo to bring up the rear.

"Nothing like Mongol enthusiasm," Remo muttered as he watched them descend on Sayn Shanda.

He rode after them at a steady pace, his brow wrinkled in thought. He wasn't looking forward to the confrontation with Fang Yu. But there was no other way.

Remo rode through the streets of Sayn Shanda. Cars and bicycles gave way before him. Occasionally a person on the sidewalk would shout, "White tiger! Freaking white tiger!"

at him in English. Word obviously travels fast among Mongolians, he thought. He felt like the star in the final reel of a King Arthur film.

As he rode along, Kula's horsemen—his horsemen, he realized with a start—were practically going house to house, trying to find Remo's black limousine.

Remo decided they had the matter well in hand and took a street he recognized would lead him back to the Genghis Khan Hotel. A Cyrillic-lettered Pepsi sign was an unmistakable landmark.

The street was long and lined with relatively modern shops and office buildings. Only the native costumes and braided hair of the women—that and the frequent Genghis Khan posters—made it seem not unlike a small American town.

Drumming hoofbeats lifted over the muted background noise of the city. They were riding hard, and coming this way.

The deep roar of a car, intermixed with a squeal of speeding tires, warned Remo of approaching trouble.

The black limousine raced up a side street bisecting the avenue. It flashed across so fast, to Remo it seemed unreal. Hot on its rear deck were a score of Mongol horsemen in full cry, Kula leading.

Remo spurred his horse.

"*Hayah!*" he said. Smitty responded, his hooves pounding the cobbles, eating up blocks.

The roar and clatter of hoofbeats changed, and grew.

Suddenly, from the opposite direction, the limo streaked across the avenue, one street closer to Remo. The Mongols plunged a length behind it. They seemed to have lost some horses along the way.

When the chase reappeared, one street closer and going in the opposite direction, Remo thought he saw a pattern forming. He slowed as he approached an intersection. Another couple of passes and the limo would have to get by him.

Remo pulled up and waited for the next violent crossing. He had time.

The limo didn't appear at the expected street, or the one below that. But the squealing of tires and the clop of hooves wasn't far away. In fact, it seemed very close.

Remo glanced down his intersection. "Oh-oh," he said.

For the familiar broad silver grille suddenly surged around a corner, Mongol horsemen hot on its burning rubber wake. It came at him like a battering ram.

Remo reined Smitty back. Just in time.

The limousine tore past him, only feet in front of his pony's snorting nose. Smitty reared up in fear. Remo calmed him with a squeeze of his strong legs.

Kula's Mongols whipped by next. Remo joined the fast-riding horsemen.

"We found it, white tiger!" Kula shouted exultantly.

"No fooling."

"It was parked before your hotel. The Chinese woman Fang Yu emerged from it. We let her alone and gave chase. Was that a good thing to do?"

"It is if we catch up to this freaking maniac," Remo told him.

"No maniac can elude Mongols, not even a freaking one," Kula shot back as pedestrians dodged back before their ponies' driving hooves.

The limo cut up a street. They went around the corner too. One pony skidded on the turn and wiped out. The others kept going.

Up another street, the limo slid like a black ghost. They negotiated the corner with difficulty. Horses were not made for racing through twisting city streets at full gallop.

On the next straightaway, a gleaming silver tube slid out from the rear deck.

Remo raised his voice in warning just as oil squirted out. Too late.

Several of the unshod lead ponies ran into the oil slick. Their hooves went every which way, except the direction they had been going. The horses stumbled and collided. The snapping of bones was audible.

Remo yanked his mount aside just in time. Kula's reflexes were equally adept. But they lost several horses. Leaving their riders to put the crippled ones out of their misery, Remo led those horsemen still in their saddles around the sprawled panicky ponies painting the street with their blood.

They followed the tire tracks around the next corner.

The street was a cul-de-sac, ending in a high stone wall flanked by ordinary shops, where the tracks stopped dead.

They reined up, looking every which way.

"Where did it go?" Kula demanded angrily.

Remo pointed to the tracks. "Through that wall," he said. "Come on. I think this is where it's going to get complicated."

They dismounted outside the wall.

Remo leapt from the back of his mount to the top of the wall. He balanced there, looking down.

"What do you see?" Kula shouted up.

"Nothing!" Remo said bitterly. He was looking over a walled courtyard. The tire tracks picked up on the inner side of the wall. But they stopped dead in the middle of the windswept snow that covered the empty courtyard.

Remo jumped down. He knelt on the half-exposed stone flags, while Mongols clambered over the wall, brandishing knives and short swords. Some of them wept silently. They were those who had lost their ponies to the oil slick.

"This is impossible," Kula said, looking around with bewilderment flattening his bronze-gong face.

The blank walls of several low buildings faced them on all three sides.

"It's under this slab," Remo said. He was digging around in the flags for a fingerhold. There was none, so he made a few with sharp blows of his hand.

"I could use a hand," Remo suggested.

"To do what?" Kula wondered.

"To turn this slab over."

Kula translated for the others. The Mongols looked doubtful.

"Are you going to help or not?" Remo demanded.

The Mongols fell to it.

With Remo providing the main power to turn it, the Mongols helped tilt the slab up. It was perfectly balanced. Once they got it moving, it turned without complaint or resistance, although they could sense the movement of free-turning gearing.

When the slab had been reversed, the black limousine was exposed in all its long sleek terrible beauty to the suddenly wide eyes of Kula's Mongols. Claws held its wheels fast.

"I have never seen such magic," Kula said hoarsely.

"This guy must have setups like this everywhere he goes,"

Remo snapped, going around to the driver's window. He peered in.

The seat was empty. He went to the back. The windows were tinted. Remo placed an ear to the pane. He detected no heartbeat or sound of respiration.

"Damn!" Remo said. He turned to the others. "Okay, everyone give me a hand. We're going to turn it again."

"Why?" Kula asked in a reasonable voice. "We have the machine you seek."

"But not its owner. There must be a secret tunnel or hiding place under the courtyard. Let's do it!"

They got the slab revolving again. When it was balanced perpendicular to the ground, Remo called, "Hold it! Right here. Just keep it right here."

Remo looked down into the recess below. It was dark. He jumped in anyway.

The space was cold. He felt around the sides and walls. A section of stone sounded hollow to his tapping touch. He exerted pressure on it. It turned. It was hung on a pivot. One side went in, the other coming out.

Beyond it lay a dark tunnel.

"I found a tunnel," Remo shouted up. "Who wants to join in the fun?"

It was a foolish question to ask of Mongol fighters. With a single cry, they all jumped down. The heavy limousine pulled the slab down into place, limousine-side-up. Darkness overtook the underground recess.

"Didn't anybody think to stay back?" Remo said sourly.

"Mongols never shy away from danger," Kula said, sober-voiced.

"Let's go," Remo said. He led the way.

The tunnel ran in a straight line, then took a jog to the left. Remo peered around the edge, and seeing nothing but unrelieved blackness, went into it.

Another bend, this one right, brought them to a dead end and a ladder leading straight up.

Remo went up, finding a hatch. He levered it up with the palm of one hand and poked his head up, looking in every direction.

He saw another courtyard, covered with snow.

"What is there?" Kula demanded.

"Nothing," Remo said unhappily.

"Then why do we delay?"

"Okay, okay, come on," Remo called down.

He held the lid back as Kula's men clambered up, swords at the ready but nothing to stick them in. The Mongols looked disappointed.

"What do you think?" Remo asked Kula as they stood in the emptiness of this new courtyard.

"Tunnels," Kula muttered darkly. "This is the work of a Chinese. They love tunnels."

"We'll see." Then he noticed the footprints in the snow.

They led to a door on a nearby wall. They reminded Remo of the footprints of the black-masked chauffeur.

"Come on," Remo said. He led them to the door. Without hesitation, Remo kicked the door in.

Better to take the enemy by surprise—or as much surprise as possible, considering his entourage, he reasoned.

Inside, yellow desert dust covered sheets draped over long glass display cases. It was a market of some type, not in use.

Remo followed the footprints to a set of stairs. They went up, in silence.

At the top they found an apartment, it too covered by drapes.

Remo looked around hurriedly. The Mongols upset the furniture like schoolkids. They ran swords and knives through overstuffed chairs, examining their withdrawn blades for blood. The absence of gore made many of them grunt unhappily.

"Nothing," Remo said at last. "Wait a minute," he said, looking out a dingy window.

On the sidewalk below, he spotted footprints. The chauffeur's. They led away from the building.

"Let's go!" Remo shouted. "He's getting away!"

The Mongols raced to the door, nearly dismembering one another trying to plunge down the stairs with swords in hand.

Remo was the last one out of the room. The stairs were choked with Mongols, so Remo cleared them with a single leap. He kicked the front door open when he reached it, hitting the sidewalk without breaking stride.

Remo found the street empty in both directions.

His eyes scanned the snow at his feet. The Mongols piled out, ready to do battle.

"Hold up!" he said, blocking Kula with a hand. "Check it out!"

The Mongol looked down. There were two sets of footprints now—one going and one coming.

"Enlighten us, white tiger," Kula said.

"This second set wasn't there a minute ago," Remo explained tersely. He backtracked them.

They led him back into the house through the broken door.

"This is the guy from the back of the limo," Remo told Kula. "I recognize his footprints from New Rochelle."

The sinister name "New Rochelle" buzzed from Mongol lip to Mongol ear. Lips tightened. Daggers were clutched more tightly.

"He must have slipped inside when we were upstairs," Remo added. "Come on. We'll nail him."

They ran back into the building. This time they turned the place upside down in their fury. Display cases were overturned and their glass kicked loose under frustrated sheepskin boots.

Remo went back upstairs.

"There is no one here," Kula shouted up from below.

"Check for secret passages, tunnels, anything!" Remo shouted down. "He's in here!"

The Mongols grunted and ran the walls through with their blades, until every vertical surface resembled crumbling Swiss cheese.

They found no sign of life. There was no basement, no attic—just two deserted and now disarrayed floors.

Remo came down the stairs dejectedly.

"I don't get it," he growled.

He went outside. "He had to come here while we were upstairs," Remo said aloud to the nearest Mongol. "So where did he go?"

The Mongol shrugged. He couldn't understand it either. Or Remo. He didn't speak English.

"Perhaps he is a ghost," Kula ventured. "We have ghosts in Mongolia, just as you do in demon-haunted New Rochelle."

"I've never seen a ghost in Mongolia *or* New Rochelle."

Remo decided that following the chauffeur's footprints was his only sensible course of action.

His Mongols at his heels, Remo made his way through a maze of alleys.

The footprints—both pairs—paralleled one another, although going in opposite directions. They led back to the first courtyard, which was once more empty.

"I thought you guys left the slab down limo-side-up," Remo complained.

"We did, truly," Kula said.

"Well, it's gone."

To be certain, they upended the slab again. The limousine wasn't on either side of the revolving surface.

But Remo noticed that the tracks of the passenger as well as the chauffeur stopped at the edge of the slab—one going and the other coming.

"This doesn't make sense," Remo told no one in particular. "I checked the car before I went down the tunnel. It was empty."

"Yes?" Kula said.

"No driver. He took off through the tunnel, right?"

"Correct. Absolutely."

"But the passenger seat was empty. I could tell from listening. So how could the guy in back walk away after we left the car and go into the house? He wasn't in the car in the first place—I'd swear to that—and he didn't end up in the house. But his footprints say he was."

"The answer to this conundrum is quite simple," Kula said sagely.

Remo looked up expectantly. "Yeah?"

"It is Chinese sorcery."

"It is bullshit," Remo snapped.

29

Remo Williams led Smitty clopping through the streets of Sayn Shanda. He had sent Kula away with his men, to await orders.

They would need to gather more men if they were to head off the approaching Mongol horde.

But for now, Remo had a date with Fang Yu.

He stabled his horse and noted that Fang Yu's bay was still in its stable.

He rode the elevator to his floor in silence, feeling suddenly strange in his native costume. He wondered what Chiun would say if he saw him now. Perhaps before the day was over, he'd find out.

Remo went directly to Fang Yu's door. He knocked twice.

Fang Yu opened the door a crack.

"Remo! Where you been? I been looking for you."

"I had to catch a train," Remo said, pushing the door in. Fang Yu stepped back, her mouth open in mute surprise.

"Train?" she said. "Where did you go that you still in Sayn Shanda?"

"Beijing ordered the Twenty-seventh Army up by rail," Remo said in a harsh, brittle voice. "Kula and I stopped them outside of town. They won't be killing any more Chinese—or Mongolians."

He watched Fang Yu's face for reaction—anger, horror, fear.

Instead, she surprised him by breaking out into a wide smile.

"You defeat Twenty-seventh Army? Remo, that wonderful! You be hero to Chinese people. Twenty-seventh Army butchers. Very bad."

"There'll be more," Remo added. "I've got to stop them if I can."

"I will help."

"Why?"

Fang Yu blinked behind her tortoiseshell glasses. "Say again, please?"

"I know you're not Ivory Fang," Remo said in a flat voice.

Fang Yu said nothing. Her face lost its color. It went as bloodless as old bone.

"So what's the truth," Remo said flintily. "Who are you really working for?"

Fang Yu swallowed. "For West. For Democratic China."

"Liar!"

"Not lie to you!" she retorted, her eyes hot. "I do so work for new China. Ivory Fang is my husband's code name. He sick, so I take his place. We do this from time to time. This way, Security Bureau never sure if Ivory Fang man or woman. Keep us safer longer."

"You're *married*?" Remo asked, surprised at his own disappointment.

Fang Yu turned away. "Husband understand."

"But I don't. I thought you cared about me."

"I do care for you, Remo. You very brave, very American. I admire American men very much. You good in sack too."

Remo decided to cut to the chase. The truth wasn't coming fast enough.

"You haven't seen me at my best," Remo said, low-voiced, stepping closer.

"What you do?" Fang Yu asked uneasily.

"You said I'm good in the sack," Remo returned. "But I've been holding back."

Fang Yu stepped back suddenly. "You have?"

"Exactly."

"Then you should not hold back. You should take me."

"Exactly what I had in mind . . ."

Remo did it by the numbers this time. He took Fang Yu's wrists in one hand. The other forefinger started its rhythmic irresistible tapping.

Fang Yu wet her lips. Her eyes squeezed in the first tormenting rhythms of the Sinanju sexual technique. Remo watched the play of emotion across her face, smiling. In a matter of moments, she would tell him everything she knew.

Then, and only then, would he take her. And then only if he still felt like it. The truth came first.

Fang Yu stepped closer to Remo, her chest against his. Her breath was quickening, pushing her small but rising breasts into his chest.

"Oh, Remo," she breathed, lifting her hands to his shoulders. Her fingernails dug in. Her eyes squeezed into catlike slits of turmoil. Her smell was in his nostrils, her breath mingling with her rose-petal scent.

Her breath smelled of pork.

It was the last smell Remo remembered. The very last thing he recalled was the touch of her slim fingers on the bare skin behind his ears, and suddenly he was swimming in blackness.

Fang Yu stepped back, her eyes hard. Remo fell back onto the bed. He bounced once, then lay still.

Fang Yu trembled on her feet. Every nerve quivered in anticipation of the consummation Remo had started. Her eyes were angry, her mouth dry.

She hurried into the bathroom and masturbated herself into a semblance of calmness.

Only then could she bring herself to go to the telephone. "*Jiao-Shi*," she reported, "he is my slave."

A sibilant voice said only, "Await the coming of my Blue Bees." And the line went dead.

30

They were ten thousand strong as they neared Sayn Shanda.

Night had fallen. They rode four hours more, until the moon was high and the wind like knives of cold glass in their *dels*.

"This is a good place," the Master of Sinanju said.

Boldbator Khan wheeled and gave the order to pitch camp.

An hour later, the last of the Mongols in the rear received word. *Gers* were set up, first the expandable trellislike wicker walls to which doors were hung. Roof spokes were fitted over this. Then came the layers of blankets and felt which transformed the skeletal circles into cocoons of warmth in the gravel-and-sand desolation.

Boldbator personally erected Chiun's tent.

Inside, their body heat began to warm the cool air. Zhang Zingzong made tea.

"We could have reached Sayn Shanda before dawn," Boldbator told the Master of Sinanju. It was statement, not a challenge. The Master of Sinanju was many minutes in replying.

"Word out of Holodo Suma troubles me," he said.

Boldbator grunted. "The Chinese sent an army by rail. It is a very Chinese thing to do. And they have failed, which is also very Chinese. It is a good augury."

"Two questions trouble me," Chiun continued. "Who commands the force that stopped them? And how long before Beijing sends more of their green ants?"

"There is talk of one called the white tiger."

"Do you know of such a Mongol?"

"No. It is said he is a Westerner."

Chiun's eyes narrowed in the candlelight.

"A white—commanding Mongols?"

"They say he fights like a tiger. That he has killed wolves with his bare hands. And brought down an entire Chinese train. You have lived among Westerners, Master. Is there any among them that can accomplish these things?"

"None who matter," said the Master of Sinanju dismissively as he accepted tea from Zhang Zingzong.

Zhang retired to a corner, where he lit a cigarette.

"Take that outside," Chiun snapped impatiently.

"But these are Double Pleasure brand," Zhang protested. "An excellent tobacco."

"I am sick of your stinking tobacco," Chiun said.

Zhang went outside to smoke.

"He is more trouble than he is worth," Boldbator snorted.

"He was a hero once. Perhaps he will show these qualities again. But I doubt it."

They drank tea in silence. The hours passed. Zhang returned to fix dinner—rice for Chiun, a boiled lamb's head for Boldbator.

They were about to retire when a guard slapped the door, disturbing the inner blanket covering.

"Enter," Boldbator commanded.

A tall man in a Mongolian army uniform entered and bowed. He was one of many the Golden Horde had collected along the way. Sent from Ulan Bator to investigate the migration of horsemen, they had invariably succumbed to the call of nomad blood.

"A woman approaches," the Mongol reported. "A Chinese woman, on horseback."

"Tell the man who captures her that she is his to do with as he desires," Boldbator grumbled.

"She has asked to meet with the Master of Sinanju," the Mongol guard continued. "She says she bears an important message for him."

"From whom?" Chiun demanded.

"I am not certain, O Master. Her Chinese is not the dialect I know. But it seemed that she said her message came from the One Without a Name."

The Master of Sinanju paled visibly. Boldbator noticed it and his heart quailed. What manner of being, he wondered, did the Master of Sinanju fear?

Chiun rose up in silence. "Lead the way," he said. "I would speak with this Chinese woman."

Boldbator followed the Master of Sinanju out. Zhang Zingzong trailed curiously, even though he had no idea what had been said. His grasp of the Mongolian tongue had not improved during the many days of contact with them.

The Master of Sinanju walked the great distance to the outer picket in silence. He stopped when he came to a bay horse, on which a young Chinese woman sat nervously, surrounded by Mongols on foot.

"I am the Master of Sinanju," Chiun intoned, tight-voiced.

"I am called Fang Yu," the woman returned in the accent of a citified Chinese. "My teacher, who is known to you, demands your presence."

"I recognize no demands," Chiun said haughtily.

"We hold one whose fate is of moment to you."

"I know of no such person," Chiun said stubbornly.

"I have brought proof." Fang Yu extracted something

from a pocket and tossed it at the old Korean's sandaled feet.

Chiun looked down. It was a lock of dark brown hair tied by a blue ribbon.

"Do you recognize whose hair this is?" Fang Yu asked.

"No," Chiun said coldly.

"My teacher has certain demands. One, that you come with me to Sayn Shanda. And the other, that the Chinese fugitive Zhang Zingzong accompany you."

Zhang caught up with them at that moment. He caught the end of the conversation. His slit eyes glared at Fang Yu. Fang Yu smiled cruelly.

"*Ze-me le*, Zhang Zingzong?" she asked mockingly.

Zhang spun on the Master of Sinanju.

"Kill her!" he hissed. "Do not let her take me! She is an evil person!"

Chiun lifted a commanding hand. "Silence," he said.

To the Chinese woman he said, "Your teacher . . . perhaps he is known to me. Speak his name. I might meet with him if his reputation for wisdom promises enlightenment."

"I cannot speak his name, for it is unknown to me. But he is known to you as Wu Ming Shi."

Chiun's beard trembled in a manner that was not caused by the wind. Boldbator noticed this, but none of the others did.

At length Chiun said, "I know him. I will go with you."

"And him," Fang Yu said, pointing to a nervous Zhang Zingzong.

"He will come too. Await me here."

Zhang protested. Chiun nodded to the Mongols. They seized Zhang roughly.

"How can you do this?" Zhang said angrily.

"Silence!" Chiun thundered in a voice greater than his wispy frame could possibly contain. "Have our ponies saddled. We ride. And let the word go out. We ride alone. No one follows us."

Boldbator looked to the Chinese woman and the retreating Master of Sinanju, his face stricken. He followed Chiun.

"I do not understand."

"Hush, son of the steppes," Chiun whispered. "After I have gone with this woman, prepare your horse Mongols. If

I do not return by daybreak, surround Sayn Shanda and ransom me if you can."

"Ransom?" Boldbator croaked. "But you are the Master of Sinanju."

"And he is the Nameless One," Chiun hissed.

He went directly to his *ger* and removed the teak box from his traveling trunk. He presented it to Boldbator.

"With this, and nothing less, you will ransom me. Will you do this if necessary, Boldbator Khan?"

"My life is yours," swore Boldbator Khan, kneeling.

31

Remo Williams thought he was dreaming.

He dreamed he swam in a dark void of warm ink. The ink filled every wrinkle in his brain, covered his eyes with impenetrable blackness, and clogged his nose and lungs with a rose-petal perfume that reminded him of a woman.

He couldn't remember the woman's name, no matter how hard he tried.

Then his eyelids came open. They felt sticky, the lashes matted as if with clotted honey.

As his vision cleared, Remo found himself staring at a fan of red-lacquered bamboo rods that formed a ceiling. His eyes flicked down. He saw the toes of his bare feet. His eyes flicked left. A blank wall. Right, and he caught a rustling movement beyond his peripheral vision.

A man in a blue silk robe bent over a table. He held a syringe in one hand. The other balanced something round and flat and flesh-colored on the tip of one finger.

The finger was long and pointed and blue. It gleamed like a metal talon.

When he turned his head to see better, Remo's neck sent shooting pains into his brain, so he never completed the action.

His slight movement caught the attention of the tall robed man as he finished pumping a poisonous orange solution into the round skinlike pad.

An incredibly wrinkled face turned in Remo's direction. Eyes like obsidian chips regarded him with reptilian steadiness.

The dry mouth parted. Words like the rustling of a viper through autumn leaves reached his ears.

"Please do not attempt to rise," the voice said.

And to his surprise, Remo obeyed. He didn't know why. He wanted to get up very much. Instead, he watched helplessly as the tall man—he was Asian, Remo saw as his face hovered over him with clinical detachment—reached behind one ear.

Remo heard a ripping sound and wondered if those blue talons were tearing at his skin.

Then the other hand reached behind his ear and the warm ink swept over his brain again.

He seemed to see in his mind's eye rills of black liquid collect in his brain crevices. They looked evil—like spreading black veins. But he knew this was impossible. How could he see his own brain? It was behind his eyes, not in front of them.

Wasn't it?

32

The first thing the Master of Sinanju noticed, as his pony topped the rise and the provincial capital of Sayn Shanda lay revealed, was the activity in the *gers* studding the surrounding pastureland.

Mongols moved between the tents, grooming their horses for battle. Chiun's hazel eyes narrowed.

"What transpires here?" he demanded of the Chinese woman.

"The Mongos have been incited by foreign elements," Fang Yu told him in a disinterested voice.

They were not challenged as they rode into the city.

Fang Yu led them to a run-down section of town where saffron-robed lamas walked the grounds of a dilapidated monastery, which looked as if it had been closed for the seventy-odd years Communism had held sway over Outer Mongolia.

Shaven-headed lamas stabled their ponies. Two helped Zhang Zingzong off his horse. He needed help because his hands were tied to the pointed pommel of his saddle with cords of braided bamboo. He had resisted being led to Sayn Shanda until two Mongols fell upon him and bound him to his horse.

After that, he was quiescent. An unlit cigarette dangled between his lips.

"Follow me, please," Fang Yu said as Zhang was set on his feet.

The three of them walked into the monastery through a heavy wood door studded with iron spikes.

Chiun's nostrils recoiled at the strong odor of incense that permeated the dim interior. Under it was the heavy cloying weight of must.

The lama gestured them to follow. He carried a yak-butter candle in an ornate brass stick. It threw light on the colorful walls—idealized paintings of the Buddha and other religious subjects. Here and there, sections of wall lay exposed, where gold or inlaid panels had been ripped free by looters.

Through twisting passages they walked, the lama's feet making slipper sounds on the stone floor. Zhang Zingzong walked with the heavy tread of a condemned man, his head hung low. No sound attended the Master of Sinanju's footsteps. He had left off his Mongolian attire, and wore instead a tiger-striped kimono. The play of candlelight on its shifting silken stripes was like the muscles of a great cat rippling under a true tigerskin.

They came at last to a great double door of hammered bronze panels depicting a looping dragon battling a fiery phoenix.

Outside the door stood a wiry man in a black chauffeur's uniform. He stood proud as a caliph's eunuch, his arms folded, his head slightly bowed, so his black cap shadowed his features.

As they approached, he lifted his face, exposing a domino mask of polished onyx. His eyes showed through the almond slits like black opals that had been sanded of their luster. They looked dead.

The black-masked chauffeur turned and threw open the doors with a double-handed flourish. He watched stonily as they passed by, then fell in behind them.

The room was a great vaulted chamber. At the far end, a throne of ivory and rosewood stood on a low stone dais. And on this throne sat a man.

Old he was. His eyes were sunk into their sockets as if retreating from all sound, all light. They were black and filmy, but their bright intelligence showed through the film like dim diamonds.

The old man stood up with a feline grace, causing the silken folds of his filigreed mandarin gown to fall and shift. The golden hem of his gown touched the floor, making him resemble a pillar of green-gold flame with a human head on top. On his head rested a black mandarin's skull cap decorated with a tiny coral button.

The Master of Sinanju stepped forward, his face impassive.

The black-masked chauffeur leapt to the dais protectively. The tall Asian motioned toward him with long fingers tipped with intricate nail-protectors of blue jade.

"Sagwa!" he hissed.

The one addressed as Sagwa subsided. Chin lifting proudly, he folded his arms and took his place at his master's side.

Without a word, Chin got down on his hands and knees in the prescribed full bow of Asia. His forehead touched the cold stone floor twice. His face was as cold as the stone, and harder.

He stood up and his lips parted, but barely moved as low words came out.

"To behold you with these old eyes," he intoned, "is to hear thunder from a clear sky. I had believed you ashes, Wu Ming Shi."

"Paper cannot wrap up a fire. It served my purposes to have Asia believe this for a time," said the mandarin Wu Ming Shi. His wrinkled vellum countenance barely moved with his words. It was like the preserved mask of a mummy actuated by mechanical assistance. "The Communist Revolution crushed my hopes to assume the ancient Dragon Throne as China's next emperor. I knew that they would fail, so I slept until a time when revolt troubled the air. Now."

"Your wisdom is boundless. Even I, your former servant, thought you no longer among the living."

"You honor me, you who are in your way as great as I am in mine."

Chiun inclined his head toward the unmoving chauffeur.

"I see you have a new servant," he remarked.

"A former pupil of your late nephew. He was to have been the first of a new line of night tigers, I had hoped."

"He knows Sinanju?" Chiun asked in surprise.

"Some. He is no Master. His true expertise is in the White Crane school of kung fu."

"Ah, I have heard of it. It approaches the perfection of our art."

The chauffeur's proud chin lifted slightly. It fell at Chiun's next words.

"The way a candle approaches the glory of the sun," Chiun finished. "Still, to one unfamiliar with it, it is formidable enough. Why is he masked?"

"In the time I slept, he allowed himself to become famous through playacting in films. This was a mistake. I had his death arranged so the world would think him no more. Now that I am free to move among men once more, I find the mask a regrettable necessity. It also reminds him of his errors, for he came into prominence dressed in these servant's clothes and wearing such a mask. It is a conceit that pleases me to have him play the part of a mere chauffeur in actuality."

Wu Ming Shi's vellum lips twitched slightly wider. The teeth showed as brown as old corn.

"I have brought the one known as Zhang Zingzong with me," Chiun said. "What is it you wish of him?"

"I have promised him to the butchers in Beijing, in return for certain concessions." Wu Ming Shi directed his stained smile toward the trembling Chinese. "They want his head very badly."

"I have certain obligations to this man," Chiun said quietly.

"Obligations which you may see fit to put aside, for I have something to offer you in return for this man."

"This is unlikely, for as you know, my word is sacred to me."

The return nod was imperceptible.

"I have in my possession a man known to you by the curious name of Remo," Wu Ming Shi went on. "Might not his life hold more value to you than your word?"

Chiun's eyes squeezed into walnut slits. His voice was controlled when he next spoke.

"No man's life is more important to a Master of Sinanju than his word," he said tightly. "The one you speak of is a former servant of mine. No more."

"He has journeyed a long way to seek you. He has suffered through storm and the deception of the female heart." The blue nail protectors gestured to Fang Yu, who stood with her head meekly bowed.

"Through unavoidable circumstances, I left him owing money," Chiun said casually, adding, "the matter that has brought me to Asia was pressing. No doubt he seeks his severance fee."

"Then you will not object to my doing with him what I will?" Wu Ming Shi suggested in a dry voice.

"I have some sentimental attachment to him. For he served me well—for a big-footed white man."

"Fang Yu," the mandarin Wu Shi Ming hissed, "bring the foreign devil here."

Fang Yu bowed and padded away. The mandarin Wu Ming Shi directed his strange gaze toward the Master of Sinanju. His nail protectors clicked as he gestured.

"While we wait," he intoned, "there is much catching up we must do. In Beijing, it is whispered that you now work for the American government. Can this be so, Master Chiun?"

"Their gold is as yellow as that of any emperor, and exceedingly bountiful."

Wu Ming Shi nodded. "The Communists would rather pay in lead than gold—even to those who work for them. And they buzz among themselves that the people do not appreciate them."

"The North Koreans are not so bad," Chiun said. "But they have no work for Sinanju, being reliant upon their armies and their Communist lies."

"They ride a tiger that will eat them if they dare dismount. It is true in Pyongyang as well as Beijing."

"Once the Chinese people devour their leaders, what then?"

The blue-jade nail protectors flashed. "In Beijing," Wu Ming Shi said, "I have allies even among the high bureaucrats. I have been meeting with them. Through them, I hear of a new Golden Horde led by a modern khan. It is said their numbers have swollen to seven thousand."

"Beijing looks through the world from the bottom of a well," said Chiun. "And your information is old. Ten thousand is their present number."

"Abiding beside vermilion stains one red," Wu Ming Shi said flatly, eyeing his chauffeur. "Near ink one is sometimes stained black. I am told, Master of Sinanju, that Mongols are gathering for war outside this very city. Are these yours?"

"I know them not," Chiun said stiffly. "My Mongols are camped twenty *li* from this place."

"In Beijing, they fear your horsemen seek to retake China."

"I am going only to Inner Mongolia, and not to conquer."

"I know what it is you seek in Inner Mongolia, Master of Sinanju, for I know you possess the Silver Skull of Targutai."

Before the Master of Sinanju could reply, the bronze doors folded open and the Chinese girl, Fang Yu, came in leading Remo Williams, wearing an unwashed white T-shirt, by one hand.

The Master of Sinanju's sudden indrawn breath was sharp. For Remo's eyes were as dull as paper cutouts, his expression slack and listless.

33

Remo Williams came awake like a fist unclenching.

An oval face floated before his watery vision.

"Fang Yu?" he croaked.

"You are welcome." The voice was light, mocking.

Remo's vision cleared. "What's going on?"

"Stand up."

Remo hesitated—in his mind. His body lifted itself painfully.

"You will do exactly as I command," Fang Yu said imperiously.

"Screw you," Remo snapped.

Fang Yu smiled tightly. "Follow me."

"No chance," Remo said.

But as Fang Yu started from the room, Remo's legs carried him after her. It was as if he were a lodestone drawn in the wake of the Chinese woman's personal magnetic field.

Remo had all his faculties. His brain was alert. His reflexes seemed fine. He took in the sights and sounds of the twisting corridors Fang Yu led him through. But he was completely powerless to resist her command to follow. Once a maroon-robed Asian with a shaven head withdrew into a stone niche and allowed them to pass in silence.

"I gave at the airport," Remo said dryly. His humor fell flat on his own ears.

They came to an ornate double-valved bronze door.

"Open these," Fang Yu said, gesturing.

Remo took the great handles and flung them back. Heavy as the doors were, they flew back, causing yak-butter candles in nearby niches to flutter and go out.

"I guess I still have my strength," Remo muttered as if he found it hard to believe.

"But I own your will," Fang Yu said, taking him by one thick wrist. She led him into a great vaulted chamber adorned with Buddhistic religious wall paintings.

All eyes turned in his direction, Remo saw. There was Chiun, hands in his sleeves, more resplendent than usual, in tiger stripes. No flicker of expression, not surprise or sympathy, disturbed the network of wrinkles that comprised his visage.

Zhang Zingzong hovered beside him, looking frightened.

And on a dais stood the black-masked chauffeur, his arms folded like a bottle genie in modern regalia. Next to him stood a thin Chinese man in greenish-gold robes. He reminded Remo of a taller, older—if that were possible—version of Chiun.

Remo recognized him as the mysterious occupant of the black limousine, the one whose comings and goings were so inexplicable.

His eyes flicked to the man's feet, seeking an explanation of those puzzling footprints in the snow. But the robe's gold hem hid his feet from sight.

Remo noticed he had trouble focusing his senses on the tall Chinese. It was as if the man were not really there.

Remo tested his hearing. One by one, the heartbeats of those in the room came to him—Fang Yu's was normal, Chiun's strong and deep. Zhang's was accelerated. Pitching his hearing beyond them, Remo was surprised at the heartbeats he picked up. The chauffeur's heart was drumming three times the normal rate. Then he zeroed in on the tall Asian.

Nothing.

Remo blocked the others' out. Still nothing. The man on the dais either had no heart—or it did not beat.

Remo allowed himself to be led into their presence.

The tall Chinese spoke.

"I am known as Wu Ming Shi. In Mandarin, this means Nameless One, for no one knows my true name. This is as I wish."

"Maybe you should be wearing the mask," Remo remarked. His voice was hoarse, robbing it of its acid quality.

"He has spirit," Wu Ming Shi told the Master of Sinanju.

Chiun shrugged unconcernedly.

"He is too spirited, which was why I was forced to let him

go. I find the company of Mongols more to my liking. They respect who I am and obey without question."

"You might at least have left a freaking note," Remo said.

"Quiet!" Chiun thundered, his crackling voice reverberating off the metallic ceiling.

"I am told, white man, that there is unsettled business between you and the Master of Sinanju," the mandarin Wu Ming Shi suggested.

"I'll say there is," Remo growled, eyeing Chiun. He was angry. The hurt was no longer in him. He felt only a cold anger in his stomach. It was like bubbling ammonia.

"I have offered the Master of Sinanju your life in return for certain things of value, including the life of this Chinese man, Zhang. The Master of Sinanju has refused my generous offer."

"I'm not surprised," Remo said, glaring at Chiun. "He always puts his own interests first."

Wu Ming Shi nodded. "So you must die," he said, "having no value in these negotiations." Wu Ming Shi directed his voice toward Chiun. He barely moved on the dais, being more like a statue than a man. "Have you any objections to this, Master of Sinanju?"

"Yes. One."

"Speak."

"I owe this one a fee," Chiun announced to all. "I cannot allow him to die with the debt unpaid—any more than I would a dog I had promised to feed."

The mandarin Wu Ming Shi absorbed this in silence. The rising tone of the Master of Sinanju's words was not lost on him. His eyes glittered momentarily.

"Conclude your business, then, so that we may finish our own."

Chiun turned and padded toward Remo. Fang Yu withdrew.

From one sleeve of his tiger kimono, Chiun withdrew several gold coins. He offered them to a dumbfounded Remo.

"Here is your ten percent, which I was unable to give you, owing to the urgent nature of my business here," Chiun said loudly.

Remo threw the coins away.

"What happened to my not earning—"

"Our business is done!" Chiun said quickly. "I am sorry that you followed me here, for it would have been better had you not done so. For your life is forfeit."

"What are you talking about?"

"Farewell, faithful servant," Chiun shouted, turning away from Remo. Out of the side of his mouth he spoke. "Do not shame me before these Chinese barbarians," he whispered. "And remember this: one hand lies while the other tells the truth."

"What kinda crap is this?" Remo demanded.

"Please," Chiun said in an offended tone.

Remo arched a puzzled eyebrow. "Please?"

"This is a place of holy men." Chiun withdrew.

He stopped before the dais and bowed slightly. "The debt is paid. You may execute him now."

"Execute!" Remo barked, his muscles tensing. He started to back toward the door.

"Stay," Fang Yu snapped. Remo obeyed. He didn't want to obey. His mind knew he should not. But his body refused to go along. He was helpless.

And on the dais, the hauntingly familiar black-masked chauffeur stepped off, light as a dancer, and approached Remo with the sure catlike grace of a tiger approaching a staked goat.

He lifted his hands, circling around Remo. His lips peeled back in a satisfied grin of anticipation.

"Observe how like the white crane attacking the fox," Wu Ming Shi intoned, "Sagwa hops on one leg."

"So does a dog when it relieves itself," Chiun said.

"The arms are held high like wings, and like beaks the hands are prepared to strike at his opponent."

"This other man is a vassal, not an opponent," Chiun pointed out.

"He has will except when countermanded. The result of a certain drug introduced into his system through a Western conceit called a skin patch."

Skin patch? Remo thought, remembering the tearing sound behind his right ear. He reached for it.

"No!" Fang Yu cried. "Do not touch behind your ears." Remo obeyed.

"This is not a fair fight," Chin said emotionlessly.

"You object?" Wu Ming Shi demanded quickly.

"It is no longer my concern, for the debt has been settled."

"The other man wears a similar patch. For he is high-spirited. Thus, they are equal, both obeying my commands, but also capable of attack or defense."

Chiun nodded. A little of the tension that had deepened his facial wrinkles relaxed.

Remo didn't notice any of this. He heard their exchange as if from far away. All his concentration was on the black-masked chauffeur. He circled Remo warily, looking like an absurd black crow as he hopped on one foot.

Remo circled with him, waiting for the first blow.

None came.

"I guess I go first," Remo said. Then Sagwa feinted with one hand. Remo faded back. Then he lunged forward.

Sagwa leapt aside. One arm straight as a rod swept downward. Remo slid under the blow, feeling the push of compressed air driven by the stroke.

He swung on the rebound, using his elbow as a striking point. But it encountered only the faint afterthought of Sagwa's body warmth.

The gap between them was too great, and Remo instantly understood the theory behind this unfamiliar fighting style. Don't strike first. It kept the opponent at a disadvantage. In order to strike, Remo would have to come in on an inside line. But the chauffeur was like a repelling force on a pivot, prepared for any attack. There were no openings, because he refused to attack. He would only defend himself.

Remo watched the man's hands. They were like beaks undulating above his head.

Then, grinning, the chauffeur made a fist with his right hand. Remo watched it closely.

"Where have I seen you before?" Remo asked the man.

"In your nightmares," Sagwa spat. The fist flattened out, fingers straight. The other hand now formed a fist.

"One hand lies, the other tells the truth," Remo muttered. "But which one?"

He decided to find out.

Remo jumped back until his spine touched the closed bronze doors. Using them for leverage, he propelled himself with a backward kick.

The maneuver sent Remo shooting into the air, sailing over the chauffeur's twisting head.

A gloved fist shot up, clipping Remo's left calf.

It felt like a sledgehammer. Remo saw stars. He landed on one foot, the other held off the ground. He hopped three times before he found his balance.

The chauffeur came around, still hopping on one foot.

"Okay," Remo said. "Now I know which hand tells the truth."

Remo hopped back as the chauffeur advanced. He sensed the power of Chiun's inner essence hovering near him.

His whispery voice floated to Remo's ears. "Remember, do not shame me."

Remo hesitated. Why should he listen to Chiun now—after all that had happened? Then again, Chiun had warned him about the lying hand.

Remo put his foot down. It hurt. He stepped forward, limping slightly. "Damn!" he said.

The chauffeur hopped before him, not advancing, not retreating, but taunting him. Remo watched him maneuver. He saw the opening he wanted.

Remo went in low, his body bent at the waist.

With a victorious cry, the chauffeur brought his right fist down. Remo countered with crossed wrists. A mistake. The other hand, straight as a spear, caught him in the throat.

Remo rolled with the blow, coughing. As the chauffeur approached, Remo retreated, scrambling to keep his feet. This brought him close to Chiun.

Pitching his voice so only Chiun heard it, he demanded, "What happened to one hand lies, the other tells the truth?"

"He is Chinese, and therefore devious," Chiun whispered back.

"This guy is no kung-fu dancer," Remo growled.

"Nuihc gave him the benefit of certain knowledge," Chiun said.

"He knows Sinanju?" Remo said in surprise.

"He knows many styles, some worthy, some not," Chiun said. "But listen to his heart. He is empowered by drugs."

"That explains why he's faster than me."

Chiun turned to Wu Ming Shi suddenly, lifting his voice. "It would seem that our servants are equally worthy."

"You have taught yours more than a few defensive tricks."

"A servant needs to protect his Master," Chiun returned.

Remo hopped closer, lifting both hands in imitation of the chauffeur's tortured stance.

"Your guy seems to know what he's doing," Remo taunted. "Why don't I try it?" He made a fist. "One hand lies," he mocked, "the other tells the truth."

For a moment, Sagwa's black eyes grew worried behind his mask. Then his arrogance asserted itself.

"You are a fool!" he hissed.

"Maybe, but you're the guy who thinks he's a whooping crane."

Remo feinted, more to test this unfamiliar style than anything else. It felt awkward, but he instantly appreciated the advantage of the long-arm style. Joints and wrists locked, it imparted pile-driver power to the blow because the entire of the body was behind it.

Respectfully the chauffeur danced out of the way of Remo's first clumsy blows.

Remo moved in, hopping. He danced to one side, hopped into reverse. All the time, he watched his opponent's hands, looking for the truth and the lie.

The chauffeur did the same. His arms went back and forth, and Remo opened and closed his fists alternately.

And while his opponent's eyes were mesmerized by the play of fingers, Remo suddenly put his weight on his bad foot and lashed out with his good one.

The blow was low and elegant. It caught the chauffeur in the kneecap, splintering it.

Sagwa screamed. And in the instant he balanced in mid-air, Remo countered with a closed fist to the other knee. It broke like a plate.

The chauffeur landed on his ass. Remo stepped up and brought one foot down on his left elbow. The joint cracked like a walnut.

Pain warped the chauffeur's masked face. He grabbed for Remo's restraining ankle. Remo deflected the off-balance stroke with a casual slap of his hand. Then he reached down for the mask, saying, "It's midnight. Time for all good little trick-or-treaters to unmask."

"Stop!" commanded the mandarin Wu Ming Shi.

Remo's hand froze. Gritting his teeth, he willed his straining fingers to touch the mask. They held fast, as if encountering an invisible wall.

"Stand back from my Sagwa," Wu Ming Shi ordered.

Obediently Remo stepped back. He swore under his breath.

"Sagwa. Rise to your feet."

Sagwa, sweating and straining, attempted to get up. He used his one good arm to lever his body up. But his legs refused to take his weight. Three times he tried to get to his feet. And then, exhausted, he fell back sweating and breathing hard.

His heart rate was tremendous, Remo heard. It accelerated to the point where Remo wondered if it would burst the heart muscle itself. The man's yellow face turned red with exertion.

Finally Wu Ming Shi spoke up.

"Enough! You have failed me, Sagwa."

Sagwa stared at the high ceiling. Tears welled up from his eyes. They overflowed the close-fitting onyx mask.

The mandarin stepped off the dais. He walked stiffly, clumsily, as if his old joints were unaccustomed to movement.

He stepped up to Sagwa's side. Remo listened for a heartbeat. He heard one. Just one. Then, no more. He wondered if he was mistaken.

Wu Ming Shi looked down upon his servant.

"You can no longer serve me," he said coldly.

"I am sorry," said Sagwa plaintively.

"Silence!" The mandarin Wu Ming Shi took two steps toward Remo. His black button eyes were cold and venemous.

"You are worthy, for a white man," he said.

"Suck eggs," Remo said.

No emotion flickered over those vellum features.

"Finish what you have begun," he told Remo.

Remo hesitated.

"One blow! To the face! Now!"

It was as if Remo stood apart from his body. He turned to Sagwa. One hand drew back. It struck the chauffeur in the face. The black mask broke in sympathy with the skull beneath.

All the tension left Sagwa's body as if he had been unplugged from the universe.

Remo straightened. His expression was furious.

Wu Ming Shi called over to the Master of Sinanju.

"Now that my servant is no more, I have need of a strong one like this," he intoned.

"It is no concern of mine," Chiun said coolly.

Wu Ming Shi turned to Remo. "You are my slave from this moment on."

"Make me," Remo spat.

"Bow."

Remo, face grimacing with exertion, fell to one knee.

"No, the full bow. Both knees. Forehead touching the floor."

Remo fell into the position. His forehead touched the cold stone floor.

He was so surprised he said nothing. He felt like a human puppet manipulated by unseen strings.

Chiun padded over. His sandals stopped at Remo's left hand.

"This is remarkable," Chiun said.

"A depressive alkaloid known as Burundanga," Wu Ming Shi said sternly. "It produces complete hypnosis in its victims, making them susceptible to any verbal commands. Should I order this man to step in front of a speeding car, he will do so without hesitation, although his brain will scream in protest until the last synapse dies."

"He responds to your voice?"

"Clearly."

"Stand," Chiun said suddenly.

And Remo stood.

"He knows no loyalty, it seems," Chiun said to Wu Ming Shi.

"The drug is not so specific. A flaw. But perhaps I will overcome this with certain refinements of the alkaloid."

Chiun nodded. "Drugs are no substitute for ability—or loyalty," he said. "I wonder if you will ever learn this."

"I will miss my Sagwa," Wu Ming Shi said slowly. "For he amused me, he who once considered himself so far beyond my power that he dared to make of himself a mere movie star." His eyes left the body to fix Chiun's gaze with his own.

"We have much to discuss, you and I. But not now, for I fear this excitement has put a strain on my heart. I must rest."

Chiun bowed. "This former servant of mine was recalcitrant. I would enjoy having his obedience until we speak."

Wu Ming Shi considered this in silence. "I will hold Zhang Zingzong as a guarantee," he suggested.

"So be it," Chiun said. To Zhang he instructed, "You will do as this man bids. No harm will come to you, for this is a man of his word."

Zhang Zingzong hung his head in meek submission.

"Fang Yu will show you to quarters," Wu Ming Shi announced.

Fang Yu approached and said, "Come."

The Master of Sinanju looked down at Remo.

"Rise, O slave, and follow me," he said imperiously.

Remo Williams came to his feet as if in a dream. The Master of Sinanju padded by him. Remo fell in line behind him, going through the bronze door and into the incense-filled corridor.

"This isn't funny, Chiun," he hissed.

"These are not funny times," Chiun retorted. "You should never have followed me here."

34

Fang Yu escorted them to a simple stone room, a monk's cell. There were no windows, only a bare cot and floor rugs for warmth. A yak-butter candle guttered in a wall niche.

"Leave us, cat-eater," Chiun told the Chinese woman coldly.

Fang Yu withdrew, her face turning crimson.

"Enter, O slave," Chiun said.

Remo did as he was told.

"Sit."

Remo sat on the cot.

"I like you better this way," Chiun cackled, closing the door behind him. "Heh heh heh."

Remo said nothing.

"Have you nothing to say?" Chiun murmured.

"How about blow it out your backside?"

"How about you keep a civil tongue!" Chiun spat. "No," he added quickly, "you will keep a civil tongue, Remo. I command this. No more will you insult me. In fact, you will immediately apologize."

"I immediately apologize," Remo said humbly.

Chiun blinked. "No, say 'I apologize profusely,' " he said.

"I apologize profusely."

Chiun started. "This is unbelievable. Have you no harsh words for me?"

"I have plenty," Remo growled, "but you won't let me say them."

Chiun raised a long-nailed finger. "Awesome Magnificence. I prefer to be addressed as Awesome Magnificence."

"Awesome Magnificence," Remo said flatly.

Chiun approached. He looked Remo over carefully. Pushing back one ear, he felt the skin. Remo couldn't feel his probing nail, so he knew it was the skin patch Chiun touched.

With a tug, Chiun removed it.

"Ouch!" Remo complained, reaching for the back of his neck.

"This is a strange device," Chiun said, examining the circular Band-Aid-like pad.

"It's a skin patch," Remo explained. "People wear them when they're seasick. They time-release drugs through the pores."

"Are you still under its wicked influence?" Chiun wondered.

"I don't know."

"Clap your hands," Chiun commanded.

Remo clapped.

"It must wear off eventually," Chiun said. He replaced it, saying, "For now, I will leave it there. Say thank you."

"Thank you, Awesome Magnificence."

"Do you mean this?"

"No!"

"Then you are not welcome," Chiun sniffed. "This is not like you, Remo."

"Not like me!" Remo said hotly. "You're the one who took off to Outer Mongolia without even leaving a freaking note!"

"Ah," Chiun said. "I have much to explain to you."

"I don't want to hear it."

"Speak your heart."

"I'm dying to hear every word, Awesome Magnificence."

Chiun beamed. "Then I shall enlighten you," he said, going to the door. He listened intently. Hearing no eavesdroppers, he settled onto the rug. He patted the bare spot before him and said, "Sit at my knee, Remo."

Remo obeyed.

Sitting face-to-face, their legs locked in identical lotus positions, the Master of Sinanju began to speak.

"Think not I abandoned you, or America, through spite or neglect or any of those base motives."

"Why did you?"

"When you told me of the impossible footprints, I had an inkling that the mandarin Wu Ming Shi still lived. And knowing that he sought Zhang Zingzong, I knew his motives must be weighty. I confronted Zhang and wrung from him the secret of the teak box he carried with him from China."

"Yeah?"

"It contained the silvered skull of Targutai, one of the advisers of Temujin, known to you as Genghis Khan. For when Lord Genghis died, he was buried in a secret place atop Mount Burkan Kaldun. And those who attended him in life—indeed those who knew of his burial place—were all put to the sword to hide forever the sacred burial place of Temujin."

"Wouldn't it have been better to cremate him and scatter his ashes over the water?"

"Mongols are very traditional. It is not done." Chiun's eyes twinkled. "I like that about Mongols."

"They're okay," Remo said. "Except for Kublai."

"What do you know of Kublai Khan?"

"Oh, I've picked up some pointers," Remo said easily. "We *are* in Outer Mongolia, you know. Or is it Inner Mongolia?"

"Outer. But they are no different," Chiun said thoughtfully. He resumed his tale. "Temujin died a wealthy man, and did not fully trust his sons, especially Kublai, who is as hated among modern Mongols as Genghis is revered."

"Unlike Ogatai, who's not big with Koreans."

"Who told you about Ogatai?" Chiun hissed.

"Oh, I've heard some loose talk," Remo said laconically. "You know what incorrigible gossips these Mongols are."

Chiun stroked his beard thoughtfully. He went on. "Now, Genghis ordered that the greatest part of his treasure be buried in a secret place so that when a truly worthy descendant of his came into the world, he would seek it out and take up the good work. Many tried. None succeeded. For no one could find the fabled Silver Skull of Targutai, on whose brow was inscribed a riddle which would start a seeker on the path to Temujin's glory. Legend has it that it was secreted in the Great Wall of China, but no one knew where. Until, by sheer luck, Zhang Zingzong found it. And although unable to decipher the riddle, he carried it with him as he attempted to escape China. Many Chinese helped him. But some of these were servants of Wu Ming Shi, of whom Zhang knew nothing. One of these informed Wu Ming Shi, and he gave chase all the way to America. The rest you know."

"Like heck," Remo said. "It doesn't explain the disappearing footsteps. And do you know that he has no heartbeat?"

"It beats but once a minute. I have listened. This is how Wu Ming Shi survived into the modern world. He knows the secrets of slowing down breath and heartbeat, using less energy, consuming less food, and stretching the moments of his life. For he is, if I calculate correctly, over two hundred years old!"

"What!"

Chiun nodded. "He was old when I first encountered him, and I was not a young man then."

"What is this man to you?"

"You talk like a Mongol," Chiun commented.

"It rubs off. Answer the question."

"Who is the Master here?" Chiun sniffed. "Speak truly."

"You, Awesome Magnificence."

Chiun smiled. He went on.

"When last we spoke," Chiun said, "you asked me about the emperors I served before America. Let it be known that the heartless mandarin was my last client before the gold of America was placed in my hands."

"He's an emperor? He looks like Fu Manchu." Remo stopped. He blinked. "Fu Manchu! Is that guy Fu Manchu?"

Chiun shook his aged head. "Wu Ming Shi," he corrected. "He coveted the throne of China. He has always coveted the throne of China. His aims were thwarted by the Communists and the Nationalists before them. This is when he vanished. I worked for this man, as the Master before me and the Master before him. At first, he was a good client, his gold flowed like rain, and the work was worthy, even during the first Idiocy of the Barbarians, known to some as World War One.

"But one day, Wu Ming Shi summoned me to his place of exile and asked that I extinguish the life of a boy prince he saw as a rival in his aims. You know, Remo, because I have taught you this, that in Sinanju the lives of children are forever sacred. No gold, no honeyed promises, may dissuade us from this. We are assassins, and some criticize us for this, but we are no better than mere murderers if we do not adhere to certain precepts. Not killing children is the greatest of these."

"I know," Remo said quietly. That was his second thought. His first was an acid, "No checks." But he decided against it. Chiun's story was more important than getting in a zinger.

"I refused this instruction and Wu Ming Shi sent me away," Chiun continued. "When I returned to the village of Sinanju, I found the women weeping and the men enraged. For Wu Ming Shi had done the unthinkable. He had dispatched his Blue Bees to Sinanju to steal away certain children."

"I thought you said Fu Manchu—I mean Wu Ming Shi—never used bugs and reptiles, except in books."

"He does not. The Blue Bees are his servants. They can be found in all cities, for he has a worldwide network of adherents."

Remo thought back to the first time he had met Fang Yu. She had worn blue. And he suddenly remembered the blue-clad Chinese workers he had seen in every Mongolian town.

"I know what happens next," Remo said. "You cleaned his clock for him—right?"

"No. For I was in a place of no comfort. I could not kill children even to save other children, although I considered this. Carrying my pride before me, I ventured to the place where Wu Ming Shi held forth in exile and attempted to ransom them. I demanded satisfaction, and Wu Ming Shi refused, saying that the children of Sinanju were in another place, and would not be harmed so long as he was not harmed. I knew this to be true, for above all, Wu Ming Shi is a man of honor. I begged, and still he refused. Finally I went away, after first making clear to Wu Ming Shi that so long as the children of Sinanju lived, so would he. And he vowed to me that if I ever moved against him or his political aims, his Blue Bees would attack Sinanju on the first day I left it unguarded."

"So it was a standoff," Remo said.

"Not quite. For the honor of Sinanju was at stake. I could not kill this man, so in retaliation I inflicted upon him a certain insult. Then I returned to Sinanju, vowing never again to venture from it. For I had no heir, and I knew this man's cold-bloodedness knew no bounds. So long as I remained with my people, Remo, Sinanju was safe. But I could not work, and so the years slipped from me and the hard times came."

Chiun bowed his head recalling the sadness.

"You never told me this."

"It was ancient history," Chiun said, "or so I thought. In time, the Communists overran China. Wu Ming Shi was forced to retreat, for he was known to Mao. It was in these days that I first began training the one known to you as Nuihc, my nephew, for the line of Sinanju had to go on."

"Big mistake."

"I have told you the tale of Nuihc, Remo, but I never told you all. I trained this deceiver and he took new work. But the work came from Wu Ming Shi. I knew this after Nuihc went into the world and shortly thereafter the children of Sinanju, no longer children, were returned. That was all the village ever saw of Nuihc's work. No money came from his efforts and I was unable to venture forth to investigate this matter because then there would be no one to protect the children from Wu Ming Shi, who ached to avenge the insult I inflicted upon his person."

"What insult?" Remo asked curiously.

"A minor unimportant detail," Chiun said. "And so it was for many years until word reached me that Wu Ming Shi had passed from this earth, his long-deferred dream unattainable. Nuihc found other clients. Still no money came. This was the early days of what you called the Cold War. I had resigned myself to remaining in Sinanju, the last worthy Master of Sinanju, when the American Conrad MacCleary came, offering gold if I would train a white. It was an insult, but after so many cruel blows, what was one more? I had trained a traitor, why not a white? Or a monkey? It was all the same to me. Sinanju was over. I would accept the gold so that the village would survive a few years longer. The rest you know. Nuihc found us and now Nuihc is no more. But Wu Ming Shi lives."

"Why didn't you tell me any of this when you found out he wasn't dead?" Remo wondered.

"I dared not. Wu Ming Shi threatened all that was dear to Sinanju before. I knew that if he knew of your existence, he would threaten you in order to make me his vassal once more, now that Nuihc had perished."

"Really?" Remo said. "All this was to protect me?"

Chiun nodded. "Truly. I pretended to this man that you were an unimportant servant."

"But he was going to execute me, and you were going to stand by."

"Do not be ridiculous, Remo. You—executed by a hopping masked lacky? This Sagwa is better than one might expect, having been trained by Nuihc. But you would have figured out his trickery in time. As you did."

"With your help."

Chiun nodded. "With my help. This is a subterfuge we must continue, for the time being. Until I know the full extent of Wu Ming Shi's power. No doubt he had servants who are under orders to strike at Sinanju should he come to harm at my hands."

"So what's next?"

"Wu Ming Shi covets the treasure of Temujin, no doubt for the same reason Zhang Zingzong does. Both men see it as the instrument through which they will impose a new order on China."

"So you're going to cut him in for a piece?"

"No, I will make a present of the final skull to him."

"You, willingly giving up a treasure?" Remo asked incredulously.

"It is the only solution. I will offer this to him to atone for the insult done to Wu Ming Shi, and all will be well."

"You think so?"

"Of course not! But I will pretend otherwise. And when the time is ripe," Chiun said, standing up suddenly, "I will harvest this heartless mandarin like wheat before a thresher. This I vow."

"Think he'll go for it?"

"It will appeal to his vanity that I, the Reigning Master of Sinanju, should offer him atonement. His ego is so monstrous he will undoubtedly accept my generous offer."

"Then what?"

"In this land, they speak of the Wheel of Life. I sense the Wheel turning, Remo. Perhaps it will exalt us, perhaps it will crush us. Perhaps nothing will change. Who can say with a wheel?"

And admonishing Remo to stay alert, the Master of Sinanju departed from the room, leaving Remo to contemplate the story he had been told and the guttering yak-butter candle.

35

Two hours past daybreak, Boldbator Khan rode up to the outskirts of Sayn Shanda, an ornate teakwood box under one padded arm.

He rode into the camp of *gers* north of town, where Mongol horsemen waited expectantly, their horses saddled, bows and blades in the open.

"Ho, Mongol brothers!" Boldbator cried. "I am Boldbator Khan."

He was ignored the first three times he cried his greeting. His wide face was still. This was not the greeting he had expected.

"Have you not heard of me?" he asked a man.

"We ride with Kula," the man replied without enthusiasm as he rubbed down his pony. "And we serve the white tiger."

"Where do I find this Kula?" Boldbator demanded.

The Mongol gestured to a *ger*.

Boldbator rode up and dismounted, clutching the teak box. He pounded on the *ger* door.

The Mongol who emerged was stout-boned and grim of face.

"*Sain Baina*, Kula. I am Boldbator Khan, here to ransom the Master of Sinanju from the Nameless One."

"I have never heard of such a person," Kula grumbled.

Boldbator blinked. "Then why do you assemble for war?"

"We have lost the white tiger, a mighty warrior."

"What has befallen this white tiger?"

"A Chinese wench named Fang Yu made off with him. They are in the city, but we know not where. Not even the priests know, and priests always know every dirty little town secret."

"The Master of Sinanju rode off in the company of a Chinese woman named Fang Yu," Boldbator related.

It was Kula's turn to consider. He waved Boldbator inside. The *ger* door spanked shut, and the rising sun inflamed its scarlet-and-gold designs.

It was not long after that that the Master of Sinanju rode into the camp astride a pony, calling, "Boldbator the Mongol! I seek Boldbator the Mongol!"

Word reached Kula's *ger*. Boldbator emerged, Kula behind him.

Mongols of every stripe gathered around to listen to this Korean man who spoke the high Khalkha Mongol of the old empire days with the fluency of a herdsman.

"You are safe, O Master," Boldbator said happily. "I had feared I would have to ransom you."

"It is good you have come, Boldbator Khan," Chiun returned in stiff tones. "For I will need what is in that box to ransom myself."

Boldbator Khan hesitated. "What this box contains rightfully belongs to the Golden Horde, in part measure. As agreed."

"A share that I, Chiun, vow will be yours," retorted Chiun. "You have my word on this."

Boldbator handed up the box. Chiun took it. He placed the box on his saddle pommel and worked the designs until the lip popped. Then he extracted the cracked skull. He took it up in both hands, running his long-nailed fingers over it searchingly. Satisfied, he held it so that he looked into the skull's empty sockets, his thumbs touching its temples.

Boldbator Khan watched in silence. The Master of Sinanju stared long into the skull as if into eternity. Then he gave it a twist of his hands. Boldbator heard the abrupt scrape of bone. Chiun spat on the skull's ancient brow.

Then the Master of Sinanju returned the skull to its resting place.

"I go," he intoned, "but I will return. Do not seek me, Boldbator Khan. But await me here."

Chiun turned to the audience of Mongols.

"This holds for you all, sons of the steppes," he said, stern-voiced. "No one of you will follow me where I go, or you will face the wrath of your khan."

The Mongols looked back with hard bronze expressions.

Their gimlet gaze followed the bouncing haunches of the Korean's pony as it cantered back into the heart of Sayn Shanda.

Kula turned to Boldbator. "Who was that man that he orders Mongols around like mere Manchus?"

"That was the Master of Sinanju," Boldbator said. "There is none greater."

Kula snorted. "You have never ridden with the white tiger."

"I have never heard of this white tiger," Boldbator grunted.

"And I have heard the Master of Sinanju is a myth, not a man."

36

The mandarin Wu Ming Shi sat on his rosewood-and-ivory throne like an entombed prince. His eyes were shut, the lids so brown and waxy they looked as if they would never open again.

They remained closed when the double bronze door valved open and Fang Yu padded into the room, trailed by the Master of Sinanju.

"Honorable teacher," Fang Yu said with quiet force.

The eyes came open like unveiled secrets.

They flicked to the black back of his chauffeur, standing with arms folded on the edge of the dais, and then to Fang Yu as she rose from her bow. The Master of Sinanju stood beside her, his clear eyes on the chauffeur. Wu Ming Shi's eyes were on the teakwood box.

"Bring the box of Temujin to me," he hissed.

Fang Yu accepted the box and brought it to the edge of the dais, where she raised it to the chauffeur's outstretched hands.

"Bring it to me, Sagwa," he said.

Helpless, Remo Williams accepted the box and carried it to the man seated on the throne.

"Thank you," Wu Ming Shi said.

"Shove it up your ass," Remo Williams said.

"Return to your place, insolent slave," Wu Ming Shi said. "And still your tongue."

Obediently Remo returned to the dais edge. He folded his arms. The uniform was too tight for him. His back itched. He looked at Chiun, who avoided his gaze, thinking at least he didn't have to wear that stupid black mask.

Wu Ming Shi carefully removed his nail protectors, revealing curved talons. Taking care not to break the brittle nails, he solved the secret of the teakwood box within seconds. The lid sprang.

"I first learned of this," Wu Ming Shi said, "when one of my Blue Bees gave refuge to the so-called people's hero, Zhang Zingzong. The inscription on the skull was reported to me, but without the skull itself, it was of no use."

Wu Ming Shi stopped. His eyes locked on the skull's cracked brow.

"This is not the Skull of Targutai!" he said with sibilant violence.

"True," Chiun said smoothly. "That skull led to the broken dragon, whose skull bore an inscription which led to another skull buried in Karakorum. That skull is the one you now hold in your hands. You have my word on this."

The hateful glitter in Wu Ming Shi's eyes faded. His narrow chest rose and fell with his slight breathing.

"Five-Dragon Cave," he murmured. "I know it well."

Returning the skull to the box, he rose to his feet painfully, clutching the box like a square football.

"Know, Master of Sinanju, that with this gift you erase the memory of the insult that was done to me so long ago. I vow to you that from this day forward, the village of Sinanju and all who dwell within need fear naught from the mandarin Wu Ming Shi."

"If you will so inform your Blue Bees, I will consider our business done," Chiun returned with a slight stiff bow.

"They will be so informed before we leave."

Chiun's wispy beard trembled. "We?"

"Many *li* separate Sayn Shanda from Five-Dragon Cave. The Gobi is overrun with Mongols, stirred up by a new khan. I will need protection if I am to reach the place I seek."

"I have not offered my protection."

"But you will give it," Wu Ming Shi said with a cracking of his lips into a brown smile. "Else my Blue Bees will hear nothing from me before we leave. I know you will not wish me to depart Sayn Shanda without word going out—and you will happily see me to my destination. For I am without my faithful Sagwa."

Chiun considered. "I agree. On one condition."

"And this is?"

"Your new servant. I wish him back, for without the treasure of Genghis, I will be forced to return to America. He is not the best servant I have had, but he is at least somewhat housebroken. You may have Zhang Zingzong for him."

Wu Ming Shi looked to his chauffeur. "Ah, so he *does* mean something to you."

"It is as I have said," Chiun insisted quietly.

"Yes. This can be arranged. Prepare to ride." Wu Ming Shi turned to Fang Yu, saying. "Let the Blue Bees of the world know my directions. And assemble a group of them for the journey."

Fang Yu bowed and padded away.

37

Remo walked ahead of the mandarin Wu Ming Shi only because the mandarin Wu Ming Shi commanded him to do so.

The long black limousine was parked outside the monastery. Before it, over forty blue-clad Chinese workmen sat on short-legged Mongolian horses, in rows four deep. Directly behind the limo, the Master of Sinanju waited astride a pony, as did Zhang Zingzong and Fang Yu. Zhang's head was bowed, his wrists bound to his saddle. Fang Yu sat proudly, attired in a blue work uniform.

"My Blue Bees," mandarin Wu Ming Shi said proudly.

"I'll bet they're good little Doo-Bees, too," Remo told him.

"Open the door for me."

Remo obliged, hating every second.

The mandarin Wu Ming Shi paused at the door. His dead brown teeth showed in an ugly smile.

"You are silent," he hissed. "Good. You learn."

Remo decided he had enough. He brought his foot down for where the mandarin Wu Ming Shi's instep should be. To his surprise, he stomped the hem of the mandarin's gown flat without encountering flesh and bone.

"Where do you keep your feet?" Remo asked, dumbfounded.

Wu Ming Shi swiftly eased into the limo interior, his guttural, "Close the door and take your rightful place," coming as if from a well.

Remo obeyed and climbed in behind the wheel.

The horses started off, and Remo, unable to resist the orders coming through the glass partition behind his head, followed them.

They rode south, out of Sayn Shanda and into the hard desert. Remo doubted the car would handle the rough terrain, but then he realized that was why the so-called Blue Bees rode ahead. Their pony hooves packed down the sandy gravel so the car's tires found traction.

They passed several clusters of *gers*, and while curious Mongol eyes followed the procession, none followed them with their bodies.

They made good time, the horses cantering, the limo moving at a steady pace. Occasionally its tires would hit a gully. The Blue Bees hastily dismounted, and wielding brooms and shovels, filled in the rough spots. And they would continue.

Remo drove monotonously. After a few hours the mandarin laid his head back against his seat and fell asleep, his head tilted back, his mouth open, as if in rigor mortis. He looked dead, his face a varnished death mask.

Remo discovered that the black seat rest beside him had a lid. He lifted it, exposing two rows of shiny black buttons. Each button was labeled in Chinese, but he guessed they controlled the limo's defensive array. He shut the lid.

Shortly after that, the Master of Sinanju cantered up beside him and Remo rolled down the car window.

"I didn't know you could ride a horse, Little Father," Remo remarked.

"Koreans are the finest horsemen in all of Asia," Chiun sniffed.

"The Mongols don't think so," Remo said.

"What do you know of Mongols?" Chiun demanded.

"Enough to clear out of their way when the dinner gong is struck," Remo said. Then, "It was all true, wasn't it, from Amelia Earhart to Fu Manchu?"

Chiun nodded. "How did you know I would be in China?"

"Smith, who else? He found that note in a bottle Zhang threw overboard."

"What! There was no note!"

Remo frowned. "He knew about Temujin too."

Chiun frowned. "It is another of Smith's sneaky listening insects." He spat. "That man is more duplicitous than the fictitious Fu Achoo."

"I thought we pulled all the bugs from the house?"

"*You* must have missed one," Chiun said pointedly.

"Never mind. Why does he call me Sagwa?"

"It is not a name, but a Chinese insult. It means Stupid One."

"At least I'm trusted to drive the family car," Remo snorted. "Are you really going to give up Zhang to the PLA?"

Chiun did not reply. "When the evil one awakens," Chiun said, "do not obey his orders."

"And how am I supposed to disobey?" Remo complained. "I feel like Howdy Doody!"

"Just do as I say. Obey him until we reach Five-Dragon Cave, but after that, do as I say."

Fang Yu rode up, hissing, "Return to your place in line, Old Duck Tang!"

"She's calling you Donald Duck," Remo supplied.

"And you are Old Mouse Mi," Fang Yu laughed. "That mean—"

"Mickey Mouse," Remo said unhappily. "I get the picture."

"I return," Chiun said haughtily, "but only because I do not wish to listen to this female cat-eater."

"What you know? You Korean! They eat of dog!" Fang Yu spat after Chiun's departing form.

"I'm so glad you two are getting along," Remo said acidly.

Fang Yu matched her pony's gait to the car's smooth pace.

"You were lying to me all along, weren't you?" Remo asked.

"Not all lies. You good in sack. Better than husband."

"So you really are married?" Disappointment tinged his voice.

Fang Yu nodded. "Zhang Zingzong is my husband—the fool!"

Remo almost lost control of the wheel. "What!"

"When Zhang find skull, he share with me. Zhang not know I was a Blue Bee, just as you not know I was not Ivory Fang. I tell him about this. But he not want to become Blue Bee. He flee with skull, but not know that Blue Bees are everywhere, even in US FBI."

"What happened to the real Ivory Fang?" Remo asked.

"Real Ivory Fang got out of way. I not really spy for West. I serve my teacher, my *Jiao-Shi*, who will one day restore China to greatness. He is a great man, Remo. He save me from orphanage. Has worldwide swarm of Blue Bees, and many cars like you drive now, and hiding places for them all over. Blue Bees in America find Zhang, and through him, the Master of Sinanju. But *Jiao-Shi* arrive too late to catch them. He know this Korean would come to China, so we wait and watch. My task was to be with you because everyone know Sinanju work for American now."

"So you kept him up on what I was doing?"

"Some. Teacher was hearing own reports of Old Duck Tang. I meet with him that night in Beijing, tell him about you. But when I learn you seek Master of Sinanju too, I understand my teacher had to know this. I know teacher had gone to Sayn Shanda. That is why I suggest we go there, not for other reasons."

"Well, thanks for the ride."

Fang Yu laughed with childish cruelty. "You very welcome, Sagwa."

"Don't mention it," Remo growled. "I don't suppose you'd care to enlighten me as to how your teacher manages his disappearing acts. Every time I follow his footprints, I end up where he isn't."

"Perhaps he walk backward," she said with a tinkly laugh. "You not think of that, Sagwa?"

Fang Yu pulled back and let the trailing ponies catch up. She joined them. Remo rolled up the window to shut out the cold.

At the border of the two Mongolias, frontier guards looked on stonily as they rode by like a funeral procession.

They followed the Great Mongolian Road to a small town and then with the Blue Bees beating a path, into the snow-dusted steppe and toward the foothills of a nearby mountain range.

Here, the driving became rough. The car jumped and jounced, waking the mandarin Wu Ming Shi in back. He looked like an animatronic mummy coming to life. Even awake, only his eyes looked alive.

They moved through a narrow pass between rising hills. As had been the case since leaving Sayn Shanda, Remo couldn't see where they were going. The line of horse rumps made sure of that.

Finally, with hills rising sheer on either side, the Blue Bees broke ranks and Remo hit the brakes.

He looked around. They were in a pass beside the entrance to a cave. Before them, the road led to a narrow iron bridge fording a wide river. Behind was the pass. There was no other way to go, Remo thought worriedly, except over the bridge or back the way they came.

The mandarin's voice in the speaker tube said, "Attend me, Sagwa."

Remo hesitated. The urge to obey the short command was not as strong as it had been. He looked to Chiun. Chiun nodded. He got out, wondering if he could have disobeyed the command.

As he opened the rear door, Remo's eyes shot to the mandarin's emerging feet. But the settling gown hem had already covered them—if they even existed.

Wu Ming Shi levered himself to a standing position. His heart beat once and was still. It made the hair on Remo's neck stiffen.

All around them, the Blue Bees were dismounting.

Fang Yu hurried up, carrying a teak box in both hands. She extracted the cracked skull and presented it to the mandarin.

With glittering eyes, Wu Ming Shi read the inscription on the skull aloud.

" 'Now that you have beheld the seat of my mighty power, go to the lands that I have conquered. In Five-Dragon Cave, you must not walk the left path, or the false path will claim you.' "

He looked over to the Master of Sinanju, who sat patiently on his pony.

"Do you swear to me that this is the skull you found at Karakorum?" he called, crack-voiced with effort.

"I do," Chiun intoned.

"Then I am done with you."

He signaled to Fang Yu, who retreated to the limo and gave two long blasts on the horn.

From both ends of the pass came the roar of starting engines and the drumming of booted feet.

All eyes turned to the narrow iron bridge. From behind low hills came the clanking murmur of T-55 tanks and other motorized infantry.

Chiun's hazel eyes, blazing anger, sought the mandarin's face.

"You gave me your word that there would be peace between us!" Chiun said vehemently.

"It saddens me to break it," Wu Ming Shi said brittlely, "but I have grown very, very old and I can no longer indulge my honor at the expense of my dreams of empire."

"You have abided by ink too long," Chiun spat.

"Come, my trusted Blue Bees," Wu Ming Shi said. "We shall now claim our glory, and when the time is right, these tools of Beijing—which I shall restore to its ancient name of Peking—will also feel your sting."

"Not so fast!" Remo said, reaching for the Chinese's brocaded shoulder.

"Sagwa!" the mandarin hissed. "You will remain in this spot, rooted like a locust tree, and when the green ants of the PLA come for you, you will not resist them."

"Wanna bet?" Remo said. His fingers dug into bony flesh.

"Look above you," Wu Ming Shi said without concern.

Remo looked up. PLA soldiers had appeared on the rock walls above them. Scores of AK-47 muzzles were directed at Remo's face.

Before they could fire, the Master of Sinanju's cold voice rang in his ears.

"Remo, you will do as you are told!"

Remo let go. He stood in place dutifully.

The mandarin Wu Ming Shi looked to Chiun. His betel-nut-brown smile showed through parted lips.

"Our debt is now truly canceled," he intoned.

Then, his Blue Bees gathering around him like workers around a queen bee, the mandarin stalked stiffly and with ginger steps into the yawning mouth of the cave. Their horses followed after them.

As the tanks rolled closer, Remo's eyes sought the ground. Scores of foot- and hoofprints tracked the dusty snow. But mingled with them one single contrary pair—toes pointing in the wrong direction. They ran back to the spot next to Remo, which the mandarin had just occupied. Remo looked down. A single pair of footprints were pressed into the snow. But they faced the car. Wu Ming Shi had been facing away when he stood beside Remo.

"Chiun, maybe you can explain this to me," Remo said.

"Not now. We must deal with the so-called People's Liberation Army."

"I can't pitch in until you countercommand me."

"Remove your skin patch, Remo Williams," Chiun said, "and do what you can to hold that iron bridge. I will take the other end."

"Great!" Remo tore the patch from behind one ear. He shucked off his tight chauffeur's jacket, exposing a white T-shirt.

"No!" Zhang Zingzong spoke up. "Master, I beg you. Let me do this. I will buy you all the time you need for escape."

Chiun's hazel eyes narrowed. "You wish this?"

"Very much. I must know if I am truly brave, as everyone says."

"Then go," Chiun said, rending Zhang's bonds with a slicing fingernail.

Shaking off the braided bamboo bonds, Zhang wheeled his mount and went racing for the narrow iron bridge.

Zhang Zingzong slapped his pony's flank with one hand. The bridge neared. Just short of it, he reined up and threw himself from the saddle.

He ran, and as he ran, he fumbled out a cigarette. One last smoke would do the job. He lit it with his Colibri lighter, reaching the bridge as the first dome-turreted T-55 rattled onto it, making it shudder in sympathy with the mighty engine of death.

Zhang walked across the bridge to meet it. His heart beat high and fast in his throat. He sucked in a brain-reviving cloud of tobacco smoke. It was just as it was after Tiananmen Square, in the moment that he had electrified the world. Except this time Zhang Zingzong was not burdened with bags of groceries in each hand. And here, there was no place for the tank to turn aside. It must crush him or back down.

The driver of the T-55 was a peasant from Shenyang. He was a good soldier, belonging to the Fortieth Army, which had refused to move against the prodemocracy demonstrators. He saw the man standing alone on the bridge, refusing to cower. It reminded him of another Chinese man and another Chinese tank not long ago.

He braked. He would not run this courageous man down.

Unfortunately, his tank commander had no such scruples. After a furious exchange, he reached forward into the driver's pit from the turret and pulled the stubborn driver out. He got behind the controls and sent the T-55 lurching ahead.

Still, the lone Chinese refused to back down. A second tank rolled onto the bridge behind him.

The commander hesitated. Beijing had told him that he would find the infamous counterrevolutionary Zhang here. The one who had faced down a column of PLA tanks. His orders were to take the man alive, for a propaganda trial. He grinned. What better propaganda than to force the man to back away, undoing his supposed feat?

He inched the tank ahead. Zhang Zingzong took a step forward too. The tank tracks gained another few inches. And Zhang matched them. He was not going to back down.

The tank commander hit the gas. The T-55 lurched ahead suddenly. Taken by surprise, Zhang flinched. The tank commander grinned. He would back down now, he knew. No mere student could face an oncoming tank. If not, there was plenty of time to stop.

Zhang Zingzong took a last puff of his Double Pleasure cigarette. He flicked it at the slitlike driver's periscope slot. It shed sparks going in.

The tank commander got a face full of embers as the butt bounced off his chin. He swatted it away angrily. It hit the floor. He stepped on it with his free foot.

And then his eye returned to the periscope. There was no sign of Zhang Zingzong.

He grinned. The coward had retreated. He sent the tank surging ahead with a heavy boot.

The grinding splintering sounds came from directly under his feet. His grin turned to a grimace of horror. He heard a muffled *pong!* and suddenly he had a vision of his own head dropping into a wicker basket—the penalty for giving the prodemocracy insurgents a greater propaganda tool than they had had in the living symbol of resistance that Zhang Zingzong had become.

Zhang Zingzong, the martyr.

The T-55 refused to go on. Somehow, those splintered

bones had wedged in the tracks, freezing the tank in the middle of the bridge, and cutting off the others from access to the pass.

It would be up to the other unit now.

The tanks rolled around the bend and stopped, blocking the other end of the pass. Charging before them were PLA regulars, with bayonets fixed on their lunging AK-47's.

"C'mon, Little Father," Remo said. "I'll show you how to play pong."

"Really, Remo! Ping-Pong at a time like this?"

"Not Ping-Pong. Pong. Just watch me."

Remo rushed in to greet the first group of soldiers. Their fixed bayonets told him they were disinclined to shoot. That was a lucky break for him, but not for the soldiers whose green helmets were no protection from the rapid series of double-handed slaps that closed on them with jackhammer force.

Pong! Pong! Pong!

Three PLA soldiers dropped in their tracks, their heads crushed within the suddenly mangled shells of their duty helmets.

The sight of this had a profound effect on the soldiers directly behind them. They stopped dead in their tracks. Some started to back away in fear.

Remo turned to Chiun, saying, "See? Pong."

The Master of Sinanju floated up beside him. He took out two flanking soldiers with snapping circular kicks, landed lightly, and split the larynx of a third with a long fingernail.

"This is no time for games," Chiun said loudly.

"Why not? There's only a couple dozen. We can take them easy."

"Twenty-four here. Many on the walls above. Probably a hundred if not a thousand in reserve. For this is a land of a million green ants. We cannot fight them all."

The tanks, forming a bulwark that jammed the pass, began to creep forward. Remo looked back over his shoulder. He lost his cocky grin. The lead tank on the bridge was bearing down on Zhang Zingzong.

"Can you hold then a little while?" he asked Chiun.

"Can a duck swim?" Chiun asked indignantly.

"Just hold that line." Remo rushed back to the limousine. He got behind the wheel and sent the limo charging in a circle. Bullets from the sharpshooters on the walls above drummed the roof and pocked the windshield. The limo was obviously bulletproof.

Out of the corner of his eye, Remo spotted Zhang Zingzong. The man was crawling under the bridge tank. Then it lurched forward, gnashing treads making a clattery sound on the bridge.

Remo tried to shut out the splintering-of-bone sound. Then he heard the distant, too-familiar *pong*!

Teeth clenched, Remo sent the limo's blunt nose toward the bulwark of T-55's, muttering, "Why didn't I think of this before?"

He raised the compartment lid beside his seat, exposing the twin rows of shiny black buttons.

The Master of Sinanju was dodging tanks. They lurched and lunged at him without success.

"Chiun!" he shouted. "Back away—now!" Without waiting, Remo began stabbing buttons. The sound of hydraulics toiling came from under the hood and greenish gas spewed from the grille. Remo cranked up his window, as PLA soldiers dropped in their tracks.

He hit more buttons, and other things began happening. From his driver's seat, he couldn't tell what exactly, but there came a spray of sparks from somewhere low on the front end, a jolting recoil, and streaks of fire ripped the air between the limo and the tank line.

Explosions began peppering the tanks.

"Rockets?" Remo said. He stabbed the button repeatedly. He got the same result. "Rockets," he said happily. Each stab discharged flame-tailed rockets. The constant recoil jammed him back in his seat, but he didn't care. He was having fun.

Remo veered away from the now-blazing tank line and pulled up at Chiun's side. "Get in," he said.

The Master of Sinanju leapt inside, saying, "We are still trapped here, and outnumbered."

"Us—outnumbered?" Remo said, looking through the windshield. The ground was littered with PLA bodies. Some dead, others actually snoring from the green gas. Bullet strikes from the sharpshooters above were visible all around them.

"The Chinese are inexaustible. We are not." Chiun sounded very worried.

Remo sent the car around in a circle, looking for a way out of the trap. His eye brightened at the cave entrance. It looked wide enough to accept the limo.

"Can't hurt to try," Remo muttered.

"No!" Chiun said abruptly. "Do not go in there."

"Why not?" Remo demanded. "It's shelter, isn't it? I'll just back in and hold 'em off with rockets."

Remo changed his mind when a cloud of dust rolled out of the cave mouth in a slow, dusty exhalation. He braked suddenly. Then came a low rumble and screaming from deep within the cave.

"What the hell happened?" Remo said, trying to see past the bullet-starred windshield.

"The mandarin Wu Ming Shi followed the instructions on the skull. He took the right tunnel and so he has perished."

"But the skull said to go right, didn't it?"

Chiun raised a wise finger. "One should not believe everything one reads—even if it is graven on a skull by Genghis Khan."

"I'd say *especially* if it was written by Genghis Khan." Remo frowned. Soldiers were climbing over the tanks stalled on the bridge. Others were trying to get past the blazing tank line, with less success. Spurred on by shouted orders, a few plunged through the flames. Their uniforms caught fire. They ran a few steps, then threw themselves into the snow, rolling and screaming while trying to put the flames out.

"I don't think they're in a mood to give up," Remo said.

"If we must make our last stand here," Chiun said, throwing off his kimono sleeves to reveal bare splindly arms, "then so be it. Many Chinese will perish before we breathe our last."

They got ready to jump from the car.

Then, over the din, came a low approaching sound. The growing thunder of a thousand hooves trampling the ground.

"Mongols!" Remo said.

"This is impossible!" Chiun squeaked. "My Mongols gave their word not to follow me."

"Maybe they're not your Mongols," Remo suggested lightly.

"Then whose Mongols would they be?"

"Maybe they're my Mongols," Remo said airily.

"Your Mongols!" Chiun exploded. "You do not have any Mongols!"

Then from out of the foothills they came. Howling and shouting, hurling walls of arrows before them. They swarmed over the tank line at the bridge. Their ponies splashed into the cold river and lunged up the banks, wild-eyed and sweating. Sharpshooters began falling off the high walls of the pass, feathered with willow shafts.

"That's our cue, Little Father," Remo shouted. They jumped from the car as Mongol horsemen formed a protective circle around them.

Kula led them. He reined in before Remo and Chiun. Jumping down, he ignored the Master of Sinanju and clapped his hands on Remo's shoulders in the traditional Mongol greeting.

"Ho, white tiger!" he cried. "I see we are in time to succor you."

Chiun stepped between them. "Remo, do you know this lunatic?"

Kula looked down at Chiun. "White tiger, is this old one with you?"

"White tiger?" Chiun said. His eyes narrowed.

"It's just a nickname they hung on me, kinda like the Lone Ranger," Remo offered. "How'd you know where I was, Kula?" he asked the Mongol.

"I heard that the Blue Bees had taken you. We tortured one of them until he told us where you would be found. That would-be khan, Boldbator, refused to join us, but Kula's men were not afraid."

"He was not afraid!" Chiun insisted harshly. "He was under obligation not to follow me. He is a Mongol with honor—unlike you."

"I am not under your obligation, or Boldbator's," Kula spat. "I serve the white tiger, the greatest warrior in all of Mongolia."

Remo turned to Chiun. He smiled broadly.

"I guess you had to hear it sometime," he said seriously. "It's true. I am the greatest warrior in all of Mongolia."

"You?" Chiun exploded. "You are no white tiger, but a pale piece of pig's ear!"

At that, Kula drew his knife. "Who are you to insult the white tiger?" he growled.

"I am the Master of Sinanju," Chiun said proudly, drawing himself up to his full five-foot height.

"That is what Boldbator swore," Kula returned. "I did not believe him, either."

Chiun's tiny mouth formed an outraged O. "What manner of Mongol are you that you do not know of the Master of Sinanju when you stand in his awesome presence?" Chiun demanded.

Kula gestured to his horse Mongols, as they drove the last of the surviving PLA out of their tanks and back into the hills with exultant whoops of joy.

"The kind who would lead his men into the teeth of the Chinese Army and hurl them broken into the wind," he said with pride.

"I think that translates as my Mongol can beat your Mongol," Remo whispered.

"Remo!" Chiun snapped. "Tell this man who I am!"

"Happy to." Remo turned to Kula. "Kula, this is Chiun. Chiun—meet Kula."

Kula regarded the Master of Sinanju stonily. Chiun turned to Remo, "No, tell him I am the Master of Sinanju."

"It's true," Remo said. "He is."

Kula's gong of a face looked Chiun up and down.

"There," Chiun said haughtily. "Now you may kneel. I will not require the full bow because you have assisted us."

"He is very small for a Master of Sinanju," Kula told Remo. "In the time of Lord Genghis, Masters of Sinanju were great robust men who rode magnificent ponies."

"I am an expert rider!" Chiun shouted.

"Then why did you ride this machine?" Kula asked, slapping the black limousine.

"Remo, tell this barbarian to kneel!"

Remo threw up his hands in a what-do-you-expect-me-to-do? gesture. "Hey, he's a Mongol. He's gonna do what he wants."

Chiun turned on Kula, pointing a furious shaking finger.

"You, horse Mongol!" he shouted. "Summon your men. In this very cave lies the treasure of Temujin. I will pay ten percent of all we recover to the men who help me carry it back to the village of Sinanju."

Kula looked to the cave mouth, where the dust still rolled out, carrying with it the tang of blood and other bodily secretions.

"What is to stop me from going in there and wresting the treasure for myself, old dragon?"

The Master of Sinanju's wrinkled face smoothed out in sudden shock. He leapt to the cave mouth, spreading defending arms.

"No man will cross this threshold but at my leave!" he warned. "Else he dies!"

Remo caught Kula's eye. "Believe him," he said.

"Ten percent for the use of your horses," Chiun called.

"Try for twenty," Remo suggested, *sotto voce*.

Kula lifted his voice. "Twenty and no less."

"Twelve!" Chiun shouted back.

They settled on fifteen percent, but only because the rest of the Mongols rode up, having driven off the last PLA stragglers.

They went inside carefully, batting the dust away from their faces as they felt their way along the high inner walls. They were covered with ancient dingy murals, depicting Buddahs, Chinese demons, and dragons. Remo counted five of the latter, which explained to his satisfaction why it was called Five-Dragon Cave.

"This is the fork," Chiun said at a split in the tunnel.

The dust was coming from the right-hand tunnel. The entrance was jammed with broken rock, dirt, and other debris. Dusty, blood-caked limbs projected from the choke of rock. Some were human, and some equine.

"How are we going to clear all that away?" Remo asked, trying not to think of Fang Yu buried under all that crushing rock.

"We will not," Chiun said, striding on to the left-hand tunnel.

Remo caught up. "I thought the skull said not to take the left fork."

"No. It instructed the reverse. Before I presented the skull to Wu Ming Shi, with my nails I incised the word not in a certain place. Blinded by greed, he neglected to examine the riddle closely for signs of doctoring. And so he perished."

They came to a high-ceilinged vault of rock. Mongol yak-butter candles lit the area with shuddery yellow light.

"Dig," commanded the Master of Sinanju, pointing to the wide flat ground before them.

Not a Mongol moved.

"Go ahead," Remo said quietly.

The Mongols threw themselves into their work with enthusiasm.

"You gotta know how to handle these guys," Remo said with a straight face.

Chiun fumed wordlessly.

As they dug, Remo spoke up. "One thing I still don't understand."

"There are many things you do not understand," Chiun said testily.

"Wu Ming Shi. When he walked, he left the screwiest tracks behind him."

"Ah," Chuin said, gesturing Remo back to the tunnel fork.

There he pushed aside loose rock with a sandaled toe and uncovered a foot encased in a soft black slipper, the toe pointing up.

"That is Wu Ming Shi's foot," Chiun pronounced. "Examine it and see how foolish you feel after you behold the sublime truth."

Remo knelt down and removed the sandal. The exposed foot was wrinkled and leathery brown, the nails curved like blunt talons. The ankle skin was withered like a huge twist of beef jerky.

"He could have used a good foot manicure," Remo remarked, "but that's about it."

"Extract the cadaver," Chiun suggested.

Remo shrugged. He pulled away more rock and debris, exposing a second foot. Taking the corpse by both ankles, Remo pulled. He had to twist and turn, because the body was really stuck. He got most of Wu Ming Shi pulled loose from the rock. The body was missing an arm and the head.

But that wasn't what made Remo abruptly drop the body as if it were contaminated.

"What the hell?" he said in surprise.

For Wu Ming Shi's remains had landed chest-down, even though the toes pointed upward.

"This is crazy!" Remo blurted out. "His feet are on backward!"

"Truly," Chiun beamed. "It is the insult I inflicted upon the wicked mandarin Wu Ming Shi, lo these many years ago."

"You turned his *feet* around?" Remo said incredulously.

"It is a simple trick. Perhaps one day I will show it to you."

Chiun padded off, the high carriage of his head telling Remo his pride had been restored.

A call came out of the left-side tunnel. Chiun picked up his skirts in his haste. Remo flashed after him.

They plunged into the candlelit vault.

"Behold!" Kula said, lifting a dirt-clotted skull from the wide hole his Mongols had excavated.

Chiun snatched it from him, wailing, "Another stupid skull! What manner of Mongol trickery is this!" He spanked the dirt from the bony forehead, revealing Mongolian script. Chiun read it with narrow suspicious eyes.

"What does it say?" Remo asked.

"It says, 'Know, O hasty one, that the tortoise has more than one egg.' "

"What's that mean?"

Chiun's eyes suddenly lit up. He turned to the waiting circle of Mongol faces.

"To your steeds, sons of Temujin! We ride to Karakorum!"

The Mongols regarded the Master of Sinanju with identical metallic expressions.

"Why should we do this?" Kula asked in a reasonable voice.

"Because that is where the treasure truly lies!" Chiun hissed.

"You swore that it lay here, where we dig," Kula returned, unmoved.

"I was deceived!" Chiun flung back. "The *Khagan* was having a last jest on us all. We did not dig deep enough at Karakorum. It is there!"

The Mongols folded their arms stubbornly.

Remo stepped up. "Tell you guys what. We gotta get out of here before the PLA comes back. What say we ride up to—" He turned to Chiun. "What did you say that name was?"

"Karakorum," Chiun muttered darkly.

"Karakorum," Remo repeated.

"To Karakorum with the white tiger!" the Mongols shouted.

They stampeded from the cave, forcing Chiun to float out of the way of their booted feet.

"I love Mongol enthusiasm, don't you?" Remo asked Chiun.

"Pah!" Chiun spat, storming from the cave.

"Guess you gotta know 'em to love 'em," he muttered happily.

38

Elements of the People's Liberation Army made several abortive stabs at interdicting the Mongol column as it moved northward. Mongol war cries discouraged them. A snowstorm came up, rendering pursuing tanks useless. A few jeep forays ended in overturned jeeps with Mongol arrows feathering tires and Chinese bodies alike.

No Chinese had any stomach for a fight after that.

Chiun drew his horse up alongside Remo's.

"How did you learn to ride so quickly?" Chiun asked.

"*Fahrvergnugen*," Remo said coolly. Receiving no response, he asked, "You know, you led me on quite the merry chase this time."

"It was to protect you. And you did not do so badly, pale piece of tiger's ear."

Remo laughed. "Was Wu Ming Shi really two hundred years old?"

"It was closer to two hundred fifty, I understand. He was an evil man, but he knew many terrible secrets. Now they have died with him and a debt to the House of Sinanju has been finally settled in full."

"Too bad we lost Zhang," Remo said as the snow squall died.

Chiun shrugged. "Zhang's life was his to throw away."

"He went out a hero—which is more than I can say about

Fang Yu." Remo's face was hard, his eyes bleak as chips of age-darkened bone.

"It is better to live, Remo," Chiun told him. "I could have been a so-called hero and eliminated Wu Ming Shi many years ago, but others would have suffered for it. Remember this if you ever face such a choice."

"Point taken. Listen, did you really do Amelia Earhart?"

Chiun nodded grimly. "It was during a time when Wu Ming Shi had no need of Sinanju. The Japanese were only a slightly less odious client."

"I can't believe you did that. She was an American hero."

"Heroes are destined for a young death. Remember this too."

"Yeah, well, when I'm head of the House, I won't stoop to taking that kind of work."

"It is too late, Remo. For you have already killed one who is a hero to some—although he was but a kung fu dancer."

Remo looked doubtful. "Who?"

"He was called Bruce. His last name escapes me, but years ago, he enjoyed some minor notoriety in absurd Chinese movies."

Remo blinked. "Not the chop-socky star?" he said hotly. "Little Father, that guy's been dead for years."

"No, he perished in the monastery. You knew him as Sagwa."

"Sagwa!" Remo snapped his fingers. "Wait a minute. The guy I'm thinking of got his acting start in a TV show called *The Green Hornet* back in the sixties. I remember watching it. Yeah, it comes back to me now. He played Kato, the chauffeur with the mask." Remo's eyes widened suddenly. "That so-called Chinese limo! It was the car Kato used to drive. Black Beauty."

"Black Ugly," Chiun sniffed.

"No wonder he looked familiar, even with the mask. And that's why I recognized the car." Remo stopped. "Oh, my God," he croaked. "I killed Kato."

"No," Chiun corrected. "*We* eliminated that upstart. For all Masters rightfully share in all credit."

"Trade you a chop-socky actor for an aviatrix?" Remo asked sheepishly.

Chiun beamed happily.

* * *

They linked up with Boldbator's Golden Horde outside of Sayn Shanda after nightfall.

An argument immediately broke out over rights to the treasure of Genghis Khan. Boldbator claimed ten percent. Kula claimed fifteen. Boldbator demanded of the Master of Sinanju why this Kula, a mere bandit, should get five percent more than he, who was the New Khan.

"Because I foolishly made a pact with him to carry the treasure away," Chiun said petulantly.

"But you made the same pact with me—for less."

"But he was at Five-Dragon Cave, not you."

"You commanded me to remain here," Boldbator thundered.

"I know that!" Chiun flared. "But how was I to know the treasure was not in Five-Dragon Cave after all? Oh, this is ridiculous." He turned to Remo in exasperation. "You were there, Remo. Explain it to this nomad."

"Don't look at me," Remo said, backing away. "He's not my Mongol."

The argument raged all day. War threatened to break out between the opposing camps, each claiming to be the ordained bearers of Temujin's treasure, until Remo took Chiun aside and said, "Look, how much of a percentage did you promise Zhang?"

"Half," Chiun whispered conspiratorially. "But only because it was his skull to start with."

"Fine, so if you cut Boldbator in for fifteen percent to match Kula's share, that's only thirty percent, right?"

Chiun eyes gleamed. "You are right, Remo. I am left with seventy percent for myself."

"Actually, sixty," Remo said.

"What do you mean?"

Remo wagged a finger in Chiun's face. "You forgot my ten percent. You made a big production of trying to give it to me back at the monastery. I have witnesses."

"All dead," Chiun retorted. "And I only said that to deceive Wu Ming Shi. Besides, I referred to the television show reward, not the magnificent treasure of Temujin."

"Hey, if I don't get my commission, I won't let my Mongols play with your Mongols. No happy jaunt to Karakorum."

"Then I will get eighty-five percent!" Chiun crowed.

"Not if my Mongols beat your Mongols to Karakorum,"

Remo pointed out. "That's a big group you got there, Little Father. All those camels and wagons and yurts. I don't think they can ride as fast as my guys."

Chiun pulled at his hair. "This is blackmail!" he shrieked.

"No, this is horse trading," Remo shot back. "I hear it's an honored Mongol tradition."

"What do you know of Mongols?" Chiun said indignantly.

"Not a lot," Remo said, gazing over the sea of felt tents spread before them. He grinned. "Maybe ten percent worth."

"Done," Chiun clucked glumly. "Now, let us set out for Karakorum."

Remo cupped his hands around his mouth. "*Ai yah!* Let's ride!" he shouted.

Dozens of Mongols jumped to their mounts like Sioux about to raid a rival village.

The rest looked to Chiun with the blank expressions of a sky full of yellow moons.

"Your turn," Remo said lightly. "I think these slow guys are yours."

Two days' ride later, they were camped on the plains of Karakorum. Mongol tools were prying up the earth's crust as Remo and Chiun, perched on the stone tortoise, watched over them.

"*Ai yah!*" The cry came from what had become a crater large enough to hold a three-ton meteor.

A rotting chest was passed from hand to hand until it was deposited at the Master of Sinanju's feet.

Chiun fell on it, flinging open the lid. His eyes widened at the piles of emeralds and rubies and pearls heaped within.

"Look at this, Remo!" Chiun squeaked. "Is it not fabulous?"

"It's a start," Remo said nonchalantly.

All through the night, more chests were hauled up, along with other trophies—golden gongs, jade figurines, and personal mementos of Genghis Khan. Chiun let the Mongols divide up these last, telling Remo, "It means so much to them."

"Bull," Remo countered. "You know it's not as valuable as gold or jade or any of this other stuff. Except to a museum. Actually, to a museum it would be worth more than gold."

After that Chiun insisted upon his rightful share of the Khan of Khan's personal effects.

The treasure made a huge pyramid in the middle of the plain.

"Rich! I am rich!" Chiun cried to the star-dazzled Mongolian sky.

"I don't see what you're so excited about," Remo put in soberly. "You were already rich."

"One can never be too rich," Chiun countered, examining a jade wand for flaws. He found one. It went into the Mongol pile.

No one slept that night. By dawn they had every camel and creaking cart loaded with treasure.

Remo and Chiun mounted their horses and took the lead. Boldbator, raising the nine-horsetail standard of Genghis Khan, and Kula, sipping *kaoliang* wine from a bladder, took positions on either side of them.

Remo lifted one arm, mimicking an actor in a cavalry movie.

"Sinanju—ho!" he cried, bringing his hand down. The New Golden Horde started off. It was a full two hours before the ponies in the rear were able to move.

As they made their hoof-drumming, wheel-creaking, yak-grunting way east to Korea and the village of Sinanju, the Master of Sinanju cast a worried look to the army that marched behind them.

"Something wrong, Little Father?" Remo asked.

"All these Mongol mouths," Chiun squeaked. "How will my poor village feed them when we reach Sinanju? We have no mutton!"

Remo laughed. "Tell you what, Chiun, you just feed your Mongols and I'll worry about mine."

"I have been thinking, Remo," Chiun said slyly.

"Yeah?"

"I have so many Mongols, and you have so few. Perhaps I will give you some of mine."

"Your generosity underwhelms me, Little Father." And Remo laughed again. It was good to be back in the saddle again.